THE JESTER'S MAGICIAN

ALSO BY KEN PRATT

The Royal Potter's Shop

When the Wolf Comes Knocking

The Jessup County Chronicles

The Gypsum Creek Massacre

Caustic October

The Matt Bannister Series

THE JESTER'S MAGICIAN

THE JESSUP COUNTY CHRONICLES
BOOK 3

KEN PRATT

CKN Christian Publishing
An Imprint of Wolfpack Publishing
1707 E. Diana Street
Tampa, FL 33609

www.cknchristianpublishing.com

Paperback ISBN 979-8-89567-890-9
Ebook ISBN 979-8-89567-861-9
LCCN 2025944715

Dedicated to Cathy, my wife.
For always being supportive, loving, and for your sacrifice, which
allows me to write.
Thank you.

THE JESTER'S MAGICIAN

PROLOGUE

BRANSON, OREGON, 1934

CHRISTINE BANNISTER FOCUSED ON THE AGE spots and thinning skin on her hands as she brushed her long silver hair into a neatly formed bun. Her husband, Matt, sat in a padded chair in front of Christine's wheelchair, holding a mirror for her. They hadn't gone to church that particular Sunday morning because Christine had suffered from a migraine the night before and had slept in later than usual. The migraine had faded, and now she was preparing to meet Alex Wentworth for another story for his article in the Jessup County Chronicles.

Christine gazed at her hands quietly before leaning closer to the mirror and squinting to focus on the lines around her eyes and mouth. Her hair had lost its dark pigmentation many years earlier, and now she saw the reflection of an elderly woman. A faint lifting of her lips followed a distant memory of her grandmother. "I look old," she said without any further explanation.

1

"Ahh, looks are deceiving," Matt replied, gently shaking his head to reassure her.

She looked at her husband with an appreciative gaze. "I look in the mirror, and I see an old woman, but I feel as alive and young inside as I ever have. I feel like I could go to the old dance hall and dance all night like I used to. Well, at least my spirit feels like it could, but I look in the mirror, and no one would want to dance with me now." She exhaled with a resigned sigh.

"That's not true. I'd dance every dance with you," Matt said.

She smiled. "I know you would. I'm talking about the young and handsome men in town."

"My lady, are you looking for some young buck to start having an affair with? Do I need to start keeping an eye out for you sneaking around?"

Christine smiled at his teasing and gently slapped his hand. "I don't think it would do me any good, Matthew. My body doesn't work the way it used to. Even if the dance hall was still open and I went down there, I couldn't dance even if I wanted to. Matt, do you know how frustrating it is to hear some music and want to dance, but I can't even stand on my own two feet? I look in this mirror, and I doubt our grandchildren would believe that once upon a time, I was the most sought-after and highest-paid dancer in Bella's Dance Hall. They wouldn't believe men used to spend a lot of money just for one dance with me. Now, when I look in the mirror, I know the men would pay money not to dance with me if they were being forced to." Her eyes narrowed slightly when she noticed a wry smile on Matt's lips. "Don't you say it."

He chuckled. "My gun belt still fits if you want to earn some money. I'll force them to dance with you."

"You're terrible. I remember when I was young, I thought my grandparents were so old, and they were barely fifty. Now, I'm twenty-some years older than they were. Sometimes, my spirit feels so young, free, and adventurous that I wish I could go outside and dance barefoot in the rain once again. I used to love doing that. But I sit here in this wheelchair and have to face the facts: I'm just an old, crippled woman."

Matt tilted his head. "Christine, you're still just as beautiful as the day I met you."

She smiled sadly and laid a hand on his arm affectionately. "Thank you. It's always nice to hear that. But I think you have to say it because you're so much older than me." She smiled lovingly.

Matt nodded. "That's why I can't take you to town anymore. I'm tired of always being accused of robbing the cradle."

Christine laughed.

Matt continued, "The Bible says the spirit is willing, but the flesh is weak. I know Jesus said it in the context of temptation, but the same could be said about getting older. I have this tough and dangerous reputation even after all these years, but just trying to lift a hundred-pound grain bag is about all the fighting I can do. Don't tell anyone, it might ruin my reputation, but I doubt I could whip half of those young bucks that run around town causing trouble. If they wanted to dance with you, I might end up looking as lost and helpless as that Leonard fella did when he was watching your friend Mary dancing with that magician years ago. Remember? I could still whip maybe more than half of the young bucks out there. My spirit is more than willing to butt heads, but I'm not as spry or limber, and I don't hit quite as hard as I used to. Even old lions have a day when they need to step down and let a stronger lion reign."

Christine chuckled. "Matt, my darling husband, you're in your eighties. I doubt you could whip any twenty-year-old, even if you think you can."

"Hogwash. Some of these young men nowadays seem mighty soft. I doubt some could fight their way out of a paper bag without hurting themselves."

"It seems I remember hearing Uncle Charlie say something similar about our generation."

Matt paused for a moment to reflect on his youth. "Yeah, I'm sure he did. Time keeps moving forward day by day until too many years go by, doesn't it? Before you know it, one generation is being born as another passes into eternity. It's just a revolving cycle of time."

"It does go by too fast," Christine said in a soft, reflective tone. "You mentioned something that I think would be a good story for Alex today. I had forgotten all about Mary and that magician until you mentioned it. What was his name? Handy Andy or something like that?"

"Landy Jandy. The poster for that show is upstairs, hanging in a spare bedroom. I was looking at it the other day while I was in there."

"That's right," Christine replied, recalling slowly. "Do you remember his magic rope trick? The standing rope of time, or whatever it was called?"

"I do."

"Matt, I know you planned to tell Alex a different story, but will you share the story about Landy Jandy? I'd like to be reminded of that one myself."

———

BEFORE LONG, Alex Wentworth sat in his usual spot across from Matt and Christine. He talked to Christine while Matt excused himself to go upstairs. He returned carrying a framed copy of a poster announcing the arrival of a traveling show. It was a vividly colored poster featuring a beautiful woman singing with outstretched arms, accompanied by smaller pictographs of other acts. Bold red letters proclaimed:

The Amazing Hennessy Brothers Traveling Show presents the Golden Voice of world-renowned singer Hellee Montrese. Also featuring Gus Miller and his trained monkey, Bart; Darlene Smith, the "That's impossible" contortionist; the music of the Hennessy Singers; and the mysterious magic of the World's Creepiest Magician, Landy Jandy.

"Wow, that brings back some memories," Christine said as she looked up at Matt. "Are you going to tell him about everything? Even the family stuff?"

Matt shrugged his shoulders. "I don't see why not. It happened."

"What's this?" Alex asked, holding the poster to read it.

Matt sat at the end of the davenport to be near Christine, who was in her wheelchair. He took her hand. "That is today's story. I think you'll find it interesting. As the date states, it was November 1884. It all started when Bella and Dave, the owners of Bella's Dance Hall, entered my office..." He paused. "You might want to write this all down because I can promise you that this is a story very few people know about."

CHAPTER ONE

BRANSON, OREGON, 1884

THE US MARSHAL'S OFFICE WAS A SINGLE-STORY granite-block building, twice as long as it was wide. The front featured two large bay windows with the words *US MARSHAL* in decorative gold on the glass. An awning covered the front, and a white sign with black lettering proclaimed *US Marshal Matt Bannister*.

Inside, fine mahogany paneling adorned the walls. Immediately within five feet of the door, a three-foot-tall partition spanned the width of the office, featuring a gate at its center. This partition served as a barrier, separating visitors from the deputies' desks, which were covered with sorted papers and ink wells. Beyond the desks, a heavy metal door with a lock led to the jail cells. Midway back, a private office had windows draped with curtains.

Along the opposite wall stood a beautiful, securely locked gun cabinet housing half a dozen rifles, next to a handsome wood stove heating a pot of coffee near a long dining table with six chairs. A set of cabinets stored coffee and other supplies, while a coat rack held a lone garment. A bulletin board filled with wanted posters of scoundrel-looking faces hung next to a map of the Pacific Northwest, and portraits of mountain scenes, as well as one of a bright sunflower, were arranged neatly around the office.

US Deputy Marshal Phillip Forrester wasn't what one would expect upon entering the marshal's office. He was a twenty-six-year-old man who wore suits, seldom donned a gun belt, and had no calluses on his soft hands. Phillip was soft-spoken, friendly, and gentle in spirit. He had short, neatly combed light-brown hair and kept his oblong face clean-shaven, with a pair of wire-rimmed spectacles resting on the bridge of his nose. Phillip seemed more at home in a business office than as a lawman. Fittingly, his responsibilities included managing office affairs and ensuring the prisoners were fed and cared for.

Phillip carried several sealed envelopes to the table where Matt sat, waiting with his three deputies: Morton Sperry, Truet Davis, and Nate Robertson. Phillip distributed the envelopes based on the names written on them. "It's payday, gentlemen."

Truet leaned back in his chair and clasped his hands behind his head. He looked at Morton Sperry, who opened the envelope and counted the money. "Mort, you better get moving and rush that money home to your wife before she skins your hide. My horse is right outside if you want to run it home."

Morton stuffed the envelope into his shirt pocket. "No kidding. Raising four kids and another one on the way is not for the weak. I'll tell you, though, if there is anything Audrey does well, aside from cooking, it's budgeting. I could never save a dollar myself, but she has cured me of that."

Matt Bannister was in his mid-thirties, lean with broad shoulders and a muscular build. His square-shaped face was handsome, featuring a well-groomed short, dark beard and long dark hair pulled back in a ponytail. His brown eyes shone with kindness and sincerity as he said, "You married yourself a fine woman, Morton. Audrey is great at everything she does."

"That she is," Morton agreed.

Truet Davis stretched his powerful arms. "Well, fellas, I am heading to Willow Falls for the weekend. I suppose I'd better get going if Morton isn't going to borrow my horse to run that money home."

Morton waved toward Phillip. "Phillip's the one who wears a dog collar, not me, Truet."

"Dog collar? What do you mean?" Phillip asked.

"It means your wife holds the reins and controls everything you do like a dog."

"She does not," Phillip protested.

"She does, too," Truet agreed. "You know Matt and his family always tease his brother Steven about being henpecked, but oh, man, you make Steven look like Stonewall Jackson."

Phillip's cheeks reddened slightly as the others laughed. "Say what you will, Truet. You and Morton like to tease me, I know, but we all know Audrey sets the rules at Morton's house, and Christine does at Matt's. So, talk big, Truet, but when you marry Annie, you'll be saying *yes, dear,* more than any of us."

Matt laughed lightly. Annie Lenning was his younger sister who was engaged to Truet.

"He's got a point," Morton said to Truet. "Annie's the toughest woman I've ever met."

"He might," Truet admitted. "Annie's a bit headstrong, I won't deny that. But that's what I love about her. She's got fire and sass."

Phillip said, "I love my wife. And I want to treat her right, so say whatever you want to say, but we are happily married and I want to keep it that way."

Matt glanced at Nate Robertson, who appeared distracted. "Nate, what are you looking so sad about?"

"Well, since you all are talking about women, I suppose I'll share with you that Angela and I had a fight. She's mad at me about something so darn dumb that I don't understand."

"Do tell," Truet encouraged. "You're among friends."

Nate gazed at Truet questioningly. "I was at the dance hall last night, and Rose was wearing a very pretty dress. It was new, apparently, and Angela asked if I thought Rose's dress was prettier than hers..."

"Oh, no," Phillip said softly.

"Yeah," Nate said to Phillip. "I told the truth. Yes, it was a prettier dress. Angela got mad and told me off. She said that since I liked the dress so much, I should court Rose. Then she told me to leave and wouldn't talk to me anymore."

Matt chuckled. "Phillip, you never admit that anything is nicer than your lady's. It's the pinnacle of courting wisdom. When she compares anything to another woman, you always say no. It's the safest route home."

Truet added, "Always say no when that happens. Every husband of a happy wife knows that. Huh, Mort?"

"It's common sense," Morton said, looking dumb-founded.

"I was just being honest," Nate replied.

"Well, now you've learned your lesson. Say no next time."

"I will. So, how do I fix this? Should I apologize?"

"Too late for that," Morton joked. "She'll be bringing that up for the next three years."

"She'll get over it or she won't," Truet reasoned. "Maybe it's her week of...well, you know. Or maybe she was just in a bad mood. Nonetheless, she'll apologize, most likely for overreacting. I wouldn't worry about it. And if she's still upset, drop her and court Rose."

Matt and the others laughed as the door swung open, ringing the cowbell. Bella and Dave, the owners of Bella's Dance Hall, stepped inside. Dave held what looked like rolled-up posters in his hand.

Matt stood. "What are you two doing here?" he asked with a friendly smile as he approached the partition behind which they stood.

"I wanted to verify that you're still alive," Bella teased with her raspy voice. She was a stout woman with broad shoulders and a no-nonsense expression that made her seem rough, blunt, and hardened. In truth, her heart was golden, and she cared for her dancers as if they were her daughters.

Matt explained, "Christine keeps me on a tight noose."

Bella smiled. "I'm glad to hear it. We're going to stop by your place and visit with her on the way back. I'm sure you've seen the posters around town for the Hennessy Brothers' Traveling Show that's coming to town this weekend. They're performing two shows, Friday and Saturday night, at the dance hall. I was wondering if I could put a poster in your window?"

"Of course."

"Good." Dave pulled out a poster from the rolled-up copies. "Here you are," he said.

Matt unrolled the poster, read it, and examined the pictographs. "That sounds like it could be fun. It's taking place on the dance hall stage and not in the community hall?"

"Yes," Bella answered. "I invited them here, so why not have them perform at the dance hall? It will be good entertainment and beneficial for our business. Since you married our best singer, we decided we had to do something. Hellee Montrese is quite talented. I heard her sing once when we lived in Denver. I'm excited to meet her and hear her sing again. I made arrangements for the Hennessy Brothers' group to stay at the Monarch Hotel, where they should arrive sometime today. I expect to see you and Christine there."

Matt nodded with interest. "I'm sure we'll be there."

Dave quipped, "Christine's ticket is free, but we have to charge you. You'll understand we consider Christine like our daughter, so for her, it's like coming back home."

"And I'm the unwanted son-in-law."

Dave grinned and nodded. "I knew you'd understand."

Matt chuckled while shaking Dave's hand. "It's good to see you two."

"Well, you know where to find us," Dave said.

Bella jabbed a pointed finger at Matt. "You better bring Christine home to see that show."

"I will. I'll see you both there."

Truet Davis took the poster from Matt and read it. "The magical mystery of the World's Creepiest Magician, Landy Jandy. Hmm," he grunted. "It sounds like the perfect place to take your sister."

"The creepy or magical part?" Matt asked with a wry smile.

"A little bit of both," Truet answered quietly. "I'll bring her back here on Saturday to watch the show."

———

SAL GABLE WALKED into the lobby of the Monarch Hotel and approached the reception desk. "I see you're still working here."

"Of course," Pam Collins replied with a friendly greeting. She peered at the gentleman, trying to remember him. The man appeared to be in his early thirties, wearing a brown suit with a pink vest featuring black trim and buttons. He removed his derby hat, revealing his short, neatly combed brown hair. A well-groomed, thin mustache rested on his upper lip. Pam did not recognize him. "I take it you have stayed with us before?"

"This past summer, for a few nights, don't you remember me? I used to come and go in and out of the lounge to gamble. I'm Sal Gable, and your name is Pam. I remember you," he said with a flirtatious nod.

"I apologize, Mr. Gable, but I don't recall you being here, but we have people come and go in here every day. Unfortunately, if you want a room, we are booked over the weekend. I apologize, but we have no vacancies." Pam was in her early forties and the assistant manager of the hotel. She wore her straight brown hair in a bun at the back of her head. Although she was rather plain-looking, her sparkling blue eyes and friendly smile caught Sal's attention.

"No vacancies? Seriously? You have more rooms than rats in a whorehouse's cellar."

"Usually, we have a vacancy, but we have a traveling show coming to town, and they've rented all the rooms. They're supposed to arrive today."

"I wanted to stay here so that I could gamble in the lounge. Is it possible that I can still do that if I stay elsewhere?"

Pam wrinkled her nose. "Unfortunately, not without a membership."

"And how do I go about that?"

"The member's fee is fifty dollars a year, paid upfront." The Monarch Lounge was a private club exclusively for men, welcoming both hotel guests and lounge members. The lounge offered a discreet environment for drinking, smoking cigars, and engaging in gambling. Although not publicly known and kept in strict confidence, a few select women had rooms in the back reserved solely for members.

"Fifty dollars!" Sal exclaimed. "Does that include free drinks or a discount on the prices?"

"No. It just allows you membership without staying here," Pam said.

"That's a whole lot of money just to walk through a door."

William Fasana, the hotel security guard, walked behind the counter to grab a set of keys. He chuckled as he overheard Sal's complaint. "It keeps the riffraff and penny-ante gamblers like you out. How are you, Sal?" He shook the man's hand.

"William, you rat. It's good to see you. I wanted to whip your hide on the poker table, but fifty dollars upfront is a whole lot to ask when you haven't got a room for me."

William leaned his hands on the desk, his long, curly blonde hair hanging freely. His weathered face and blue eyes peered at Sal. "How long are you in town for? The last I heard, you were going east."

"I'm back for a while. It depends on whether I can take enough from your customers to make this place my home."

"That's my job," William chided. "Well, if you have a pocketful of money you want to give away, I'll let you have a weekend pass into the Monarch Lounge until you're broke or a room opens up. I don't mind taking your money. As for staying here, you'll have to find somewhere else until Monday."

"I can do that. You just have a fair deck and those cards ready."

William watched Sal leave the hotel and said, "Sal Gable is one of those sharp-looking show-offs who talks a larger game than he plays. Don't fall for him, Pam. You could do better."

"I'll try not to," she replied, glancing sideways at William.

"Well, I know the last time he was here, you were panting like a puppy every time he walked by. I'm just telling you, you could do better."

She grinned. "That's odd, because I don't remember that, William. In fact, I don't remember him at all."

William took a deep breath and exhaled. "Dang, I wish I could do that."

"What?"

"Forget about those who broke my heart as easily as you can."

Pam laughed. "Get to work, William."

THE BRANSON SHERIFF, Tim Wright, ascended the steps to Solomon Fasana's home and knocked on the door. He hated to bother him at home, but Solomon was the only undertaker in the county. It took several sharp knocks for the door to open.

"Sheriff Wright, what brings you here?" Deloris Fasana asked, her brow furrowing. She had been in the kitchen preparing her favorite chicken and dumplings for dinner.

"I hate to bother you and Solomon, but Mrs. Poole passed, and the family would like her body taken to the funeral parlor. I would have taken her there myself, but I strained my back the other day and don't want to lift anything heavier than my saddle."

"Oh, that's unfortunate," Deloris said. "Who are the Poole's?"

"An older couple who live out in a little shack about a quarter mile outside of town. She went to take a nap and didn't wake up. I suppose that's how I'd like to go if I had to."

"Well, we all are going to have to take that plunge sometime. I'm married to a mortician, so it's common around here. Dying in your sleep is certainly not the worst way to go."

"Is Solomon here? I'll take him back out there. Mr. Poole doesn't want to sleep with her corpse tonight."

"Solomon is, but he is indisposed at the moment. He's not been feeling well lately and is presently...well, as I said, indisposed. Would you like to come inside and wait?"

———

SOLOMON FASANA WAS MISERABLE, suffering from nausea, stomach cramps, vomiting, and diarrhea. He wasn't certain where he had contracted the illness. It could have come from any customer in his furniture store, situated above the mortuary, or from one of the families he served during a funeral. It was even possible that he had picked up something from one of the bodies he handled. Whatever the illness was, it would pass, it always did.

His stomach cramped even though he had just finished emptying his bowels. He entered the house, longing to lie in bed and rest without needing the chamber pot or hurrying outside to the privy. He swore to himself that as soon as water was piped through town, like some of the bigger cities were doing, he would invest in one of those water closets inside his house, no matter the cost.

He furrowed his brow upon seeing Tim sitting in the family room. "Tim?"

"You look terrible," Sheriff Wright said, startled by how pale and sick Solomon appeared.

Solomon was in his mid-fifties, tall and thin, with a square face adorned by a well-groomed gray beard and short, thinning black hair flecked with gray. "I feel terrible. Why are you here?"

"I got a dead body for you to pick up. Mrs. Poole passed."

Solomon shook his head and braced his arm against the back of the davenport to steady himself. "I can't do it. I'm sicker than I've ever been. Get your deputies, Matt or someone, to help you. I'll give you the keys to the mortuary door. You know where to put her. I'm sorry, but I must lie down."

"Have you seen the doctor?"

"No, but I'm thinking about it. I'll give it another day or

two. Deloris, will you hand him the keys to the mortuary? I need to lie down."

"I certainly can. Sweetheart, go lie down," she said with concern. "I will bring you some water and an apple to keep you hydrated."

He gave a slight nod and walked slowly toward the stairs.

Sheriff Wright turned to Deloris. "He looks bad. You need to have the doctor come look at him. He could have cholera or some other outbreak that we need to stop from spreading while we can."

"Yes, I will do that. I'll get you the keys. Tim, put the woman in the mortuary, and make sure to lock the doors and bring the keys back."

Tim's expression was filled with concern about a larger outbreak. "I'll do that. Seriously, you need to get him seen by the doctor before whatever he has spreads throughout town and we all end up dead."

"I promise I will do that."

CHAPTER TWO

Later that afternoon, three colorful carriages with painted sideboards displaying bold red lettering reading: *The Hennessy Brothers' Traveling Show* parked outside the Monarch Hotel, and several people climbed out. A fourth and a fifth wagon pulled onto Rose Street to unload the stage curtains and other props needed for their show.

A hefty man with broad shoulders and a large belly stepped out of the first carriage, stretching his back as he examined the hotel's granite block and brick trim construction. He had a round face with blue eyes and thick, dark brown eyebrows. His chubby cheeks were framed by a thick but short beard and mustache. He scanned the building and the main street with a scowl. "It doesn't look too flea-bitten anyway. Let's get this show done and move on to Portland before the snow begins falling. The last place I want to be stuck is in this two-bit hellhole."

"Be nice, Bud. We need these folks to want to come see

us, not be turned away by your negativity," a taller, leaner man said as he stepped out of the carriage, ready to assist his wife like a gentleman. He wore a gray suit and a matching derby hat, while his wife stretched her back after the long journey.

Bud glanced at his brother. "If we make enough from these peasants to pay for the hotel, I'll be shocked. We're better than this, Ian. We don't have time to stop at little pissant villages like this one. This is a waste of time."

Ian Hennessy was in his late thirties and traveled with his wife, Barbara, who led the all-women's group, the Hennessy Singers. Four women stepped out of the second carriage and joined the two brothers. They were married to the men in the Hennessy Traveling Show's band, which provided all the music during the performances. Traveling as married couples created a more cohesive troupe. Although one band member's wife was not part of the musical group, she kept herself busy by collecting tickets during the show and ensuring that other details were taken care of. Everyone had a role to play to ensure the show's success.

Ian looked at the businesses up and down both sides of Main Street. "I think we'll do okay, Bud. How about you get us all checked in? I'll help get the luggage."

"Fine," Bud said under his breath. He was in a foul mood after four nights of trying to sleep on the ground and hard traveling over rough terrain. Sharing a tent with people he didn't like didn't help much either. "I just hope we don't get bedbugs, lice, or the heebie jeebies from staying here."

"Oh, you'll be fine, Bud," Ian said, waving his hand. "Just get us checked in."

Hellee Montrese joined them after stepping out of the

third carriage, clad in a fur coat and a black hat with black lace covering her face. "The mountains are pretty," she said to no one in particular.

Overhearing her, Bud stopped at the door and exclaimed, "Pissant towns surrounded by pretty mountains bring nickels, cities of concrete and steel bring dollars. I swear, Ian, this is a waste of time." He yanked the door open and walked into the hotel.

"Well," Ian said to the ladies, "let's check into our rooms, freshen up, and get some dinner. The fellas will be here shortly once the wagons are unloaded."

———

BUD HENNESSY STOOD at the curved front desk inside the hotel lobby, glaring at Pam impatiently. "Can you count? The reservation is for eight rooms. Do you have them or not?"

Pam tried to maintain a kind expression as she explained, "Of course, we have eight rooms for you folks. That's not what I was explaining. I cannot give you eight room keys without registering the rooms and keys to a person..."

"For crying out loud, I am a person!" Bud complained. "Give me the keys, and I'll hand them out to my people. Any damages are paid by us anyway. You don't have to make this complicated like an incompetent woman."

"Mr. Hennessy, for the third time, when you sign the register book for *your* room, I will give you your key, and then the next guest can sign the register book for a key to *their* room. That's how it works here. I will not hand you eight keys to distribute randomly."

"Why are you being such a—"

Ian abruptly exclaimed, "Bud! Sign her guest book, take your key, and go get some sleep. Making a scene isn't going to help anything."

"Fine!" He scribbled his name in the register book. "There! I signed it," he spat out at Pam. He picked up the ledger and shoved it in her face. "Can you see that? Huh?"

Pam forced a kind smile and held out his room key. "Thank you. Your room is…"

Bud dropped the ledger onto the counter, ripped the key from her hand, grabbed his trunk, and walked abruptly toward the stairs. "I can count!"

Ian exhaled. "I apologize for my brother. It's been a long trip, and he needs a nap and some food. He gets grumpy when he's hungry and tired. I'm sure he'll apologize later."

"No, he won't," Barbara Hennessy stated.

"Don't worry about it, I've experienced worse," Pam said with a slight wave of her hand. "There are seven rooms left. If I could have one person in each room sign for the room key and list who else is staying in the room, I will gladly hand out the keys."

"I am Ian Hennessy. This is my wife, Barbara. We'll be sharing a two-bedroom suite with J.D. and Amanda White. This is Amanda here."

Pam gestured toward the stairs. "Is anyone sharing a room with your brother?"

"No." Ian chuckled. "He's better off alone."

Pam handed out keys until only two remained. A woman wearing a long fur coat and a black veil covering her face spoke softly, "I'm Hellee Montrese. I should have a room as well."

"Yes. You have a lovely room on the top floor. I think you'll like it very much. If you could sign here."

"I'm sorry, but I can't sign my name."

Pam's brow lifted curiously. "Can you not write?"

"I can write just fine, but I don't sign autographs."

Pam said, "I'm afraid you're going to have to sign for a key."

Hellee explained, "Miss, have you not seen the posters around town or the one on your window? I'm the world-famous Hellee Montrese. If I sign that piece of paper, you might sell my autograph, and I wouldn't get my percentage."

Pam lowered her brow. She spoke as carefully as she could to avoid offending their guest. "If I ripped this page out to sell your autograph, I'd lose my job. I don't know that your autograph would pay my rent long enough to make it worth it, Miss Montrese."

Hellee scoffed bitterly. "Well, I never!" she exclaimed before laughing pleasantly. "I'm just playing. Good choice. I doubt you'd get a nickel for my autograph anyway. I think the world-famous part is a bit exaggerated." She signed the register book.

Pam handed her the key. "Here you are, Miss Montrese."

William Fasana exited the Monarch Lounge to speak with Pam at the reception desk. He glanced at Hellee and, noticing the black veil, said, "My condolences, miss."

Hellee sniffled and spoke through broken breaths. "T... thank you. I loved him so much."

"I'm sure you did, miss," William said empathetically.

Hellee whimpered, "It's my fault that he's dead. It's all my fault. I miss him so much." She began to sob loudly.

William glanced at Pam, uncertain about what he should do. He slowly and awkwardly raised a hand to rest on her shoulder to comfort her. "I'm sure it wasn't your fault, miss."

She turned to William bitterly. "It was to!" she snapped. "Giovanni was the best friend I've ever had. I didn't mean to...k...kill him." She sobbed loudly in the lobby.

"My sincere condolences," William said softly.

"Oh, Giovanni, Giovanni!" she sobbed. Her voice was high-pitched between the sniffles. "I swear he looked bigger than he was. How was I supposed to know a guppy filet was so small? He looked so much bigger, but there was just a little bit of meat. Fins! He was just fins. I feel so betrayed."

"What?" William asked, removing his hand.

Hellee laughed, touched his chest with her finger, and said, "Gotch you!" She giggled and carried her two carpet bags toward the staircase.

William's mouth dropped open as he watched her, dumbfounded. He turned to face Pam. "Was that supposed to be funny? That woman was wearing a veil. Isn't that what women wear to funerals?"

Pam grinned. "I think she has a sense of humor, William. That's Hellee Montrese, the famous singer who is staying here."

"I hope she's a better singer than she is a comedian. I don't think what she did was funny at all. I thought she was in mourning."

Pam watched her disappear around the second flight of stairs. "I think this is a strange bunch we have staying with us."

———

THE MONARCH RESTAURANT was located behind the receptionist's desk in the Monarch Hotel. The main dining room had plenty of tables, but there was also a private room at the back of the restaurant with two large tables pushed together, reserved for the Hennessy Brothers' Traveling Show. Sixteen chairs were closely arranged as dinner was served by two waitresses, who constantly brought plates of food and drinks to serve the hungry group.

After four days of traveling in cramped coaches and sleeping in tents, it was nice to finally reach their destination, where they could rest, bathe, and enjoy a good meal. The mood was cheerful, though they were exhausted from lack of quality sleep and traveling in the cold weather.

Bud had napped for an hour but remained grumpy with a sour disposition. "Do you hear that baby crying? Those folks are staying next to my room. I wish they'd shut that baby up. I have to listen to it upstairs and down here." A young couple at the hotel had an infant and were dining in the packed restaurant.

"It's just a baby, Bud. Baby's cry," his sister-in-law Barbara said.

"I wouldn't know about that, now, would I?" he snapped at her with a cold sneer.

Paul Jandy grinned slowly. "Are you a grumpy hog tonight, Bud?"

"I'm grumpy enough to tear your head off!" Bud snapped.

Ian Hennessy interrupted, "How about we just enjoy our dinner and call it a night? I know we could all use some rest. It's a good dinner, so let's enjoy it and call it a night."

J.D. White, the leader of the band, said, "Tomorrow morning bright and early, we'll get the stage set up. But tonight, I want to snuggle up to my wife and relax before getting a good night's sleep."

"I won't argue with that," Amanda White said, agreeing with her husband.

Gus Miller tossed a cherry seed at Hellee. "What do you say we snuggle up, huh?"

Hellee glanced at him without any interest. "Not on your life, Gus. Snuggle up with Bart. He's your pet monkey."

"Yikes," Paul Jandy said to his friend, Gus. "I think ice crystals just formed in my water, that was so cold."

Gus answered, "Irony is cruel, isn't it? You, me, and Bud are the only single men in this group, and the only single woman available wants nothing to do with any of us?" He grinned. "I suppose that means we're free to go out on the town and do whatever we want. Right?"

"I wouldn't want it any other way," Paul agreed. "While these sad sacks are kept in by their women, let's go meet a few. Except for Bud, meeting a woman is too hard for him, it's just easier to pay a whore's fee, right, Bud?"

Bud cast a stern glance at Paul but did not respond.

Gus Miller said, "If anyone wants to talk to me tonight, you'll find me in that lounge over there until I can't stand up straight."

Paul Jandy shook his head. "No, no. Women aren't allowed in there, that's where Bud will be. You and I are heading back to the dance hall to enjoy a few dances with the pretty ladies. I saw a few I'd like to get to know."

Gus agreed. "Great idea! Bud, are you coming with us or sticking to the men-only club?" he asked, knowing Bud would have no interest in going anywhere with him and Paul.

Bud glanced at Gus with a cold sneer. "I'm going to bed and getting some sleep. That's what I'm going to do."

"While you're dreaming of pulling snails out of their

shells, we'll be meeting the prettiest of the ladies over there."

Ian cleared his throat. "Gus, just eat your dinner and go do whatever you're going to do. But you better be ready to work in the morning."

"I always am, boss."

Paul leaned over the table to look at Ian. "Ian, don't you think it's about time I start headlining the show again? My act far surpasses Hellee's fair-to-middling vocals. People are falling asleep when she sings."

Hellee nearly choked on a piece of chicken. "Hardly!" she spat out.

Ian answered, "Paul, Hellee's name draws a crowd. No one knows who you are until they see you. Your day will come when you are the top act, but not on this tour."

"I should be," Paul replied.

Bud spoke firmly, "Hellee is the top act and remains so because she has traveled the world and has the audience. You are a pissant con artist." He shook his head irritably. "I wish they'd shut that damn baby up. A man can't even enjoy his meal with a screaming baby."

"The baby is fine. It's just crying because it's hungry, I imagine," Barbara said.

Bud shouted with a powerful growl to the young parents of the baby, "Hey, can you please plug that screaming kid onto your teat to shut it up! We're trying to eat in here."

The restaurant had fallen silent except for the sound of a crying baby. The young mother stood up, took her baby, and left the restaurant, leaving her irritated husband at their table.

"It's about time," Bud said, his deep voice brimming with satisfaction.

Ian lowered his head and rubbed his eyes, showing his irritation. "Bud, do you see all those people in the restaurant? You just lost potential customers."

"That was uncalled for," Barbara scolded.

"What do I care?" Bud asked. "At least I can now eat without listening to a squealing brat."

―――――

A FEW MINUTES LATER, a well-dressed man carrying a single ivory-handled Colt in his gun belt walked into the room. He had long, wavy blonde hair that fell to his shoulders and a blonde goatee on his rough, weather-beaten face. He spoke in a deep voice, "Hello, folks, I'm William Fasana. I am the hotel security here. I understand there was a complaint about a guest's child?"

Gus Miller leaned back in his chair, his face twisted into a sarcastic grin. "What? Are you a shootist? You know, a gunfighter?"

William raised his brow. "Ask around about me. Now, I heard there's a complaint about a guest's child. What seems to be the problem?"

Bud explained, "It's hard to enjoy our dinner with a screaming baby echoing in our ears. We spent good money on this dinner. Far more than they did, and we shouldn't have to listen to a screaming brat."

William spoke in a soothing tone. "Listen, I know that can be frustrating, but Mr. and Mrs. Neeley are guests here as well and deserve the same respect that you all do. Mrs. Neeley is up in her room feeding the baby as we speak, but her meal is getting cold, and her husband is eating alone. Today is their first wedding anniversary, and Mr. Neeley wanted to do something nice for his wife. They haven't got much money, and now their dinner has been ruined."

Bud shrugged his shoulders uncaringly. "So? Then she should learn to feed the brat before she eats, shouldn't she?"

"I think it would be nice if you apologized."

"I am not apologizing! Not to anyone. I'm paying for this meal."

Ian Hennessy spoke. "We will pay for their meal, and I will apologize on behalf of my brother. I am sorry for the trouble. I'll also give them free tickets for tomorrow night's show, but they need to know children are not allowed. And do me a favor and make sure they get some dessert tonight. I do apologize."

"I appreciate that. A bit of hospitality keeps the peace around here. And you," William said to Bud, "if you cause any more trouble, you'll be asked to leave."

Bud's chest puffed outward as he held his head back. "And what if I don't want to leave?"

"You'll still leave."

Ian spat out, "Bud, don't say another word! Just eat your food and keep your mouth shut."

"Sir," a woman in her mid-thirties said to William. She was an attractive woman with dark brown curly hair and mischievous blue eyes. "Thank you for the condolences earlier. It meant a lot to me." A few snickers came from several of the ladies at the table.

William narrowed his eyes as he gazed at her. He quickly realized that the snickering was at his expense. "You're welcome. I personally haven't had the privilege to try guppy yet, but I hear fine dining does come in small quantities. If you'd like to continue your fine portions, I happened to see a nice slug out back. Would you like me to boil that up for you?"

She gazed at him appreciatively. "Maybe tomorrow?"

William smiled with a slight chuckle. "I'll happily reserve it for you." He addressed the group, saying, "Again, my name is William. If you need anything, do not hesitate to let one of us know. And welcome to the Monarch Hotel."

CHAPTER THREE

Paul Jandy and Gus Miller walked to Bella's Dance Hall on Rose Street. It was a two-story pink building on the corner, filled with lively music, joyful shouts, and laughter echoing down the street. The two men had visited earlier that day to unload the traveling show's props and equipment but returned to enjoy themselves for the night. They climbed a few steps onto the porch and entered the well-lit alcove, where customers could hang their coats and hats on one of the many golden hooks lining the walls of a side room just inside the door. The new white-based paisley wallpaper in the alcove was bright and cheerful.

Above the double door leading into the dance hall's ballroom hung a plaque made of unfinished myrtle wood, with carved letters inlaid with black paint that elegantly proclaimed: *A lady is a lady and must be respected as such.* Along the right wall, hung vertically, was a matching piece of myrtle wood with bold lettering at the top listing the expected rules.

No guns or knives beyond this point.

No fighting, quarreling, or harassing our musicians beyond this point.

Our ladies are to be danced with, not touched, manhandled, or harassed at any point.

Beyond this point, dancing, drinking, laughing, and fun are the only things tolerated.

Enjoy,

Love, Bella.

A STOCKY MAN with broad shoulders and a thick brown mustache stood firmly, guarding the roped-off stairway leading upstairs and the double doors to the ballroom. The man smiled in recognition. "You two made it back. We look forward to your show tomorrow night, but until then, dance with some of our ladies and have a good time."

"Thanks, Dave. We intend to," Paul Jandy said. He was forty-two years old and nearly six feet tall, lean, with long arms and legs that seemed a bit too long for his torso. His straight black hair fell to the bottom of his earlobes. His face was long and clean-shaven, though his thick, black eyebrows were perhaps his most distinctive feature. His brown eyes appeared dark and haunting, set beneath the shadow of his eyebrows. They slanted downward toward his nose, giving him a unique, upturned gaze. He wore a tan checkered suit and hung his long black overcoat, lined with gray fox fur at the neckline and down the front, along with his short top hat, on a hook before walking through the double doors into the large ballroom. There, a bar served drinks, and a spacious dance floor was filled with men dancing with the dance hall ladies while the band supplied the music. The ladies were dressed beautifully in long, flowing gowns, while the men ranged in status from local businessmen to miners and simple farmers, all wearing their Sunday best.

Paul paused in the ballroom, allowing his eyes to scan the dance floor like a hawk searching for prey. "I like what I'm seeing."

Gus Miller tapped his friend on the arm. "I'll get us a couple of drinks." Gus was forty-four years old, five feet nine inches tall, and broad-chested. He had short, brown hair with a slight wave on top. He maintained a mustache and wore wire-rimmed spectacles over his blue eyes. He possessed a friendly, oval-shaped, handsome face that quickly broke into a smile. Dressed in a brown suit, he approached the bar and squeezed between the men standing there to place his order. With two glasses in hand, he turned to find Paul, but his arm was gently grabbed by an older woman dressed in an elegant dark maroon dress. Her eyes were glossed from having had a few too many drinks.

"You're one of the fellas from the Hennessy show that was here today, aren't you?"

"I am."

"I thought so. I'm Bella. I own the place. I had other things going on, so I didn't get to meet you. What's your name?"

"I'm Gus Miller."

"The monkey man!" Bella exclaimed. "Do you really have a monkey named Bart? Did you bring him?" Her excitement was evident in her raised brow and eager expression.

Gus's lips curled slightly. "I didn't bring Bart, no."

"But you have a monkey? Can I talk you into bringing your monkey in here tonight?"

Gus grimaced. "No. Unfortunately, that's not a good idea tonight. You'll see him tomorrow night."

"Oh, come on," Bella pleaded. "I've only seen a monkey once in my life, and I'm excited to see one up close. Do you think I could hold him? Is he tame enough?"

Gus sipped his drink. "You can hold him if you want. But you must be gentle with him. Bart can be a bit temperamental."

"That would be amazing!" Bella exclaimed. "Gus, is there any way that I could get a photograph taken with Bart before you folks leave town? It would mean a lot to me."

He chuckled. "I don't see why not. I'll need to be close by in case he gets scared by the flash and, you know, goes berserk or something."

"Of course. I'm good with animals. I'm so excited to meet Bart. So, who's here with you? Not Hellee Montrese, by chance? I want to meet her, too. I heard her sing in Denver a few years back. She's an amazing lady."

"No. She's resting. I'm here with Paul. He's just a stagehand."

"Well, Gus, have fun, and I'll get you a few complimentary dance tickets."

"That would be great."

Gus walked over to Paul's side and handed him his drink. "I met the owner, Bella. She's excited to meet Bart more than anyone else."

Paul frowned. "What else is new? Thanks for the drink. That redhead's pretty, but they all are. I think I have my eye on that pretty one in the gold and black dress."

Bella tapped Gus on the shoulder. "Here are three dance tickets for you. I told my bartender to give you free drinks tonight as a way to show my appreciation for allowing me to take a photograph with Bart. Your friend must pay for his drinks, though. I hope you don't mind."

"No, I don't mind at all. Thank you."

Paul narrowed his eyes at his friend. "She didn't even ask who I was?"

Gus chuckled softly. "I told her you were the great Landy Jandy, the famous magician, but she said stage magicians were a dime a dozen. Bart is the star of the show, followed closely by Hellee Montrese. Bella is a fan of Hellee's."

Paul shook his head and sighed in frustration. He took a drink and watched the lady in a gold and black dress laugh as she danced with a clumsy young man across the floor. "Hellee Montrese's voice gives out after four or five songs. She shouldn't even be on this tour. I still can't believe she's the headliner and not me." He paused to survey the dance floor. "Yeah, the one in gold and black is the one for me this weekend."

―――――

BONNIE GREEN LAUGHED as she received a small glass of pink champagne from the young man she had danced with. At Bella's Dance Hall, the customary obligation required the gentleman to buy the lady he danced with a small glass of pink champagne, which was actually pink lemonade, meant to keep the ladies sober and hydrated.

"Thank you, sir. You have a nice evening, and maybe we can dance again." She turned her back on the young man and made a disgusted grimace as she approached her fiancé, Jack Sperry, who sat at a table with his friends from the silver mine. She bent down to speak quietly to the men at the table. "He stank like he hadn't bathed in six months. And you think my job isn't hard."

"You look like you enjoyed it," Jack said with a slight laugh.

"That's the secret to dancing. Grin and bear it. Why don't you come dance with me, Jack?"

Jack wrinkled his nose. "I'm saving my money for the last dance auction. It's slower and lasts longer. Besides, if anyone is going to hold you close for that long, I want it to be me."

Bonnie couldn't help the smile that came from deep within. "I can wait for that." The Sperry family had an infamous reputation, and Bonnie had been warned early on against getting involved with Jack, but he had been a perfect gentleman and kept his distance from his family. She had fallen deeply in love with Jack Sperry.

"Excuse me, beautiful," Paul Jandy said, while placing his hand on Bonnie's lower back. "How about a dance? And if you need some extra money, how about coming back to the hotel room with me for the night?" Paul pulled a money clip from his pocket, revealing a twenty-dollar bill on top of a larger wad of cash. "Name your price."

In one swift motion, Jack Sperry stood, scooting his chair backward across the floor while turning to face the man who dared to disrespect his fiancée. He thrust his right fist into Paul's abdomen, nearly lifting him off the ground with the powerful blow. Paul collapsed to the floor and curled up in a fetal position, unable to catch his breath. His face reddened as he struggled to inhale. Jack kneeled, picked up the man's money clip, and shoved it back inside the man's suit jacket pocket. Jack's voice was as hard as stone. "If you ever speak to her like that again, you won't have any teeth left to speak with! That's my fiancée, and I won't tolerate anyone disrespecting her like that. Ever! You're lucky I don't kick your teeth out right now! Say it again, I dare you!"

Gus quickly pushed his way through the circle of men crowded around where Jack had risen from kneeling over Paul. "Hey, hey, hey, Paul, are you all right?" he asked, kneeling to check on his friend. "What did you do to him?" Gus asked, glaring at Jack.

"I taught him some badly needed manners."

Bella moved through the crowd of men. "Jack, what kind of trouble are you causing now?" Her tone was accusatory.

Bonnie explained what Paul had told her. "So, Jack hit him," she finished.

Bella took a deep breath and spoke firmly, "Gus, your stagehand had it coming. You need to get him out of here. It says right on the board before you come in here that our ladies are not to be harassed at any point."

"Stagehand?" Paul struggled to ask as he sat up.

Gus snickered awkwardly. "Bella, he isn't a stagehand. This is Landy Jandy, the World's Creepiest Magician. Or as we call him, the Jester's Magician."

Paul scowled at Gus as he stood slightly bent over. "Shut up." He extended his hand out toward Jack to shake. "My humble apology to the lady and you. It was a joke." He pulled out the money clip and revealed that what appeared to be a stack of twenty-dollar bills in the money clip was actually counterfeit bills glued onto the backs of folded Joker cards. "Nice hit. That one hurt," he said to Jack as he caught his breath.

Jack took the money clip and opened all the twenty-dollar bills. "That was a dumb joke that might've gotten you seriously hurt."

"It did," Paul said, cringing to stand upright. "Miss, I apologize to you most of all. I do have a dance ticket that I was going to offer you, but your fiancé is scarier than me. If you would point me toward one of your friends?"

Bonnie motioned to Bella. "I do accept your apology, sir. But you'll have to ask Bella because she kicked you out of here."

Bella was apologetic. "I didn't realize you were Landy Jandy. Of course, you can stay as long as you treat our ladies like ladies. No more dumb jokes like that one."

"Of course. You'll have no trouble from me." He looked at Jack. "To ease any hard feelings, I'd like to teach you a drinking trick I use that promises to win any bet you can make. But the thing is, you can only do it once, maybe twice, before it becomes known by everyone in your town, so save it and make it count."

"I'll take you up on that," Jack agreed.

"Good. I might get my breath back if I'm dancing, so is there an attractive lady nearby for me to dance with? Not you, though," he said to Bonnie.

Bella grasped a dancer's wrist as she walked by. "Mary, I want you to take our honored guest out onto the dance floor, please."

———

MARY WASHBURN HAD BECOME a dancer at Bella's Dance Hall three years earlier, when Bella was still in Denver, Colorado. At twenty-nine, Mary was one of the oldest women working at the dance hall. Although she was nearing the end of her dancing career, her youthful appearance and flirtatious brown eyes continued to sell dance tickets and earn a substantial amount each night from the last dance auction.

"Wait, I must ask, are you engaged or in a relationship?" Paul asked.

"No," Mary answered with a quiet smile.

Bonnie scoffed. "What about Leonard Harris, Mary?"

"He's just a friend."

"A friend who wants to marry you."

"Oh," Paul said, gazing at Mary. He didn't find her as attractive as Bonnie or the redhead or the other dancers he'd seen, but she would suffice for a dance or two. To ensure he wouldn't get hit again, he said, "I don't want to interfere with another gentleman's lady."

Bella waved her hand toward the dance floor. "Leonard is pursuing her. But he isn't here tonight, and even if he were, he's harmless. Go dance."

"Harmless, huh?" Paul questioned. "Then, miss, I hope the gentleman who asked for your hand doesn't mind me dancing with his lady." He took her arm and led her onto the dance floor as a gentleman should.

"He's just a friend. We have no official courtship."

"I imagine you want to find a husband before you leave this career, though. Am I right?"

"Not necessarily." She had observed several of her friends meet fine gentlemen on the dance floor who formed relationships that often culminated in marriage proposals. Over the past three years, Mary had met several men, but none of those relationships lasted more than a few months. Unlike most of the other ladies, Mary wasn't desperate to find a gentleman to marry. She still had a year or two to dance before she needed to worry about losing her place in the dance hall. The lady who sold the fewest dance tickets and consistently brought in the lowest price for the last dance auction was always at risk of losing her job in the dance hall. Mary consistently ranked somewhere in the middle and had no concerns about being replaced by Bella and Dave.

Mary saved her earnings like a penny-pinching miser, keeping her money in the bank for the day she might have to stop dancing. Unlike many of the other ladies in the dance hall, Mary had a good relationship with her parents, who owned a successful business back in Colorado. It wasn't tragedy or desperation to flee prostitution, or any other circumstance that brought Mary to the dance hall, she joined because she loved to dance, and it paid well in a world that offered few options for single women to earn a decent living on their own. Unlike most of the other ladies, Mary already knew what she would do when she left the dance hall. Her family owned the Washburn Carriage Company in Denver, Colorado, which built various carriages and wagons.

Mary had one suitor who had been trying to win her heart since Bella's Dance Hall opened in Branson, but she continually denied his advances. His name was Leonard Harris, and he worked for the Seven Timber Harvester Company, falling trees, and lived in a logging camp deep in the woods during the weekdays, coming to town every weekend to dance and spend time with her.

Maybe it was silly, but Mary had marriage prerequisites, and knowing how to dance well was one of them. Leonard had no idea how to dance and didn't take it as seriously as she did. Dancing was an art, one that Mary studied. She wanted a husband who appreciated the continuity of music and whose body flowed with hers like water gliding over a smooth stone in perfect harmony. Dancing with Leonard felt like being a rag doll that a dog had just gotten hold of.

His clumsy feet either tripped her or stepped on her toes while his rough hands jerked her around in improvised dance moves.

Mary had thick black hair styled in a loose braided bun on top of her head, allowing her locks to cascade down her neck to her shoulder blades. Her face was round with fuller cheeks, having gained weight over the past two years. Her dark brown eyes glinted with playful giddiness when the band began to play Chopin's Mazurka.

Paul Jandy said, "Oh, yes. This is my favorite dance. By chance, Miss Mary, do you know the mazurka?"

"I love this dance," she said, amazed that he knew the name of it.

He proved to be an exceptional dancer and one of the few men she had encountered who was familiar with the mazurka. The band played Chopin's Mazurka every weekend, and most of the men held the ladies at arm's length, stepping slowly in line with the others in the large circle. Like any other dance, they paid to dance with a lady without concern for style, technique, or timing.

However, the mazurka was a timeless and demanding dance, quite elegant, featuring several quick steps that flowed beautifully when executed properly. To Mary's delightful surprise, she found herself at the center of the circle, dancing the mazurka without interference from the clumsy men who didn't know what they were doing. To her great joy, she had finally met a gentleman skilled in dance. The two of them had become the center of attention.

When the music ended, a round of applause erupted from the other dancers and those watching the two of them demonstrate how the mazurka was meant to be performed. Mary's smile radiated as she gazed at him.

"Thank you for the dance," he said.

"No. Thank you! The mazurka is one of my favorite dances, but no one knows how to do it around here. As you can see, the men move their feet to the left or right, and if they don't stumble and fall, they call it dancing. So, thank you. I would love to dance with you again sometime. What is your name?"

"My stage name is Landy Jandy, but my name is Paul. And yours is Mary?"

"Yes. Where did you learn to dance like that, Paul? The mazurka is not a common dance here in Branson. The band just plays the music, but no one knows it's a dance."

Paul chuckled lightly. "I imagine not. My parents immigrated from Romania, and they loved to dance. It's what we did for entertainment. You are a very talented dancer, Mary. Where did you learn to dance? Not here, I'm assuming."

"No!" she exclaimed. "Dancing school. Listen, I never do this, but we ladies can invite a gentleman to stay after closing time to visit for a while. Is there any chance you'd be interested in staying after to talk and maybe dance some more?"

Paul's brow rose with interest. "I would like that, yes. But right now, I understand I'm supposed to buy you a drink. How about two drinks for dancing so beautifully?"

When the next dance began, Mary returned to the dance floor with the next gentleman, who handed her a dance ticket. Meanwhile, Paul found Gus at a table and joined him. "Well, one dance, and I have an admirer. I've been invited to stay after closing time."

CHAPTER FOUR

"WHAT'S WRONG WITH HIM?" BRIAN NEELEY asked his wife as she tried to comfort their four-month-old baby, Dylan. Dylan had woken up crying and showed little interest in nursing for more than a few seconds at a time. The baby's loud cries could not be quieted, no matter how much Francine cuddled and coddled her son or tried to soothe him. The hour was getting late, and they worried that Dylan's cries would disturb their neighbors in the hotel.

Brian worked at the Slater Silver Mine and lived in the company housing community, two miles outside of town, known as Slater's Mile, more commonly referred to as Slater's slums of shacks and rats. Brian and Francine had been married for exactly one year, and Dylan was their first child. Brian saved his money and took on extra work whenever he could, both at the mine and elsewhere, to save enough to spend their first wedding anniversary at the elegant Monarch Hotel for one night of comfort, where Francine could soak in a soapy tub of hot water, enjoy a nice meal that she didn't have to prepare, wear a lovely robe, and relax in comfort. Brian had worked hard to spoil his beloved wife, but unfortunately, Dylan wasn't giving her much time to enjoy it.

"I don't know what's wrong with him. I think he has a tummy ache. His belly is awfully tight. I don't know what to do for him." Her soft blue eyes revealed the agony of not knowing how to comfort her son.

"Let me hold him for a while." Brian took his son in his arms, tucking Dylan's legs under him to create a fetal position. He bounced Dylan gently as he walked around the hotel room. "Shhh, Shhh, big boy," he cooed softly, holding him close to his chest.

Suddenly, the wall vibrated from the loud, heavy pounding of the hotel guests next door. A deep, angry voice bellowed, "Shut that thing up!"

Startled, Francine whispered, "Maybe we should take him home, Brian."

Brian shook his head. "We're not going home. I worked too hard for this night. He'll stop crying eventually."

"Maybe we should take him downstairs to the lobby then. I don't want to disturb anyone's sleep."

"I suppose we could do that. I'll lay him down while we get dressed."

"Let me try to nurse him again."

The man next door cursed bitterly, and a moment later, they heard the door adjacent to theirs slam against the wall as it swung open. "Open the door!" an angry voice demanded as he pounded on their door with powerful blows.

Brian stared at the door, startled by the neighbor's aggression. He recognized the deep, thundering shout instantly.

"What do we do?" Francine asked, frightened.

The pounding on their door ceased. "Open the damn door!" the man demanded.

Brian handed Dylan to Francine. "Hold him."

"Brian, don't open the door!"

"I have to." Brian's adrenaline was running high, he had no idea what to expect when he opened the door. He didn't like confrontations and disliked altercations even more. He unlocked the door and timidly pulled it open.

Bud Hennessy's glaring eyes blazed with fury. His large hand thrust a finger toward Brian's face. "Shut that baby up! I'm trying to sleep."

"We're trying to, sir. I'm sorry..."

"I'm trying to sleep! But I can't with that baby screaming its head off. Your screaming kid ruined my dinner, and now you're ruining my only night to get some sleep! I paid a lot of money to stay here, and I won't have it ruined by a screaming brat!"

"We're trying to soothe him, sir. We don't know what's wrong with him."

Bud spat out, "Pour some whiskey down its throat. That will put him to sleep!"

"I'm not giving my baby whiskey." The idea repulsed Brian. "We're doing our best, sir."

"Your best is not enough. Shut that thing up or I will!"

The young man at the front desk came up the stairs. He was a large, stocky teenager with a square face, short dark hair, and a clean-shaven appearance, though he was trying to grow a mustache. "Excuse me. You need to quiet down. People are trying to sleep."

Bud turned to him with a perplexed scowl. "You're telling me that?"

"Yes, sir. You are being rather loud."

Bud pointed an accusatory finger at Brian. "They're the ones with a screaming baby! I'm trying to sleep, but I can't!" he shouted.

The young man shrugged his shoulders helplessly. "Baby's cry, sir, that's all I can tell you. It doesn't give you the right to stand in the hallway and holler at them."

"Then what am I supposed to do? I need my sleep. I haven't slept in a bed in four nights, and now I can't sleep because of them. Listen, you little whelp, I'm paying eight times as much as they are to stay here and damn it, I need my sleep! Throw them out."

The young man spoke empathetically. "Normally, I could move you to another room, but we're all booked up. There's really nothing I can do for you."

"You're not going to throw them out?" Bud's chest rose and fell with growing hostility. "Do you understand that I have been traveling for four days and need some sleep?" he shouted, taking an aggressive step closer to the young man.

The young man spoke softly. "They are not doing anything wrong. You are. I mean, baby's cry, that's just what they do. I'm sure the baby will stop crying shortly. But we can't have you out here in the hallway yelling."

"What do you suggest I do?" Bud spat out. His reddened eyes were growing more furious.

The young man hesitated to answer. "The only answer I have is to cover your ears with the pillow and try to get some sleep. The baby will quit crying soon enough, I'm sure."

Bud groaned as he began to turn away from the young man. Then, he suddenly spun back like a released spring, his open palm slapping the side of the young man's ear with enough force to send the sturdy young man crashing into the wall. The sound of the blow was loud and severe enough to immediately send the young man sliding down the wall, clutching his ear in a pain-filled grimace.

Bud stood over the young man triumphantly. "Maybe that will open your ears to hear the baby screaming. It's louder than I am." He turned to threaten Brian, "I won't tell you again. Shut that baby up, or I will!" He walked to his room and slammed the door behind him.

Brian stepped out to check on the front desk clerk. "Are you okay?"

Josh Bannister pulled his hand away from his ear and noticed blood on his palm. Alarmed, he stood up and rushed down the stairs.

Brian looked at Francine. "We need to take Dylan downstairs."

————

JOSH HEARD the yelling from upstairs and entered the Monarch Lounge to inform the hotel's security guard, William Fasana. William was playing poker and didn't want to leave the game. He urged Josh to go upstairs and handle the situation himself. Now, Josh approached the poker table in the Monarch Lounge where William was playing with a few other men. A significant amount of money was at stake on the table.

"Did you get that situation handled?" William questioned, his eyes scanning the faces, hands, and shoulders of the men at the table.

Josh's voice cracked with anxiety. "He hit my ear. It's bleeding." He showed William his hand and ear.

William protectively lowered his cards to the table while peering at Joshua's ear. His brow furrowed in anger. "Who hit you?"

"The man in number ten. I don't know his name. William, my ear is ringing." The anxiety in Josh's voice revealed the pain he felt.

"Fellas, I fold." He took his money and stood up. "Josh, I'll come out to watch the desk. I want you to run home, wake your dad, and show him what that man did. Tell Albert I'll be waiting for him."

"Should I wake up Grandpa? He's the manager."

William shook his head. "No. Just go show your dad and have your mother attend to your ear."

WILLIAM LEARNED about the situation from Brian and Francine when they brought Dylan down to the lobby, ensuring they wouldn't disturb their neighbor any longer. While checking the guest register, William realized that room ten belonged to Bud Hennessy, whom he remembered from dinner. He got a blanket for Francine to cover herself with in the lobby as she tried to feed Dylan.

"Are you going to do anything about that man hitting your employee?" Brian asked.

William shook his head slowly. "That young man is my cousin's son. I'm waiting for his father to show up. If there is anything I know about my cousin, it's that he's one of the nicest men in the world, but what happened to his son will ignite his fury, and there isn't an army in this country that will stop him from coming down here tonight. I guarantee it. Trust me, I want to go upstairs right now and knock that man to kingdom come, but I'm saving him for Albert. I haven't seen Albert get mad in years. I'll tell you what, though, I made Albert mad once when we were younger, and I'm surprised my eye still isn't black. I think

Mr. Hennessy will be sleeping in the doctor's office tonight. That's my wager anyway. Do you want to bet five dollars on it?"

"No," Brian said. "I feel like this is all kind of our fault. We don't know why our son is crying so much. A tummy ache, I'm guessing."

"It's not your fault. That man has had a bad attitude since he arrived." William's eyes lit up when he saw Albert Bannister swing the door open and enter the hotel with a wild look in his eyes.

"Where is he?" Albert asked. He was a large man with a broad, muscular chest and arms, built from years of working as a blacksmith. His dark, bushy hair fell over his ears, and a thick, full beard framed his square-shaped face.

"Room ten. These folks watched the whole thing if you want to know what happened."

"I already know." Albert quickly stepped toward the stairs, ascending them two at a time. He reached the room and banged on the door.

Bud cursed impatiently as the banging on his door woke him. He swung the door open with a loud, "What!"

A hardened fist was driven into his stomach, expelling the breath out of Bud's lungs and bending him over. Two strong hands gripped his hair and slammed his face against a rising knee that hit like a brick. The knee rose again as his face was slammed against it. Suddenly, Bud was pulled out of his room and guided quickly by the hair across the hall, and his face slammed into the wall. Albert released Bud's hair and let him crumble to the hallway floor.

Dazed, confused, and stunned by the attack, Bud tried to gather his thoughts, but a heavy boot struck him in the face. Bud turned to his side to rise to his feet, but a kick to his kidney halted his efforts with a burst of pain that paralyzed his body. The man attacking him stepped to the other side and kicked Bud's face mercilessly.

"Stand up!" the man demanded. "Why don't you try hitting me like you did my son?" Albert dropped to the floor, driving a heavy fist down onto Bud's exposed ear, which caused Bud's head to bounce off the hardwood floor. Blood splattered and smeared across the floor from Bud's bleeding nose and a deep laceration on his brow.

Albert stood and glared at Bud, who covered his ear and groaned as he slowly turned onto his hands and knees. Albert stepped over him to straddle Bud's back and grabbed his hair while driving Bud forward. He slipped his feet between Bud's legs, collapsing him flat on the floor. He forced Bud's head to the side to expose his injured ear.

"You made my son's ear bleed. Now I'm going to do the same to you," Albert sneered. With a hardened fist, Albert swung his arm downward, striking Bud's ear with all the force he could muster. Bud cried out as Albert hit him again and again. Bud tried to fight free, but he could not escape with Albert's legs under Bud's hips elevating him off the floor and Albert's body weight pinning Bud's head against the ground. Despite his desperation to break free, there was nothing Bud could do. He was helpless, and his ear felt like it was going to explode with each pounding blow.

"Hey! What's...get off him!" Ian Hennessy shouted from the other end of the hallway. Two of the ladies from the show peeked out of their doors to see what the ruckus was and hurried to Ian's room to wake him. More doors opened as people were roused from sleep.

William, enjoying what he was watching, knew it was time to end the beating when the other guests began to wake up. He stepped in before Ian got too close and said, "That's enough, Albert."

Albert, breathing heavily, turned his head to see Ian and the others lined up in the hallway. He grimaced and hit Bud's ear once more before getting off the man.

"What's going on here?" Ian shouted. He went to his brother. "Bud, are you okay?" He glared at Albert. "Who are you, and why are you attacking my brother?"

"He deserved it," is all Albert said as he wiped Bud's blood from his knuckles onto his pants.

"I'm taking him to my room. I want to see the manager! Wake him up and have him come to my room." He and a couple of men from the band helped Bud to his feet and escorted him toward Ian's room.

"How's Josh?" William asked Albert.

"In a lot of pain. You better wake up my father."

CHAPTER FIVE

Floyd Bannister had a lot on his mind. He had taken over the management position at the Monarch Hotel a month earlier, and it was going well professionally. However, his personal life had faced several setbacks over the past few months. His wife, Rhoda, was serving a ten-year prison sentence at the Oregon State Hospital for the mentally insane, where women completed their sentences. They lived in Portland, and Rhoda's son had become involved with some dangerous individuals and was murdered. The man who committed the crime was being arrested when Rhoda shot him in the head. Now that she was going to be locked up for the next ten years with no possibility of parole, she had filed for divorce. Floyd had received the papers the day before, and they sat before him on his desk, waiting to be signed.

Her letter explained that he was getting too old to wait ten years for her, and she did not expect to live that long anyway. She asked Floyd to sign the papers and to meet someone who would be a blessing in his final years, rather than waiting for her. Moving to Branson to be closer to his six children was a good decision, but he missed Rhoda. Rhoda's daughter, Maggie, had planned to move to Branson as well, but she had gone back to Portland to visit her mother and tie up some loose ends on her part.

He did not want to sign the papers. Rhoda saved him from a life of sorrow by encouraging him to quit drinking and reconnect with his children. Rhoda's influence changed his life, and his appreciation for her was boundless. Rhoda's request for a divorce for his future happiness demonstrated her love for him, and it broke his heart.

Floyd had been woken up after midnight to hear a complaint from a guest who struck Floyd's grandson, Joshua, and then faced the wrath of Joshua's father. Floyd scheduled a meeting for nine in the morning after everyone had gotten some sleep and could be a bit more reasonable.

"Uncle Floyd," William Fasana said as he entered Floyd's hotel room. "Ian Hennessy asked for the sheriff to be here. He wants Albert arrested for assaulting Bud."

"You know the sheriff better than I do. Do you think he will arrest Albert?"

William chuckled. "No. I don't think he has the courage to arrest Albert."

"Well, let's go get this over with."

IAN HENNESSY HAD TOO MUCH GOING on to deal with nonsense. He knew his older brother could be difficult, especially when he was already in a bad mood. He was blunt, loud, and easily aggravated. Ian understood that the night before had started with a crying baby, but he could not comprehend how it escalated to Bud hitting the front desk clerk and the clerk's father arriving at the hotel while the security guard stood by and watched.

Bud had gone to the doctor first thing that morning, and his head was bandaged to keep the gauze on his ear. His hearing would remain unharmed, but his outer ear would become deformed. It was a painful wound, but the pain would subside, leaving him with a permanently deformed ear. Bud's nose was swollen and bruised under his eyes, but it was not broken. He had a laceration on his brow that required sutures, yet overall, he appeared to have lost a fight and endured a significant beating. However, he would heal.

Bud sat with an angry scowl on his face, silently staring at the floor as he waited for the hotel manager and security guard to apologize. He had not slept for a considerable length of time due to his discomfort and the baby next door, who had cried for most of the night.

"You're lucky you didn't lose any teeth," Ian said irritably to his brother.

"It was a lucky punch, otherwise, that man would be the one looking like I do."

Ian's wife, Barbara, said sharply, "Bud, this is our family business, and we cannot have you shouting at babies or hitting people! You're going to cost us everything and ruin it for us with your lack of self-control. I'm not going to let that happen. You're not the only one that your decisions hurt. You're our show's reputation."

There was a knock on the door.

Barbara said, "I'm going to my room before I lose my temper."

Ian stood. "Bud, let me do the talking. You sit there and look pretty." He opened the door and invited Floyd, William, and the town sheriff, Tim Wright, into their room.

"I'm Ian Hennessy, and that's my brother, Bud," he explained to the sheriff why he was being summoned to their room as they were introduced. Tim sat down and listened while Floyd and William remained standing near the door.

Ian was quick to say, "I know things got out of hand last night, and my brother is sorry for hitting the night clerk. He knows it was wrong, and he'll apologize to the boy. But I want the man who assaulted my brother to be arrested. He didn't say a word to Bud before he hit him and continued to beat him. Bud had no idea who that man was or why he was being attacked. That's assault, and he should be arrested. We are pressing charges."

Sheriff Wright had removed his derby hat and ran a hand through his short, dark hair uncomfortably. "That man's name is Albert Bannister. He's a prominent figure here in town."

"No one is above the law, are they?" Ian asked.

Floyd cleared his throat and said, "In that case, I am thankful the sheriff is here because my grandson is pressing charges against Bud for assaulting him. My son, Albert, had a *reason* to assault your brother. My grandson may have hearing loss issues and is still dizzy from that hit. Bud had no reason to hit my grandson whatsoever. That is a larger crime than Albert beating the hell out of the man who hurt his son. Without cause, I will add."

Bud spoke without looking up from the floor. "I shouldn't have hit that boy. I know that. I hope his hearing recovers."

"Thank you," Floyd responded. "It's a little late for apologies, though. The damage is done. So, here's the deal: if you want to press charges against Albert, go ahead. I believe anyone who hears what happened will pardon him and convict your brother, especially here in Branson, where Albert is a member of the city council and a well-respected citizen. Keep in mind that Albert's brother Lee owns this hotel and other businesses in town, and his brother Matt is the US Marshal. As a matter of fact, when Matt hears what happened to his nephew, I'm sure he'll pay Bud a visit, too. You hit the wrong boy," Floyd said firmly. "My point is, you won't win."

Ian was clearly frustrated. He waved at William. "You're supposed to be the security guard. Where were you when that baby was crying?"

"I was in the lounge, keeping an eye on things. I couldn't hear a baby crying in there."

"According to Louie, who is a member of our band, you were playing poker with him and two others when that boy came in and told you about the arguing upstairs. You told him to handle it." He shifted his focus to Floyd. "Did you know that? Your security guard told your grandson to do his job."

William shrugged before answering, "Well, you better pay Louie today or give him a draw because I took all his money. We have another game scheduled for late tonight, and I don't take I owe yous. Now, if that comment was you trying to get me reprimanded, I told Uncle Floyd that I sent Josh up there. I told his father as well. I don't hide behind my decisions. Josh is a student of fisticuffs, and I'm sure if he wasn't sucker punched, he'd box your brother half to death. I'd put a wager on it."

Bud turned his head to William and scoffed. "Bull."

Ian jabbed a finger at his brother and snapped, "Don't say another word!"

Bud groaned as he slowly stood. "Talk is cheap. I was mad, and I hit the kid. I didn't mean to hurt him. I hope his ear heals as good as new. We'll call it even. If I had a son, I'd do the same thing the boy's pa did. I'm going to my room to take a nap before I need to set up for our show."

"I'm afraid not," Floyd said. "You struck an employee, and I won't risk it happening again. Your group is more than welcome to stay, but please gather your belongings from the room and leave the hotel premises. You'll need to find another hotel."

"You're kicking me out of here?" Bud asked, his voice raised.

"Yes. You have half an hour to gather your belongings and leave our establishment. Your reactions during check-in, at dinner, and last night are more than enough to justify this decision."

MARY WASHBURN HAD COMPLETED her morning duties in the dance hall as quickly as possible and spent the next hour tending to her hair and applying a touch of blush to her cheeks, something she never wore during the day. Normally, she wore a plain house dress until evening, but today she chose a stunning purple silk dress adorned with decorative black lace around the neck, bodice, wrists, and lower hemline. Although she felt slightly uncomfortable leaving her room, knowing the other ladies would tease her for dressing up much more than she typically did, everyone was aware that she was smitten with Paul Jandy, who would be there today.

Mary seldom invited any gentlemen other than Leonard Harris to stay after hours to talk, but she had asked Paul to remain after the dance hall closed. They sat at one of the tables and engaged in a lengthy, inspiring conversation that covered multiple topics without any awkward silences. The two hours allotted for visitors flew by too quickly. Mary knew Paul was only in town for a few days, yet she felt drawn to him like a powerful magnet. For the first time in her life, she experienced the thrill of a thirteen-year-old girl with her first crush on a boy. Mary felt the same butterflies fluttering in her stomach at the thought of seeing Paul again. She wanted to make an impression that would capture Paul's attention. Taking advice from a dancer named Sherry, Mary made sure she was standing on the stairs when he walked through the door with several of his friends.

Paul paused in the foyer and gazed at her halfway up the stairs. He whistled with appreciation. "I've watched the sun rise and set all over this country, but I don't think I've ever seen a more stunning sight. Mary, I swear, you are the most beautiful woman in the world."

Her smile was delightful, radiating a warmth more soothing than the sun. "Thank you."

Paul waved toward the ballroom. "I brought the band. After we set up the stage and all the props, how about I convince them to play a little, and we can share a dance or two before setting up all the chairs?"

"I'd love to. Thanks for staying late last night. I enjoyed your company."

"It was my pleasure. I'd like to do it again if I could. However, I need to get to work right now. I'll try to find you for a dance or two."

Mary glowed when a giggle from one of the ladies hiding around the corner at the top of the stairs was heard. "I'm not hard to find. I'll be waiting."

Paul entered the ballroom, chuckling to himself as he heard Mary rush up the stairs to join a group of her friends who were secretly watching. He walked over to the stage to meet his friend, Gus Miller.

Gus said, "I can't believe you use the same lines in every town we go to. It surprises me how many women you meet who fall for that garbage. You find a new one in every town."

"Well, as long as they never talk to each other, it seems to work well. Never throw away a good line if you can reuse it. The only real trick this magician knows is how to play the part to make them think I'm falling for them." He chuckled. "The second-best trick I know is leaving them a fake address four or five states away where they'll never find me."

Gus quipped, "One of these days, when we return to one of those towns, you'll find some woman from the past holding your kid's hand with their carpet bags packed."

Paul laughed. "It hasn't happened yet, my friend. Mary's a little different, though. She might actually be worth pursuing because her family owns the Washburn Carriage Company. They're rich. She's only here because she enjoys dancing. Unfortunately, she's saving herself for marriage."

"Until you corrupt her."

"I have my doubts this time. She has a solid Christian foundation, and her morals are very high. She is an admirable lady, but she takes the religious thing a bit too seriously."

Bud Hennessy, overhearing the conversation between the two men, stepped away from his work on stage to sit on the edge near them. His head was wrapped in gauze, covering his ear and the cut on his brow. His eyes were blackened, and his nose was slightly swollen. "I bet you told her you were a Christian too, didn't you?"

"No," Paul answered. "I wouldn't lie to her like that. I told her I was raised in a Christian home, though. I mean, after all, my father was a reverend. All that is true. Is it not?"

"That much is true. But I doubt anything else you told her is," Bud said.

Paul tilted his head and shrugged. "Probably not, but I didn't know you were part of our conversation, Bud."

"I think it is beyond your capacity to respect a woman. All you think about is yourself and getting what you want. Lies come out of your mouth just like a drooling dog. You don't find that lady beautiful, but you'll get her hopes up by saying so, won't you?"

"Of course. She's cute, in a chubby, kind of woodchuck way. She's charming, but she became really attractive after I found out how rich her family is. I'm sorry to say, they don't have any sows for you to meet, hog." He finished with a devious smile.

"Paul, when this tour is over, I'm talking to Ian about not renewing your contract and you leaving our traveling show."

Paul shrugged indifferently. "Luckily for me, I can head-line my own show and tour the country selling out bigger auditoriums than you can dream of doing your stupid jester act. Gus is coming with me. I look forward to parting ways, but until then, we all have a contract to fulfill."

Bud hopped down from the stage and stepped closer to Paul. He jabbed his finger into Paul's chest roughly. "That contract is the only thing that's stopping me from firing you right now! You are a slippery snake who leaves a trail of deceived women behind and it's bad for our show's reputation. And quite frankly, I'm sick of it!"

"But slapping the hotel desk clerk is good publicity?"

Paul questioned. "Bud, I'll ignore you just like all the other times. The real question is, are you going to wear that gauze headband during the show tonight? How are we going to change the show to accommodate your failure to keep your hands to yourself? That lack of self-control is what's going to ruin this show, not my ladies." He added to Gus, "You'd think he'd learn that his words don't matter to me."

"What happened last night is none of your business! And to answer your question, I haven't missed a show yet, and I don't plan to. I'm doing my part tonight."

"You look like you got hit by a train."

"We produce a stage show. You've heard of makeup, right?"

Paul chuckled. "Yeah, I'm the only one who wears makeup. In fact, if you let me, I'll improve your appearance tenfold by painting a pig's snout on your face. Hey, you might even meet a real farm girl. Well, if you're attracted to females, I'm not so sure you are."

Bud shoved Paul backward. "One time! What I wouldn't give to hit you in the mouth just one time. That day is coming." Bud turned around and walked away.

"I really wouldn't want to be hit by him," he admitted to Gus.

Gus chuckled. "As many times as he threatens to hit you, I'd think you'd be used to it."

"I am. He's as frightening as the snarling glass wolf on my shelf back at home."

CHAPTER SIX

THE AMAZING HENNESSY BROTHERS' TRAVELING Show was not just about one performer or a specific type of entertainer. It was a collection of individuals with talents deserving of being taken on the road, including musicians who played melodies for the singers, created atmospheric humor for the jugglers and comedians, and provided dark, ominous music for the magician. The props for each act needed to be unloaded and assembled on stage, including the canvas backdrops for every performance. Setting up inside a building was much quicker than erecting a tent and stage in a field, which is how the Hennessy Brothers started their business ten years earlier.

Ian Hennessy was an actor in a Shakespearean troupe before the idea of starting his own traveling show became a reality. He and his wife were always busy marketing their business and scheduling shows in future towns. After leaving Branson, they would travel back east to the Snake River and take a sternwheeler down the Snake to the Columbia River, stopping in The Dalles for another two-night show before continuing on to Portland and San Francisco, where the tour would come to an end.

For the rugged individuals in *The Amazing Hennessy Brothers' Traveling Show*, the word *home* while on tour meant performing on stage and sleeping in hotels or a tent. They had already been on the road for five grueling months, zigzagging across the states, and now everyone was looking forward to finishing the last show and returning to their homes for the winter.

No one was more eager for the tour to come to an end than Bud Hennessy. The resentment he felt toward Paul Jandy was evident on his face as he watched Paul dance with Mary on the expansive but empty dance floor while the Hennessy Band played. Bud didn't understand how Paul managed it, but everywhere they went, Paul could meet an attractive woman and break her heart a day or two later when they left town. Paul was not what Bud would consider a handsome man, he had an unusual appearance and perhaps even seemed a bit sinister. He certainly came across that way when Paul performed his magic act, which was creepy, to say the least.

Bud and Paul had a strained working relationship. Paul's arrogance and dismissive attitude toward the others in the traveling show, especially Bud, made it hard for him to like Paul. He was disrespectful, rude, and indifferent to Bud's authority as the owner of the Hennessy Brothers Traveling Show.

It was Bud who discovered Paul's magic act and hired him for the show. They initially became friends, but as Paul's act gained success, his true nature became increasingly apparent. Paul emerged as the star attraction, and his success brought him money, fame, and a sense of entitlement to do as he pleased whenever he wanted. He had become too integral to the show's success to be let go, and everyone recognized it. In hopes of replacing him, Bud approached the renowned vocalist, Hellee Montrese, and offered her the closing act of their show. Bud anticipated that making Hellee the headliner would humble Paul enough to encourage him to quit, but he chose to stay with the show for the tour out west.

Bud's brother, Ian, often acted as the peacemaker between Bud and Paul. It was common knowledge that the two men disliked each other, but the show must go on. They didn't ride in the same wagons or sit close to each other on the trains. They avoided sharing hotel rooms and didn't socialize outside of setting up, performing, and tearing down the shows. They were not friends, but they had to tolerate each other for the sake of the show.

For the third time, Gus Miller quipped, "Bud, it looks like you had a rough night."

Bud turned his gaze from the dance floor to glare at Gus. "One more time, and you're going to look a whole lot worse than I do. I was sucker punched when I opened the door."

Gus chuckled. "You know I'm just kidding. Are you going to get some payback before we leave?"

"No. I'm just looking forward to taking a week off once we reach Portland. I plan on taking the sternwheeler to Astoria for the week to get away from you fools."

Gus nodded in agreement. "Well, you are the show's jester. You'd know about fools. I agree, though, we could all use a week away from each other. Hey, do you mind if Paul and I tag along with you?"

Bud said with a scornful expression, "Get lost. I can't stand looking at either one of you two as it is."

"For not wanting to look at us, you sure seem pretty interested in watching Paul dance."

Bud took a drink of his lemonade. "How does he do it, Gus? He's uglier than I am for the most part, and he's already got that woman gazing at him like he's the love of her life. How does he do that?"

Gus narrowed his eyes as he watched Paul dance skillfully with Mary. They moved with such elegance and grace that they could easily be part of the Hennessy Brothers' show. It was captivating to see them glide across the floor. "Bud, I really don't know. I've asked myself that quite a few times. Maybe it's part of his magic, I don't know."

"Hmm," Bud grunted. "I'm going back to my hotel to take a nap before dinner."

Gus watched as Paul slowly twirled Mary around, finishing the dance with her weight resting on his left arm. Her smile radiated as she gazed into his eyes. Gus was certain that Paul would end it with a romantic kiss, as it seemed she was waiting for that moment. Instead, he gracefully lifted her to her feet and bowed like a gentleman.

He led her off the dance floor, arm in arm, both wearing joyful smiles as the band and a few others watching applauded.

Gus clapped softly. "You two looked like you were floating on air out there."

"Thank you," Paul said.

"I think I was," Mary replied. Her eyes gazed at Paul with admiration. "You have no idea how wonderful it is to have a dance partner who knows how to dance like a fine gentleman."

Paul smiled humbly. "I had a good teacher."

Gus said, "Everyone's done here, and Gaylon, the dance hall's security man, said he'd watch over the stage. We're going to explore the town before dinner. Do you want to come with us?"

"No," Paul answered. "I think I'll stay here and visit with Mary. I'll meet you all at the hotel for dinner."

"Then, I'll see you tonight."

———

MATT MET his brother Lee on the sidewalk and learned what had happened to their nephew Joshua, who had a burst eardrum from being slapped. Matt then walked to Albert's house and knocked on the door. Albert's wife, Melissa, answered. She looked tired and worn down by heavy burdens.

"I heard about Joshua. How is he?"

Mellissa frowned as she stepped back to invite him in. "He's in a lot of pain. His ear is not bleeding anymore, but we pray his ear won't go deaf."

"Can I see him?"

She nodded toward the stairs. "He's resting, finally. You can peek in, but please don't wake him. He's been awake for most of the night. His ear is ringing, and he is in a lot of pain. I sat with him all night and this morning. I'm tired, Matt."

"I bet so. If there's anything Christine and I can do, just let us know. You don't even need to ask. We'll watch the younger ones if you want us to."

"No. They're being quiet."

Matt quietly climbed the stairs, opened Joshua's bedroom door, and peeked inside. Gauze was wrapped around Joshua's head, with a large wad covering his ear. Joshua turned his head on the pillow and smiled slightly when he saw his uncle. His eyes were red from lack of sleep. "I'm not sleeping, come in."

"How are you feeling?" Matt asked.

Josh began to shake his head but stopped as the light-headedness made him feel nauseous. "Like I can't walk straight. I've never been drunk, but I'll have to ask Cousin William if that's what it's like. I don't know why he likes it."

Matt smiled. "I don't think it's quite the same."

"I'd hope not. You've been in fights. Do you think my ear will heal right so I can lose this ringing in my ear?"

Matt's slight smile faded. "I hope so. Better yet, Christine and I will be praying so. The whole church will be. You know what the Bible says about two or more of God's children praying together. I'm going to believe that it will heal. Your job for now is to lie here and rest. Try to sleep, Joshua. Our bodies heal while we sleep. It takes time, though. I'm going to talk to the man who did this to you."

"Uncle Matt, my dad already worked him over, from what I heard. He seemed like a very unhappy man, and if Christians keep beating him up, he may never find the Lord."

Matt took a deep breath and exhaled slowly. "I'll try to be nice." He turned toward the door but paused and looked back at Joshua. "I...am proud of you for thinking like that. It shows a Godly heart, Josh. You're going to be a good man. I'll keep your words in mind. Get some sleep, kid."

CHAPTER SEVEN

MATT HAD VISITED THE MONARCH HOTEL, BELLA'S Dance Hall, and three other hotels and boarding houses with better reputations in search of Bud Hennessy before entering Shady Ben's Hotel on Rose Street. It was one of the cheapest hotels in town, primarily frequented by men drawn to the wildness and debauchery of Rose Street. Matt expected one of the owners of the traveling show to stay at a nicer, more expensive place. Somewhere known for changing their sheets at least.

"Can I help you, Marshal Bannister?" the clerk asked as Matt stepped inside the hotel. He appeared uneasy and swallowed visibly.

"Maybe. Do you have a guest named Bud Hennessy staying here?"

The gentleman behind the counter nodded slightly. "Yes, he is staying here." He swallowed. "Would you like me to get him for you?"

"No. What room is he staying in?"

"Let me go tell him you're here..." the clerk said, taking a step away.

"No, I'll announce myself. What room is he in?" Matt asked in a harsher tone.

"Room eight," the clerk responded after a brief hesitation.

Matt stood still, watching the man's nervous eyes dart away from his while he ran a hand through his hair with fidgeting fingers. "Is there something wrong?" Matt asked.

"No, sir. Why do you ask?"

"No reason," Matt said cautiously. The man's behavior raised suspicion. Nothing in the front desk area seemed out of the ordinary, but Matt casually removed the leather thong from the hammer of his Colt as he walked past the front desk.

The hotel had two stories, with the first ten rooms on the ground floor and the second ten on the upper floor. Matt walked past the reception desk and turned right down the hallway when a door opened. A man stepped out of room six, embraced by a finely dressed woman who was trying to force a kiss that he promptly surrendered to. Their kiss was deep and passionate, broken by a bit of laughter. "I don't want to let you go," she said gleefully, her eyes gazing into his. "Let's go back inside."

"I have to get back to work," he said with a laugh. He turned to face Matt and froze. "Crap!"

"What?" she asked, then saw Matt. She quickly let go of the man and turned away, covering her face with her hand.

"Ahh...Matt," the man said awkwardly. "It's...it's not what you think."

"It's not?" Matt questioned. "I'm more convinced by the kiss. Deloris, I'm betting Uncle Solomon doesn't know about this, does he?"

She turned back to face him, although her head remained low and her cheeks were reddened. "No." Her hands shook noticeably. Her eyes met Matt's. "Please don't tell him."

Matt offered a bewildered smile. "I'm not going to tell Uncle Solomon that his wife is cheating on him. You are."

Travis McKnight held up a hand. "Matt, certainly, we can come up with a reasonable agreement without breaking your uncle's heart. This would destroy him, and you know that. He's not been well for a while now, as you know."

"I don't know anything about that, but I do know he's going to find out about this, whether you tell him or I do."

"Matt," Deloris whined with emotion. She covered her face with her hands and began to sob. "This will destroy him if he finds out," she said through her hands. "This was a mistake." She sobbed. "It will never happen a...gain, I... promise. Please...don't tell Solomon."

Travis reassured Matt, "It won't happen again. You have my word on that. Listen, I know we've had our differences, but let's be reasonable. Solomon is a good man and deserves better than hearing about this. What's a little fun on the side after thirty years, you know?"

"I agree, he deserves a lot better than this," Matt said, watching Deloris. There was no trace of a tear on her face.

"Matt," Travis said confidently, "what do we have to do to keep this between us? You're a businessman, just like I am. Let's negotiate an agreement that is mutually beneficial for all of us. We already promised this was a one-time thing. There's no reason to destroy her life or your uncle's. She is his world, as you know."

"No. I don't know that. I don't think he'll be all that surprised, to be honest. What about your wife, Travis? Will she?"

Deloris's eyes hardened with offense as she dropped her hands and glared at Matt with a furrowed brow. "What do you mean Solomon won't be surprised?"

Travis's tone became firmer. "Hold on a minute, Matt. My wife can't find out about this either. Listen, between your aunt and me, we can offer you a substantial amount of money to let this go. You can't really prove anything anyway. All you saw was an innocent kiss before anything could happen."

"Nothing happened!" Deloris exclaimed, feeding off of Travis. "I thought I could go through with it, but I couldn't. I love my husband too much to betray him. Matt, please don't ruin my marriage. Solomon is the love of my life. I swear to you, nothing happened. It's not what you think. I swear it."

"The kiss was more convincing. Deloris, the next time you pretend to cry, try putting a little spit on your cheek to make it convincing. Are you sure you don't want to take Travis back inside the room while you can?"

"Go to hell!" she exclaimed. She knew she was caught and couldn't lie her way out of it.

Matt chuckled lightly. "You have until tomorrow to tell Uncle Solomon about this. If you haven't, I will. The same goes for you, Travis. Your wife will know what kind of man you are before the sun sets tomorrow."

"Matt," Travis warned, "you don't want to go there."

"Like Uncle Solomon, your wife deserves better."

Travis stammered. "What you do with your family is your business, but you leave mine alone. My family is none of your business!"

"Nor is my marriage," Deloris said with a cold edge. Her scornful eyes burned into Matt.

"I've said all I have to say. I'll see you both tomorrow."

Matt stepped past them and knocked on the next door down, which was number eight.

"Says the holier-than-thou man as he knocks on his mistress's door," Deloris said with scathing sarcasm. "Wait until I tell Christine about this!"

Matt gave her a cold chuckle. "You do that." He knocked again.

The door swung open. "What?" Bud shouted.

"Bud Hennessy?" Matt inquired.

"What do you want? I'm trying to sleep!"

Matt opened his coat to reveal the badge on his lapel. "I'm Matt Bannister. You hurt my nephew last night."

Bud felt a cold chill sweep through his spine as he took a small step back. His abrupt, rough voice softened apologetically. "Yeah, I feel bad about that. The boy didn't deserve what I did to him."

"No, he didn't," Matt said as he scanned the size, weight, and power of the man through a set of hardened eyes. "I'll be honest with you, I came with the intent of leaving you on the floor bleeding. But I stopped to check on my nephew, and he was more concerned about the condition of your soul than evening the score."

Bud took a deep breath and exhaled. "I'm sorry I hit your nephew. I really am. I don't know what else to say. I apologize for losing my temper. It wasn't his fault, but he got my wrath." He added quickly, "Your brother settled the debt I owed your nephew."

Matt's tone turned threatening. "I better not hear about you losing your temper again in my town or this side of the county line. If I do, it will be me who finds you, and I'm not as nice as my brother. That's all I came to say. Have a good day."

Bud closed the door quietly. Matt turned to see Travis

and Deloris watching him. "You can tell Christine. That's fine. You have until tomorrow at this exact time to tell Uncle Solomon because I'll be knocking on your door first."

―――――

"IF RHONDA FINDS out about this, she'll take my kid and leave. I may not love her all that much, but I sure don't want to lose her. She's a good wife. What am I supposed to do now, huh?" Travis asked Deloris as they left the hotel. The fear of his wife discovering his affair, now that they had been caught, nearly made him sick to his stomach.

"You?" Deloris stammered. "You can support yourself just fine if Rhonda leaves you. I would lose everything! I told you we can't be seen together. Too many people know Solomon's family. I can't believe this! That clerk knows Matt is related to me, why didn't he warn us like he's supposed to? Huh?" she exclaimed angrily.

"I don't know," Travis said with anxiety.

She dragged him into a narrow alley on Rose Street and pushed his back against the side of a building. Her eyes burned into him as her lips tightened nervously. "We don't have a choice, Travis. You're going to have to kill him before he tells Rhonda and Solomon! That's the only way we can keep our marriages."

"Who? What? The clerk?" Travis sputtered loudly.

"Shh! No. Are you stupid?" Deloris exclaimed. "Keep your voice down. You heard me. We need to kill Matt. It's the only way my plans are going to work. We have no choice."

"What plans? What are you talking about? We can't kill anyone."

Her expression hardened. "Then you better go home and tell your wife about me, because if you don't, Matt will! Rhonda will tell everyone in town who you chose to be with instead of her before she takes your son and leaves you. That's just a fact. You won't see your son again until he's in his twenties, if ever. You have no idea how ruthless and unforgiving a woman can be when she's betrayed. I may lose everything, but so will you. Everything that matters anyway. And just think how your son is going to feel when his father is no longer there, or worse, he'll be calling another man daddy. Is that what you want?"

Travis exhaled. "No."

"Then you better wake up and realize we have no other choice. Matt has our hands tied behind our backs if we don't do something. He's going to tell my husband and then your wife. We're both going to lose everything we care about. We don't have a choice, Travis. Matt needs to be silenced, and then we can keep what we love. It's the only choice we have, Travis, but you must do it tonight."

"Me?" Travis gasped, shaking his head. "Are you insane? I'm not a killer."

"Well, you're going to be divorced if you don't! So will I, and then I'm moving in with you because I have nowhere else to go. What other choice do we have? You tell me that. What other options are there? I refuse to end up here on Rose Street begging for change!" Her bottom lip quivered as she began to weep. "I'm scared, Travis." She leaned forward and wrapped her arms around him as she wept.

Travis held her comfortably. "I'm scared, too. I can't kill Matt. I'd be hung here on the street before I could get away with it."

Deloris broke the hug and wiped her eyes and sniffled. Her voice was firm. "You can find someone to do it, can't you? You know more desperate men than I do. Certainly, you can find someone who can do it for a price. I'll pay a hundred dollars. How much can you pay?"

"I don't know. Thirty dollars, maybe."

Deloris scoffed. "You can do better than that!"

"Rhonda watches our finances like a hawk. Thirty dollars is the most I can take out on a weekend, and then I have to tell her where it goes. You have more freedom with your money than I do. Look, I'll try to find someone, but you'll need to pay them. I can't."

"You're a lying coward, Travis! I know darn well you have money hidden away from her."

Travis exhaled heavily. "I don't want anything to do with murdering someone. Okay? I don't want it coming back on me."

Deloris glared at him as she shook her head slowly. "I don't care! We're in this together, like it or not. There are only two ways out of this situation: either we tell Rhonda and Solomon the truth and face the consequences, or we find someone who can do it for us with no risk to us. But we have to do it tonight, Travis, or our worlds are going to change tomorrow."

Travis sighed heavily. "Okay."

Deloris exhaled with relief. "You know more desperate and ruthless men than I do, so you find one. I'll go to the bank and get the money right now. If they will do it for fifty dollars, great. If not, increase the price. I'll take two hundred out of the bank. If I need more, let me know. I'll get it, whatever the price. I need you to come over and get the money and let me know who you found."

"What about Solomon? What am I supposed to say to him if he answers the door?"

"Solomon is sick. He'll be upstairs. Don't worry about

him. You just find somebody to do the job, and that's all you have to do."

"I'll do my best," he said halfheartedly. He added, "Aren't you a bit worried about getting caught? Matt's your nephew."

Deloris's expression was filled with disgust. "Matt is Solomon's nephew, not mine. I've never wanted anything to do with that family. They mean absolutely nothing to me." Deloris's lips sneered. "Travis, I'm warning you right now, don't chicken out like a little hen, either, or I swear I'll pay someone a lot more money to end your life before I end up on the street!"

Travis was taken aback by the venom in her eyes. "I'll let you know who I find."

CHAPTER EIGHT

RHONDA MCKNIGHT WAS BUSY CHOPPING vegetables for supper when she heard the door open. She peered from the kitchen to see her husband hanging up his coat. "You're home early from work. Are you not feeling well?" she asked.

"Daddy, Daddy, watch me jump. I can jump so high," a little boy said excitedly as he demonstrated to his father just how high he could leap off a footstool.

"Not now, son," Travis McKnight said, putting out a hand to stop his son from hugging his leg. He answered his wife as he entered the kitchen. "No, I feel fine. You know, work is work. I have to leave again, but I thought I'd..." Travis McKnight struggled to come up with a believable excuse for coming home early and then leaving again.

Rhonda spoke as she resumed cutting the vegetables, "Well, don't forget we're going to that show at that dance hall tonight. I keep hearing that it's supposed to be very good."

"Ohh," Travis groaned. He hadn't been allowed to enter

Bella's Dance Hall since shortly after it opened. He had no intention of taking Rhonda to Bella's and being rejected at the door for his past behavior, which Rhonda was unaware of. "Um, sweetheart, that's a two-night show. Can we reschedule for tomorrow night? I have to...well, I promised Mr. Chalkalski that I'd fill in for Roger tonight at the mill. Roger is taking his family to that show with the Chalkalskis tonight." He nearly kicked himself for not mentioning that Roger was sick, so he could use the same excuse for both nights.

Rhonda was skeptical. "Roger is just a shift supervisor, but they asked the company manager to fill in for him? You don't know anything about working in the actual sawmill, Travis. You sit behind a desk all day and look at figures and graphs. That doesn't make sense to me."

Travis knew it was a weak excuse, but once he stated it, he had no choice but to continue the lie. "Hon, it was Mr. Chalkalski who asked me. I can't turn him down. It's an exciting night for Roger, and it could mean bigger things for him down the road. I said I would fill in for him. We can go tomorrow night and probably get better seats. In fact, I'll arrange for better seats tomorrow night. Okay?"

Rhonda rolled her eyes in disappointment. "It's just another night we made plans, and you canceled them. You sure know how to ruin a good night." Rhonda's frown deepened as she gazed at her husband. "Do you not like going places with me, Travis?"

"Babe, I love going places with you. You know that. Look, I'm sorry. I just forgot we were planning to go and agreed to fill in for Roger. I didn't think about it."

"You always forget when it comes to spending time with me, Travis," she said irritably. "Supper will be ready shortly."

Travis furrowed his brow. "Dinner's done a lot earlier than usual."

Rhonda turned toward him quickly, placing a hand on her hip and narrowing her eyes into a stern gaze. "We had plans, Travis. I arranged for Sarah from next door to come over to watch Edwin. I'll cancel that too and hope she can watch him tomorrow night." The frustration in her voice was evident.

Travis put on a guilty smile as he approached her and wrapped his arms around her. "Babe, you know I hate it when we change our plans. I was looking forward to tonight. I'll make it up to you tomorrow night, I promise. I'll pay Sarah double to watch Edwin and take you out for a fine dinner too. We haven't had a night out together in a long time. Tomorrow night will be special. I promise."

"We'll see," she said skeptically.

"It will. I promise. But I must get back to work. A double shift isn't fair to ask employees to work occasionally if I'm not willing to do so myself." He gave her a quick peck on the cheek, grabbed a carrot from the cutting board, and left the kitchen to go upstairs.

"Daddy, watch me..." his little boy, Edwin, said with excitement. He stood on the footstool waiting for his father's attention.

Travis walked past his five-year-old son without acknowledging him.

———

TRAVIS SAT on the edge of his bed and exhaled. He did not know anyone willing to assassinate another human being for money. Some rough men worked in the sawmill, and even rougher men worked logging the trees, but none that he could think of were cold-blooded murderers. His blood pressure rose, accompanied by an uneasy stirring in his chest. Murder was never something that crossed his mind. He was a law-abiding citizen with a respectable career, a home, and a family. He might enjoy socializing with friends, gambling a little, and womanizing here and there, but he was not a cold-blooded murderer.

Deloris Fasana was an older woman with whom he had begun an affair after attending William Slater's Independence Day Ball at the Slater mansion. Although Deloris was not the most attractive woman in her fifties, there was something about her that drew Travis back to the same hotel room on Rose Street every Friday. She was fun, and perhaps it was a touch of vanity, knowing that Deloris desired him.

Deloris feared losing her marriage and the comfort that Solomon's two businesses provided them. Without him and his standing in the community, her world would crumble like a poorly built trestle over a canyon, leaving her destitute. On the other hand, Travis had a secure job and wouldn't lose his home or any of his financial standing if Rhonda discovered his affair and left him. But what he did fear was being left alone with no one to care for him. Although he had not kept his wedding vows faithfully, Rhonda was still his loving bride. However, what she didn't know wouldn't hurt her.

Travis didn't want any part in having Matt killed, but Matt posed a threat to his home. As long as it wasn't his money paying someone to murder Matt, his hands would stay clean. However, he couldn't think of anyone to approach with such an opportunity to earn some money. He was too afraid to reach out to anyone, fearing they would spread the word about the offer. From his time working in the sawmill, he had learned that men gossiped just as much as women did.

Travis feared that Matt would survive any attempt on his life, discover who was responsible, and come looking for him. A scar marked his forehead from the last time he crossed a line with Matt. Coincidentally, that altercation was directly linked to his ban from the dance hall. It was a painful memory he never wanted to relive. He had witnessed Matt's explosive side and never wanted to experience it again. However, if Matt were killed, he could find his way back into Christine's life just as he had before her relationship with Matt. Perhaps there were advantages to Matt's absence that even outweighed Travis's marriage.

"I thought you were leaving?" Rhonda said as she walked into the bedroom.

He stood up from the bed. "I am. I thought I left some papers in here. I guess I didn't."

"Since when do you bring papers to bed? Look in your office."

"Yeah, I will. Well, I'd better go."

Rhonda's voice softened. "Travis, you never hold me like you love me."

"What?" he asked from the door.

The sadness in her expression reflected her loneliness. "You never just hold me."

He motioned toward the stairs. "I just hugged you in the kitchen."

"Yeah," she said slowly. "You do when you're apologizing."

"I'll hug you," he scoffed with a shrug of his shoulders. He took a step forward to hold her.

She held out a hand to stop him. "No. Just go."

He grimaced, confused. "Okay. If you don't want to be

held, why even bring it up?" he asked, turning back toward the door.

"That's exactly my point," she said, watching him as he left.

Travis paused to consider her words. He turned around slowly. "Babe," he said slowly, thoughtfully. "If you were an Indian, you'd starve to death because your points are duller than a round rock. I'll hold you later." He shook his head in frustration and went downstairs.

"Of course. I'll see you tomorrow." Rhonda had to change the bed sheets in Edwin's room.

———

TRAVIS WENT to speak with the only person he knew he could trust: his best friend, Josh Slater. Josh was the son of William Slater, who owned the W.R. Slater Mining Works, a company that operated a large silver mine outside of town and was also opening a copper mine in Loveland. As the Vice President of the company, Josh and his father were no strangers to hiring men for the unsavory dealings necessary to achieve their goals.

Travis sat in a comfortable chair in William Slater's office, confessing to Josh and William about his affair with Deloris and everything that had transpired. He finished with, "Deloris wants me to have Matt killed to save her and my marriages. I don't know what to do or who to go to except you two." He shrugged. "Can you recommend anyone for me to hire, or help me out? I don't want to lose my family."

Josh sat in a chair, rubbing his face to hide his amused grin. "That's some bad timing to meet him in the hallway like that." He chuckled. "What do you say, Pa? Do you think one of the Sullivan, Hackworth, or Stone boys would do it for a promotion if they kept it quiet?"

William Slater gazed at Travis and shook his head disapprovingly. "No. You dug yourself into a hole, Travis. We're the mining company, not you. You should have left Deloris alone. She's a cockroach feeding off Solomon's money and pretending to be important in this community. Let Matt tell his uncle about her and you. I won't have any part in assassinating an innocent man, especially a man as honorable as Matt. Not for that cockroach, I won't. I have never liked her, and maybe after tomorrow, I won't have to tolerate her coming to my house to sew, bake, or read with my wife anymore. This might be a blessing for all of us."

Josh spoke on Travis's behalf, saying, "Father, his family is at risk too. Rhonda will take his son and leave him if we don't help him hire someone."

"I said no, Josh." William waved a finger at Travis. "You dug your hole, now you get to sleep in it. Go home and tell your wife what an idiot you have been. Make things right. I don't understand, Travis. You're a father. You have a wonderful little boy, and you willingly risked losing your wife and son for that old hag for how long? That's on you. I won't risk any of my employees' lives to help you take an innocent man's life to avoid the consequences of your actions. I resent you even coming here to ask that."

Travis forced a tight smile. "Mr. Slater, you're a successful businessman. Haven't you strayed from Mrs. Slater a time or two? It's something we men do."

William's expression hardened. "No, it's not. Do you think the definition of success is cheating on your spouse or excuses you to do so? No! It does not. I may have committed a lot of dirty deeds in my business dealings. I'll admit to you that I have lied, cheated, and stolen. But that is business. My marriage is sacred. No, I have never in my lifetime been unfaithful to my wife. I don't expect my son to, and when my daughter marries, her husband better never betray her or he'll end up at the bottom of a deep hole. Deeper than yours, by the way. Literally. I may not be a practicing Christian, Catholic, or anything else, but I know marriage is sacred, and I honor that. You should, too."

Travis admitted, "I don't have a perfect marriage, Mr. Slater..."

"Whose fault is that?" William Slater snapped.

Travis nodded in understanding as a wave of condemnation washed over him. He stood up. "Well, thanks for your time."

William stood as well. "Travis, do yourself a favor and go home and let the consequences of Deloris's actions play out. In the meantime, tell your wife before Matt does and beg her to forgive you. If she does forgive you, you'd better count your blessings and never stray again. Because if she's smart, she'll only forgive betrayal once. Twice is too much. And if you're too much like a dog in heat to stay faithful, then let her go so she can find someone who will treat her right. Your wife and son deserve that much from you, at least. It won't take your wife long to find a real man to fall in love with her, that I can promise you. She deserves more than you're giving her, Travis. A lot more."

CHAPTER NINE

CHRISTINE BANNISTER WAS MORE EXCITED TO return to Bella's Dance Hall and see her friends than to watch the singers and other acts from the Hennessy Brothers Traveling Show. Not long ago, she would sing for the men at the dance hall. But now, she could play the piano and sing to her husband in the comfort of her home, just like her grandmother used to for her grandfather. To Matt's credit, he enjoyed her voice and watched her with the same adoring eyes that her grandfather had when he looked at her grandmother.

Christine gave most of her ballroom gowns to the ladies when she left the dance hall. Of the few she kept for special occasions, it took her some time to decide which one to wear. In the end, she chose a blue and gold gown featuring black lace around the neck and bodice. She styled her long, dark hair into a crowning bun that exposed her elegant neck, just as she did when she danced. Christine wanted to return to the dance hall, looking as beautiful as she had during her time there.

She walked out of the bedroom and smiled at Matt. He had shaved his cheeks and neck, leaving a neatly trimmed beard, and his long, dark hair was tied back in a loose ponytail. He wore a gray suit and looked like a gentleman, except for the gun belt strapped around his waist. It seemed out of place for an evening of such expected fun, but Matt was a US marshal, and his gun belt was as essential as a carpenter's hammer when needed. His smile upon seeing her warmed her heart.

"Christine, you are absolutely beautiful. Even more so than usual."

"Thank you. Do you remember me telling you how Rose and Sherry always said I would get fat and ugly when I married you? I know it's juvenile, but I want to prove to them that I didn't. I want to go back there happier, prettier, and shining brighter than when I left. I want them to know that I'm happier now than I ever was there."

Matt gently took her in his arms. "My lady, every man in there tonight will be watching you instead of the show. Rose and Sherry are going to feel very ignored, just like they used to."

Christine smiled modestly. "Do you think so?"

"I know so because I can't keep my eyes off you. It's a good thing I'm not a jealous man, but I have a feeling that there's going to be a plague of angry wives tonight."

Christine laughed, kissed him, and broke away from the embrace to grab her wool coat. "Grab your coat. Lee and Regina just pulled up outside."

———

LEE AND REGINA BANNISTER picked up Matt and Christine in their carriage. The driver, James, dropped them off at Bella's Dance Hall, promising to return for them at a certain time. Lee wore a black suit and a black derby hat. He was a tall, lean man with broad shoulders and short, dark hair that was neatly combed to the side, along with a thick mustache that was professionally shaped and trimmed. Lee was one of the city's most prominent businessmen.

His wife, Regina, was a stunning, dark-haired woman with curly locks. She wore her hair down over her shoulders, with a white rose clip holding her bangs to one side. She donned a brown gown with tan stripes that complemented her brown eyes. Regina had only been to Rose Street once before to attend Matt and Christine's wedding reception at Bella's Dance Hall. Despite her initial reservations, she found the dance hall to be a much more appealing venue for large gatherings than the Branson Community Hall.

They entered the dance hall and were immediately greeted by Bella and her husband, Dave. They welcomed the guests inside while ensuring that no weapons were permitted within.

"Christine! Baby girl, it's so nice to see you!" Bella said, giving her a firm embrace.

"Welcome home," Dave said with a grin. "Matt, I'm counting on you to help control this crowd. We already have a few intoxicated men who might decide to cause trouble later. Lee! Regina, welcome back. I hope you all are excited to see a great show. I know we are."

"We are," Lee said, shaking Dave's hand.

"Good. Immediately after the show, we will open the dance floor for all our guests as a token of appreciation for attending. We would appreciate your help removing the chairs if you don't mind. If not, you're more than welcome to stay and dance with your beautiful wives until midnight if you'd like."

Christine looked at Matt, her eyes glowing with excitement. "Matt and I will stay and dance. What about you and Lee, Regina? You can always tell James to come back at midnight."

Regina slowly grinned as she looked at Lee. "I know Lee's tired tonight, but yes, we'll stay for an hour or two. We haven't danced since your wedding."

"Christine," Bella said, grabbing her arms with excitement. "I paid for a photographer to be here tonight. I'm getting my photograph taken with Bart, who's a trained monkey. I'm so excited! I've always wanted to hold a monkey and pet one, and I finally get to after the show. That's what I'm excited about. Oh, and Hellee Montrese is here. Do you remember I always said she'd bring tears to your eyes? She has a beautiful voice. She sings like an angel. I'm glad you're here to hear her for yourself."

It was rare to see Bella so excited about something. "That's wonderful. I hope the photograph turns out great," Christine said.

"Well," Lee said as a line began to form in the doorway behind them, "we had better hand our tickets to someone and find our seats while there are some."

Dave pointed at the entrance to the ballroom. "That lady right there will take your tickets."

Once they entered the ballroom, Christine was approached by an exceptionally attractive young lady with red hair named Rose Blanchard. "Christine, you look amazing," Rose said. Her praise was genuine and kind. "You look...happy."

"Rose, I am. I've never been happier. How are you doing?"

Rose shrugged her shoulders. "I'm the number one dancer now. The highest earner of ticket sales."

"I knew you would be. Congratulations!"

Rose wrinkled her nose. "It's not as fulfilling as I thought it would be. A gentleman was courting me for a short time, but he said I didn't have enough time for him, so he ended it. I really liked him, too."

Christine gently placed her hand on Rose's arm. "Rose, isn't it funny how we can have a goal that we think will be fulfilling, but once you reach it, you're more unfulfilled and emptier than you were before? This dance hall"—she expanded her arms to encompass the building—"is wonderful and fun, but being the highest-earning and most popular dancer only lasts for so long. Someone younger and prettier will come along, and then the dancing, popularity, and alcohol will just lead you into a deeper and darker hole day by day until you feel like you have no more purpose in life. That's why so many dancers end up going into prostitution when they leave the dance hall and eventually drink themselves to death or commit suicide. They have no sense of purpose and feel unwanted, forgotten, and that they don't matter."

"I'm not nearly that bad," Rose said with a laugh. "I'll be the top dancer, like you were for a long while still."

"Yes, you will," Christine agreed. "Rose, like I told you before, Jesus has a plan for your life far beyond dancing. He may even have a wonderful gentleman lined up in your future, but you need to follow Jesus for God's plan for your life to happen. That means taking action. I gave you a Bible: read it. And read it every day and pray. Get to know Jesus.

Listen, the show's about to start—how about we get together and talk this week?"

"Monday at noon?" Rose questioned with a hopeful expression.

"That sounds wonderful. Let's do it."

CHAPTER TEN

Iᴀɴ Hᴇɴɴᴇssʏ ᴡᴀʟᴋᴇᴅ ᴏɴᴛᴏ ᴛʜᴇ sᴛᴀɢᴇ ɪɴ ᴀ black suit with a long tail that draped from the back of his jacket to his knees. His bright white, ruffled shirt under a black vest and tall top hat made him resemble a circus ringmaster. The crowd fell silent as he spoke.

"Ladies and gentlemen, welcome to the Hennessy Brothers' Amazing Traveling Show. I promise you'll get your money's worth of entertainment, good music, wonderful singers, some comedy that will have you rolling on the floor with laughter, and even some magic that will make you wonder if it's real magic powers, sorcery, witchcraft, or just plain old trickery. But you must promise me that you won't burn our magician at the stake. Well, not without searching his body for the devil's mark and shoving an awl into every freckle, scar, and mole to see if he bleeds or, better yet, feels pain. I suppose you could tie his hands and feet together into a ball and dunk him in the river to see if he can swim. But please, if you must burn him at the stake, do those tests on him first, for my own entertainment. The great Landy Jandy made me mad today. So, torture him as you will." He paused as some of the crowd laughed.

"My name is Ian Hennessy, and I am your host. I am the founder, organizer, and, shall I say, king of the traveling show. But I am also benevolent and have asked my older brother to join me as co-owner. He has one job and one job only: to look pretty. So, without further ado, please welcome my brother, whom I look up to and love very much, Bud Hennessy."

There was applause, but Bud did not walk out onto the stage.

"Bud!" Ian shouted.

"What?" came a gruff voice from behind the stage curtains.

"Get out here. Didn't you hear me? I just introduced you."

"Do I have to?"

"Yes!" Ian turned to the crowd. "By the way, ladies, Bud is a single man and is currently accepting bridal ads for a wealthy wife with no children, at least forty acres, a half dozen horses, and a mansion. If you qualify, he promises to...what is it you promise them, Bud?"

Bud stepped onto the stage and paused, gazing out at the crowd that filled every seat in the ballroom, leaving only standing room. He was dressed in yellow tights, brown cloth shoes with pointed toes that curled upward, a green tutu, and a purple shirt that clung to his belly, revealing his flabby, hairy stomach. On his head, he wore a floppy green court jester's hat with a pair of dangling ends and bells tied at the tips.

"What in the world are you wearing?" Ian shouted.

"You're a co-owner of our show. A suit! Where is your suit?"

"Well, I figured since you are the king of *our* show, I must be your court jester, as I have no other function other than to be your servant. So, I'm your jester!" He danced from foot to foot, singing, "Derky, derky derr" like a fool. "How's that?"

Ian waited for the laughter to subside. "I am trying to promote your ad for a wife while we are in town, and you came out here dressed like that? You look like a fool."

"That's what I am, according to you. So..." He danced from foot to foot, singing, "Derky, derky derr."

"Fine, be a fool. But I'm curious, what happened to your face? It looks like you and Landy Jandy got into another fight?"

"No, that's not what happened. Well, not exactly. I was walking by Bart the Monkey, and he gave me a good whipping."

"What? Why? Bart is a well-behaved monkey. What did you do to him?"

Bud hesitated, sighed heavily, and said, "Well, Ian, I was a little hungry and just wanted a bite of his banana. He sucker punched me, grabbed my hair, and started kneeing me in the face like a coward!"

"So, a big, strong man like you got whipped by a little monkey?"

"Well, it's not the size of the monkey that matters, it's the selfishness of the monkey. Worse, he made me promise to give him a raise. I hope you don't mind, but he got a raise before he could raise another knee. Self-preservation, you'll under-stand. I'm begging you, keep that monkey away from me."

"A raise? How much more could a monkey want?"

"Your share."

"Well, Bart and I will get that straightened out as soon as I walk off stage. So, Bud, what was it you promised any rich woman with a mansion, a stable of horses, and forty acres, at least, if she marries you? Now is your chance to win some hearts, Bud."

Bud exhaled as the soft sounds of a guitar and piano played a lovely melody in the background. "I promise...I promise to love them until death do us part...or until I've sold everything they own and spent every dollar they have."

There was a roar of laughter.

"Ladies and gentlemen, I give you the Hennessy Band and singers!" Ian shouted as the black curtains opened, revealing a five-piece band and four women in matching red dresses. They sang and danced to a lively tune, and their performance, which included playful antics, drew laughter from the audience. After performing three songs, the women exited the stage to the cheers, whistles, and roars of the crowd.

Ian Hennessy clapped his hands as he walked back onto the stage. "Well done, ladies. Well done." He glanced back at the side of the stage as Bud skipped sideways onto the stage, fists clenched between his legs.

"What are you doing?" Ian asked, sounding frustrated.

"Well, I heard this is cowboy country, and I saw some fancy ladies...maybe a future bride even, so I figured I'd ride sidesaddle. You know, to build some common ground with the rich ladies here in town. They ride sidesaddle, you know. I can, too. We have that in common, you see."

"That's a...that's a good idea, Bud. You need to have some common ground, and riding sidesaddle may just be the ticket to catching the perfect rich lady's attention.

However, as you mentioned, this is some rough country, and I'm guessing the men around here don't ride sidesaddle. That's how a lady rides. The ladies here looking for a strong man might just think you look like a fool."

"Derky, derky, derr!" he sang while hopping from foot to foot. "What do you think I am? It's the role you gave me, Ian. I can't wait to get back home and tell Mother about this."

"Bud, if you want to find a good, wealthy wife to leave in the poorhouse, then you need to be a man because they probably already have a fool or two just waiting for their money. You have to be tough enough to keep them safe and ward off the snakes, spiders, and maybe a wolf, too."

"Huh!" Bud exclaimed. "I didn't realize Landy Jandy was so well-known here."

Ian hesitated. It wasn't the line Bud was supposed to say, even though it drew laughter from the audience. "Yeah, me neither," Ian said to put that unscripted line to rest. Getting back on track, he added, "Listen, it wouldn't hurt to work on that belly a bit. Or maybe change your shirt to be more manly."

"Are you calling me fat?" Bud asked, offended.

Ian nodded bluntly. "No! I wouldn't do that."

"Just introduce the next act," Bud said and stormed off the stage to applause.

"Ladies and gentlemen, it is my pleasure to introduce the lovely Darlene Smith, the *That's Impossible* girl!"

The curtain opened, revealing a young woman dressed in a thin silk dress, paired with tights and cloth slippers, casually standing beside a wooden podium. She pretended to read a book in one hand while her other hand thoughtfully rested on her chin. She was an attractive woman with brown hair styled in a bun. While still holding the book, she stretched tiredly, lifting her left leg higher behind her until her foot reached over her shoulder. As she feigned reading, she scratched her ankle resting on her shoulder.

"Good heavens! I'd crack right up the middle if I tried that," a man shouted, clearly impressed by what he saw.

The young lady lowered her leg back to the floor. She stretched her arms upward while raising the book high above her, gradually leaning backward further and further until her head was level with her abdomen, and then her hips. She continued bending her upper body until the bun on top of her head touched the floor. She never took her eyes off the pages of the book she held in her hand, pretending to read. The crowd was in awe, as "oohs and ahhs" could be heard amid comments expressing disbelief at what they were witnessing. Some younger men made a few inappropriate remarks, but Bella and Dave quickly reprimanded them to maintain the respectability of the audience.

Despite the audience's enthusiastic praise, she continued to feign reading, holding the book between her legs with her hands, followed by her arms and head. She paused as her breasts rested on the floor and her head positioned between her feet. She persisted in reading the book as if she were completely at ease, like someone lounging on a soft bed. She turned the page and continued to read while the crowd gasped.

"Her back's gonna snap like a dried twig," a man quipped.

Curled up like a ball, she ignored the comments and the loud applause. She looked up as Ian walked back onto the stage. He asked, "What are you doing, Darlene?"

"I'm just reading. What are you up to?" she asked.

"I forgot my glass of water on the podium. It gets hot in

here, and you know how thirsty I can get. Excuse me, I'll get out of your way once I grab my water."

"I'll get it for you. Will you hold my book? Don't you lose my page!" Darlene warned.

After handing the book to Ian, she wrapped her arms around her ankles and rolled forward like a ball across the stage back to the podium.

"No!" a man in the audience shouted in disbelief. The astonished audience gasped in reaction.

Suddenly, she balanced on her arms and raised her legs straight up, bent her knees, and grabbed the glass of water with her feet. Then, she walked across the stage on her hands, bending her legs behind her back at such an angle that it seemed impossible, and handed the glass to Ian with her feet. "Here you go," her soft voice said.

Ian took hold of the glass and had a long sip. "Thank you. Here's your book."

After several more displays of extraordinary body contortions, Ian walked back onto the stage, applauding. "The That's Impossible girl, Darlene Smith! Let's hear it for her." The crowd erupted in loud applause and cheers as she exited the stage, her back bent unnaturally so that her face was nearly upside down, almost near her waist. She waved goodbye to the audience, and the curtain closed.

Ian spoke loudly so everyone could hear, "Ladies and gentlemen, it is my understanding that our hostess, Miss Bella, has been waiting for this moment. Bella told me she has been waiting all her life to pet a monkey. Well, up next is Gus Miller and Bart, his trained monkey. Now, Bart is a little shy, so let's keep the noise down until his show is over. That is very important, so please, shhh. Miss Bella hired a photographer to take her picture with Bart, so the photographer is setting up his equipment on stage for Bella to have her photograph taken with the amazing Bart. Now, Bart does many tricks and is well-trained, but like any animal, he can be unpredictable, so Gus will hold on to him in case anything goes wrong and Bart goes berserk. He's a monkey, and monkeys can be unpredictable and potentially dangerous. So please, if you like Miss Bella and this fabulous building, then let's be quiet. Please."

After a moment, he invited Bella to join him on stage in front of the curtains. "Bella, are you excited?"

"Yes! Very."

"How long have you been wanting to hold and pet a monkey?"

"For as long as I can remember. I am very excited."

"Okay. Well, we talked, and we'd like to capture your excitement in a photograph. If you don't mind, I'd like to blindfold you, sit you down, and take the photograph the moment you meet Bart. Are you okay with that? I mention this because we've never had anyone so excited to meet Bart before, and I think it would be special. So, can I blindfold you?"

"I want a picture of me holding him on my lap if possible," Bella said.

"Well, if Bart behaves and likes you, then sure. However, if he is misbehaving, it would be safer not to. Monkeys can be quite dangerous, and I don't want you to get hurt, most of all. That's our number one concern." He peeked behind the curtain. "Are you ready? Okay. Bella, let's blindfold you."

The crowd fell silent as Ian looked out at the audience with a broad smile and raised his finger to his lips, signaling for silence. The curtain opened, revealing two chairs facing the photographer. Sitting in a chair next to the empty one was Gus, holding Bart.

Some audience members started to laugh. Ian explained to Bella, "Bart is quite interested in you already. I think he likes the red on your dress."

Bella giggled like a child as she listened to Bart's chatter while being directed to the chair and helped to sit safely.

Dave laughed loudly as he yelled, "I think you found yourself a new friend, Bella."

"Sssh! Keep the noise down, please," Ian pleaded.

Bella heard Gus Miller say, "Bella, when they remove the blindfold, no quick moves, okay? You don't want your photograph to be blurry or to spook Bart. So, no quick moves. Are you ready?" he asked the photographer.

"Yup. I'm ready."

"Okay, here it goes. Bella, it's my pleasure to introduce you to Bart the Monkey." Ian quickly pulled the blindfold off and moved out of the way of the camera.

The excited grin on Bella's face was captured by a blinding flash from the camera, which blurred her eyes. For a moment, she focused on the black-and-white fur and yellow eyes with black dots staring lifelessly at her.

"Oh, for crying out loud!" Bella shouted as she quickly stood up. "Bart is a puppet?" The audience's laughter roared.

"I'm no puppet!" Bart exclaimed, his mouth moving with the words. He turned his head to Gus and asked, "Is she talking to you?"

Bella's excitement vanished like water on sand as disappointment became clear on her face. She stared, stunned, between Bart, Gus, and Ian. Suddenly, she burst into laughter. "You got me! You got me good."

"Bella," Ian explained apologetically. "Before you blame me, it was your husband who came up with this idea, not us. It should be a great photograph, though."

Bella glanced at Dave and shook her head. "You're sleeping on the davenport tonight, old man!"

Gus was a ventriloquist who performed a comedic show that had the audience laughing along with Bart the Monkey.

Gus received rousing applause as the curtain closed at the end of his show. Ian Hennessy walked to the center of the stage and said, "We're going to take a short break while we set up the stage for the World's Creepiest Magician, Landy Jandy. In the meantime, get a drink at the bar, and for the next few minutes, I will leave you with my brother, Bud, who has mastered the art of juggling. He got into the art by juggling wives, lies, and innocent deceptions, but it turns out he's not a very good juggler. So, he has an ongoing ad for a rich wife, if any of you wealthy women are interested in him. I saw some big houses on the hill and around here, so I know at least one of you must be interested in him because he's handsome...to some *homely*, I mean lonely, old widow somewhere. Here's Bud."

CHAPTER ELEVEN

Bud finished his clumsy juggling and brief comedy skit while the stage backdrop was changed behind the closed black curtains. When they were ready, Bud announced, "Ladies and Gentlemen, I give you the exciting, strange, and frightening, known around the world as the Jester's Magician, Landy Jandy, the World's Creepiest Magician."

The Hennessy Band began to play a softly eerie piece of music, albeit off-key, as the black curtains opened. The music created an uneasiness among the crowd that intensified when the curtains were fully drawn back. The background was transformed into a dark screen adorned with shadowy, askew tombstones draped in spiderwebs.

A man in a black suit and a long-tailed jacket stood at the center of the stage with his head bowed. A tall black hat adorned his head. He lifted his gaze to face the audience, revealing his face for the first time. His face was painted bright white, except for the area around his eyes, which were painted black, along with his lips. The expression on his face was stoic, grim, and haunting.

His white gloves moved in a circle as he opened his show. "Time," he said over the soft yet haunting music, "crawls slowly like a stalking snake, unseen and unnoticed as it moves forward toward the end of time. That begs the question: What is the end of time? For you, it may mean something different than it does for the person next to you, your family, or friends. Every generation has a time to be born, a time to play as children, a time to grow into the teenage years, and experience that first love and that first job. Then, a time comes to start building a family, and the next generation is born. The circle of time continues as the children play, grow into teenagers, and leave home to build their families. But what about the generation growing older? The serpent is getting closer."

He waved his hands to the side of the stage and began a slow but steady hand-over-hand pulling motion. A rope about an inch thick began to slither slowly across the stage floor, moving back and forth like a snake as it came closer with every pull Landy Jandy made with his hand movements.

"Stop!" he shouted suddenly, holding his palms up to stop the rope. He faced the crowd and explained, "But you can't stop time. It moves forward, slowly stalking, slowly aging, continuously approaching." The rope continued to draw closer.

Landy Jandy looked at the rope and kneeled when it reached the center of the stage. While kneeling, he turned his palms up and flicked his fingers upward, causing the rope to begin rising. As he slowly stood, the rope climbed higher—three feet, four feet, five, six, seven—before stopping at eight feet, standing straight up by itself. The crowd was mesmerized.

Landy Jandy took hold of a solid ring and lifted it over the rope, demonstrating that no strings were holding it upright. The rope was banded with black lines in every weave of one of the braided ropes. He spoke, "This is a three-strand braided rope, with one braid being dyed black. The marks are about one inch apart. If one generation is equivalent to one inch along the rope, then that means, in the scope of time, our time, yours, and mine are very short. Despite your importance in the world, your wealth, your health, or your determination, none of us can escape the passage of time. There is an end of time for all of us that, at the very most, is only an inch or so long on this thirty-foot-long rope.

"Eternity's rope would wrap around the earth indefinitely, until the earth resembled an old woman's ball of yarn. That ball of yarn would eventually continue to grow past the sun, because eternity never stops. In fact, the universe is not big enough to encompass the width of a one-inch rope if it were measured in eternity. But your time on earth would still be one inch of that rope. All the days you play, waste, live, work, enjoy, spend time with those you love, and celebrate are yours to appreciate, for your time is fleeting before the serpent finds us at the end of our time and takes us into eternity. What you do with your one inch, or what you make of it, depends on you."

He paused as the audience applauded thoughtfully. "My father was a minister back in Pennsylvania. This rope analogy was his that he would use to try to demonstrate how long eternity is. I merely borrowed his idea, enhanced it, and added a bit of magic." He motioned to the stiff rope standing upright. "My father would ask his congregation,

'Where are you going to spend eternity?' You reflect on that because, as he'd say, 'A more important question, you'll never be asked.' Now, how about some real magic?"

———

"As I mentioned, my father was a minister, and I grew up reading the Bible and attending church services every Sunday. In the book of Exodus, when Moses stood before Pharaoh and turned his staff into a snake to demonstrate God's power and authority, I was bewildered by how the magicians in Pharaoh's court were able to do the same thing. They turned their staffs into snakes and water into blood as well. My question growing up was, by what power did they do that? Not God's and not by one of their gods. So, where did that supernatural power come from? And was it real?" He paused as the eerie music continued. "Ancient Egyptians had real magic. A papyrus scroll discovered many years ago recounts the story of a priest who could revive a decapitated chicken by magically restoring its head, and he even revived a decapitated bull. Another turned a wax figure of a crocodile into a full-sized, very real crocodile.

"Jump forward a thousand years, and history proves that magicians had great power to do the impossible. Apollonius of Tyana, in the first century AD, was worshipped as a deity due to his reputed magical abilities. It is said he could make people disappear, and once he was arrested in Rome, he disappeared...literally. Another, by the name of Iamblichus, is said to be able to levitate and walk in the air as quickly as one walks on the ground. During the Middle Ages, a girl was accused of witchcraft and executed for tearing a handkerchief into pieces and putting it back together again. In the sixteenth century, a magician named Triscalinus was at the court of King Charles IX of France, entertaining the king and his guests. Triscalinus summoned the rings off one of the courtiers' fingers. The entire audience watched as the rings floated through the air into Triscalinus's grasp.

"I started dabbling in magic after watching a magician at a carnival as a child. The funny thing is, I don't remember his name. He never became skilled enough to go beyond a small sideshow, I suppose. His tricks were mesmerizing to me as an eight-year-old boy, although I now know they were basic beginner's sleight of hand. That magician sparked my interest in magic, and I began learning about the history of magic and magicians. Some of those magicians could have been as powerful as the great priests of the pharaohs in Exodus, if we are to believe the stories passed down through history.

"Indeed, I cannot attach a severed head and bring life from death, but if I were alive during the Middle Ages..." He pulled a white handkerchief from his jacket pocket and cut it into several small pieces with a pair of scissors. He then held them in his hand. He pronounced a few unfamiliar words in Latin and revealed that the handkerchief was not only fully restored, but he dropped an egg from the handkerchief into his other hand. Despite the crowd's enthusiastic applause, he held up one finger, covered the egg with a handkerchief, said a few mysterious words in Latin, and threw his arms upward as a yellow canary flew out of his hand over the audience. He said, holding the empty handkerchief hanging from his fingers, "If I lived during the Middle Ages, I'd be burned at the stake."

The audience gasped and then broke into applause.

Landy Jandy pointed at the yellow canary flying around

the building. "But the question is, is it real magic or trickery?"

He motioned toward the rope that stood stiff and upright. "I hear we have a well-known federal marshal, named Matt Bannister, with us tonight. Do you folks trust him? Marshal Bannister, will you please come up here and inspect the rope? Tell us, is the rope standing on its own, or is it suspended in air by some fine trickery?"

"Go, see." Christine urged him to do so.

Matt rose to applause and went up onto the stage.

Landy Jandy motioned to the rope that stood straight and firm. "Please look closely without touching the rope. Are there any strings, wires, or signs of manipulation?"

Matt stood six feet tall, and the rope ended at eight feet, stretching across the stage behind the black curtain. The rope resembled any other he had ever seen, except for the black braid that appeared every other inch. He raised his hand above it to feel for any attached wires or strings, there were none. He found nothing. He peered at Landy Dandy, dumbfounded.

"Well?" Landy Jandy questioned.

Matt shook his head. "I don't... No. I can't find anything holding it up."

"Well," Landy Jandy said, then snapped his fingers. The rope fell immediately. "Now you can touch the rope. Is there anything special, different, or suspicious about it?"

Matt picked up the rope and bent it, feeling the fibers to verify that it was a standard rope. He shook his head. "It's just a rope, as far as I can tell."

"Thank you, Marshal Bannister. Matt, if you would stand right here and be a witness to the fact that I am not using any trickery. Now, can I have a volunteer—any volunteer?"

Many hands were raised. Landy Jandy hid his smile when he saw Mary with her hand up. "How about the beautiful lady right there in the purple dress? Please come on up." She walked up the stairs and approached him. "Please introduce yourself to the audience."

"I'm Mary," she said, her voice trembling with a nervous giggle.

He explained to the audience, "Now, Mary and I have already met. At the end of this trick, you will see why I chose her. However, we have not practiced this trick, and she has no idea what I am about to do. The good marshal is here to oversee and verify that there will be no sleight of hand that he can distinguish, but if so, catch me and feel free to announce that I am a fraud. That is your duty as the protector of these fine folks."

He took a loaf of bread and held it up for everyone to see. He had Mary check it and cut a slice about half an inch thick from anywhere on the loaf. Landy Jandy took the single slice and, carefully, in full view of the audience, tore a circle in the middle of it. He had Matt check the table to see if anything was there. He set the bread on the table, covered it with a black handkerchief, and said a few words in Latin.

He motioned toward the table. "Mary, please remove the handkerchief. What you'll find is a gift for you to keep as a reminder of me."

Mary took away the handkerchief and stood in awe. "Oh, my word."

"What is it?" someone in the crowd shouted.

"If I may," Landy Jandy said, carefully picking up the bread. The center circle was filled with a large golden medallion. It had his likeness stamped on one side, along with his stage name, and on the back side were the words,

"The World's Creepiest Magician." The medallion fit snugly into the hole in the bread. He tore the bread and handed the medallion to Mary. "That is for you to remember me by." He asked Matt, "Marshal, did you witness any trickery? Did the medallion fall down my sleeve or was it in my hands? Anything suspicious?"

Matt shook his head, amazed. "No. There was nothing there."

"Magic. Like I said, I'd be burned at the stake if I had the unfortunate luck of being born in Europe a couple of hundred years ago. Ladies and gentlemen, I have a few more tricks up my sleeve, but let's hear it for the Marshal and Mary."

CHAPTER TWELVE

Hellee Montrese finished the Hennessy Brothers' Traveling Show with four amazing songs that brought laughter, joy, reflection, and praise as her angelic voice won over the crowd. The applause for her performance was loud and continuous, as was the appreciation for the evening's entertainment. While several men and women folded every wooden chair and set them aside, the Hennessy Brothers' Band took a short break, promising to return and play for the guests to dance to.

Lee Bannister was curious. "There was nothing attached to that rope?"

"No," Matt reassured him.

"So, how was it standing up?" Lee questioned. "It stood by itself for a while. And that bird. Where did that come from? Were you in on the gold medallion trick?"

"I wasn't in on anything. I didn't expect to be called up there. But I do intend to ask him because I am curious about those things myself."

Regina Bannister said, "He did mention Pharaoh's

magicians and those other ones throughout history. Do you think it was really magic?" she asked Matt.

"No. There had to be a trick, but it was convincing. No strings were holding that rope up."

"Where did Christine disappear to?" Lee inquired.

Matt waved toward the bar, where a large crowd of people obstructed any view of her. "She's talking to her friends over there. These ladies who work here have been her only family for almost four years now. Bella and Dave are like adopted parents to her."

"Hennessy!" Lee called as he saw Ian step across the ballroom floor.

"Why, it's the Bannister brothers and a beautiful lady. Miss, I hope you can find better company than these two," Ian said good-naturedly to Regina. "I hope you all enjoyed the show."

Lee answered, "We did. I'm glad we came. We might even come back tomorrow night to see it again. I have a question, though. The magician's rope, how did it stand up like that?"

Ian took a deep breath and shrugged. "I get asked that question everywhere we go. I'll tell you the honest truth, Landy Jandy has been touring with us for a few years now, and he still won't tell me how it's done. I've seen Landy do some unbelievable things, though. You could ask him how he does it, but he won't tell you. Magicians are very secretive. Come back tomorrow night. He never does the same trick twice. That's part of his secret."

CHAPTER THIRTEEN

LEONARD HARRIS HAD SPENT THE DAY CUTTING timber eight miles outside of town in the Blue Mountains. The life of a lumberjack was filled with many dangers, from the obvious risk of a tree falling the wrong way to the peril of a tree splitting, which could kick back unexpectedly. There were numerous other hazards in the logging industry, but only one was known as a widowmaker. As it happened, Leonard was one step away from becoming the next victim of a widowmaker. A branch, weighed down by freezing rain overnight, snapped free just as Leonard was walking beneath it. The heavy limb slammed toward the ground, striking the side of Leonard's face. The impact knocked him to the ground, and the branch landed on top of him.

For a moment, he lay there, staring at the black gloss of a piece of obsidian that was mostly hidden in the ground. The men he worked with quickly went to his side and helped him to his feet, confirming that he was all right. The right side of his face stung as if a thousand bees were tearing away his skin while he rubbed it, feeling the slight bleeding from the deep scratches that extended from his right upper forehead down to his lower chin, including a cut on his nose.

Leonard knew he was lucky. Just a half-inch to the right, and he would have been killed by the unexpected widow-maker. Despite the close call and the discomfort of his minor injuries, he bent down and picked up the piece of obsidian. The shiny black, glass-like rock was not uncommon in the Blue Mountains, but he had never found a piece before. He had hoped it might be an arrowhead or spearhead, but it was merely a chunk measuring between three and four inches long, with a smooth curve on one end and a sharp edge on the other. He put it in his pocket, thinking it could have been used as a knife for chopping roots by some ancient Indian in the past, possibly.

He was excited because it was Friday, and he would get to see Mary at the dance hall. It promised to be a very special night because he knew Mary was not working due to the traveling show performing over the weekend. He looked forward to watching the entertainment with her, but what he was most excited about was having Mary to himself without other men pushing their dance tickets into her hands and taking her away from him. Leonard had been wanting to court her for a long time.

The week before, Mary invited him to stay after closing for extra time to visit and get to know each other even better. It was always a privilege to be asked to stay late, but last week she had a stiff neck and invited him to massage her neck and shoulders. It was a step forward in their relationship that she felt comfortable enough to ask him to rub his fingers and hands over her neck and shoulders. He was convinced that the day was fast approaching when she would agree to become his lady. Leonard knew deep down that Mary would be his sweetheart by the end of the weekend, and they would be officially courting.

He left the lumber camp with the other men on one of the wagons taking them to town for the weekend. Leonard lived with his brother Fletcher, sister-in-law Jenny, and their two children on weekends. Fletcher Harris had recently purchased his own company after working at the sawmill for years to save enough money. Now he owned the only nightmen service in Branson and was making a good living for his family. Fletcher retained the original company's name, Branson's Nightmen Service, to clean personal, public, and company privies and haul the waste away. The job was filthy, smelly, and extremely unsanitary, but it was a necessary profession that no one else wanted to undertake. Fletcher acquired the company at a fair price, and the three-man crew worked at night while the city slept. Although Leonard was offered a position with his older brother, he had no desire to scoop human waste for a living.

Leonard bathed at the local bathhouse on Rose Street and cleaned up, though he was unable to shave due to multiple scratches. Despite his injured face and a week's growth of whiskers, he hurried to Bella's Dance Hall to watch the Hennessy Brothers' Amazing Traveling Show with Mary. He had never seen such a line of townspeople, both men and women, waiting to get inside Bella's Dance Hall before. The line extended outside, and by the time he got inside, it was hard to find Mary. He could not locate her in the crowd until the magician Landy Jandy called her up on stage.

Mary looked as beautiful as ever while she climbed the stairs. Suddenly, Leonard felt the pangs of deep jealousy cut through him like the teeth of a saw blade tearing at his flesh, one tooth at a time, cutting deeper with every gaze, touch, and word from Landy Jandy as he took her hand. It wasn't verbal, and it wasn't just the contact of her hand, but something felt different about Mary. It was the way she looked at the magician with lingering eyes, and the smile on her face was different from the one she usually wore when speaking to Leonard. He suddenly realized why he was filled with an unreasonable sweltering fury: Mary gazed at the magician the way he longed for her to gaze at him.

When the show ended, Leonard helped remove the folding chairs and then tried to navigate through a large crowd to get closer to the bar. He asked Mary's fellow dancer, Sherry Stewart, if she had seen Mary.

Sherry had already had her fair share of drinks and was surrounded by four men craving her attention. "Len, your face!" she shouted with a humored laugh. "Were you kissing on a porcupine up there in those woods? Desperate times call for desperate measures. Am I right?" she teased with a laugh.

He smiled good-naturedly at the teasing. He explained, "A limb hit me. Do you know where Mary is?"

Sherry snickered, a mischievous gleam in her eyes. "With her new man," Sherry answered with a growing grin, waiting to see his reaction.

"Who?" he questioned. Her words felt as if the world's strongest man had hit him in the gut.

"The magician Landy Jandy. She asked him to stay after last night, and now she is smitten. I've never seen her so taken by a man before. It's too bad for you, Leonard. But the good news is that Loretta thinks you're handsome and would make a good wife. You should court Loretta."

"I don't want to court Loretta," he spat out, offended by such a suggestion.

"Mary's being courted by the magic man, she won't even notice you anymore. She told me that he has magic fingers when he rubbed her neck and feet last night." Sherry observed Leonard's reaction and was not disappointed by the troubled frown that sagged at the corners of his lips.

Leonard gazed around the large crowd and spotted Mary standing near Landy Jandy, looking at the medallion he had given her on stage.

———

"I LOVE IT," Mary said, gazing at the medallion. "I'll lean it against the mirror on my vanity. Thank you."

Landy Jandy was still in costume with his face painted, leaning one shoulder against the wall as they spoke closely together. "Is that so you can see my ugly mug every morning when you wake up?"

She smiled shyly. "Maybe."

"Ohhh," he teased. "I'd like to have our photograph taken so I can keep a likeness of you with me on my travels. I would look at it all the time until I either came back to you or convinced you to join me."

"Stop it." She laughed, lightly slapping his arm.

"I mean it. We have a photographer here. Let's take advantage of it while we can."

An older man approached and asked, "Excuse me, but how did you make that rope stand up?"

Landy raised his brows. "Magic."

"No, seriously. How did you do that, and what about

the bird trick? That was a live bird. It's still flying around in here."

Landy Jandy looked up to see the canary flying to a new spot to rest. He smiled at Mary. "Well, sir, if you can't explain it, then maybe you should accept that I just did...in a single word: magic. It's what I do. Creepy, isn't it?"

"Are you into witchcraft or something?"

Landy laughed. "No, sir. I assure you, not. The secret to being a magician is to keep the public guessing. Now, if you'll excuse me, we're right in the middle of a vital conversation of the utmost urgency." He noticed the man standing back, listening to them with a scratched-up face. The jealousy in the man's eyes clearly indicated he was the friend of Mary's who wanted to court her. He shifted his gaze back to Mary. "What do you say, Mary? Shall we get a photograph together?"

"Not until you wash that paint off your face. If I sent a photograph of you looking like that to my parents, they'd wonder if I was courting a clown."

Landy raised his brow inquisitively and lifted his voice slightly. "Courting? I do like the sound of that."

"Oh, stop it!" Mary said with a flirtatious laugh and a light slap on his arm. She knew she had let the word slip.

He laughed. "Okay. I'll go wash my face. And then we'll get a photograph together."

Taking the opportunity to talk to Mary, Leonard forced an awkward smile as he approached her. Her attention was focused on Landy Jandy, who strolled toward the kitchen.

"Did you like the show, Mary?" Leonard asked.

"I did. It's nice to see you." Her quick smile faded too quickly to be convincing. She turned her head back toward the kitchen, waiting.

The sharp teeth of jealousy's saw blade cut a little deeper. "Can I see your medallion?"

"Sure," she said, handing it to him.

The stamped likeness of Landy Jandy stirred a sense of disdain in Leonard's stomach. Who was he to compete with a man who carried medallions featuring his likeness? "That's nice," Leonard said kindly as he handed it back to her. "They're not selling dance tickets tonight, but do you want to dance when the music starts?"

Mary wrinkled her nose. "Not tonight, Leonard. I never get a night off to socialize and enjoy myself. The last thing I feel like doing is dancing."

"Would you like to sit down and talk? I could massage your neck."

Mary explained in her usual soft voice, "Leonard, I already promised Paul that we'd sit for a photograph and spend this evening talking. I'm sorry, but he's leaving town in a couple of days, and I'd like to get to know him better."

"Who is Paul?"

Mary held the medallion up. "Paul is Landy Jandy."

"The magician? You know his real name?" A swirling sensation in his stomach rose like vomit, carrying the bitter taste of indignation.

"Yes. I met him yesterday. He's a very nice man, and he is an amazing dancer. I haven't had this much fun dancing since dancing with my father."

Leonard grunted irritably. "I heard he stayed after closing last night."

Mary rolled her eyes. "From whom?"

"Sherry."

Mary frowned. "Of course. Well, listen, Sherry would be a fun person for you to talk to and dance with tonight. We can talk and dance next weekend."

Leonard spat out quickly, "Sherry doesn't make me feel the way you do. I don't want to talk to her."

"We can talk next week," Mary said with a growing smile as Paul Jandy emerged from the kitchen with a freshly washed face.

"Well, shall we get our photograph taken?" Paul asked. He noticed Leonard. "I hope I'm not interrupting anything important."

"No. Leonard's just a friend."

"Leonard?" Paul questioned, extending his hand to shake while scanning the man's face. "Well, any friend of Mary's is a friend of mine. I'm Paul Jandy."

"Leonard Harris." He squeezed Paul's hand in a firm grip that buckled the magician's bony fingers. He didn't like Paul.

"I see," Paul said, relieved that Leonard released his hand. He could feel the man's hostility in the aggressive, tight squeeze. He could see the jealousy boiling in Leonard's eyes. Suddenly, an idea came to him, bringing a slow grin. "May I ask what happened to your face? You're all scratched up like you lost a fight with a potato grater."

"I meant to ask you what happened," Mary said as she noticed the scratches for the first time.

"A limb fell from a tree and scraped me up pretty badly. If I had been one step to the right, I'd be dead."

"Oh, my!" Mary said. "I'm glad you're okay. Thank Jesus for that."

"Thank you," he said. "It knocked me down, and that's where I found this for you," he said, reaching into his pocket.

Paul interrupted him, "Wait! Hold that thought. I'd like to share a business idea you might want to consider. If I took the black makeup I use and rubbed it into your scratches, you could pass as a zebra hybrid, which is a close cousin to an ass. The public would believe it. That's money right there." He didn't appreciate having his hand squeezed by the stronger man.

Leonard pressed his lips together and nodded slowly. He understood it was an insult aimed at him.

Paul clarified quickly, "I didn't mean that in a derogatory way. I meant you are cut to shreds. But it gave me an idea for the show. Thank you for that," he said sincerely. "Hey, good luck finding a lady tonight looking the way you do." He chuckled and spoke to Mary, "You and I have a photograph to get taken."

"Why are you two having a photograph taken together?" Leonard abruptly questioned. "You don't know her, nor does she know you."

"Leonard, it's fine," Mary said.

Paul gazed at Leonard and couldn't help but smile. "Are you her fiancé? Brother or father?"

Mary replied swiftly, "No, he's just a friend. He's a dance hall customer. That's all."

"Well?" Paul asked Leonard.

"No, I'm not," Leonard admitted slowly. He felt dejected by Mary's response. His affection for her was as genuine as the cold rain falling outside the dance hall, however, she apparently did not feel the same.

Paul continued, "So, you're not her beau, courting her, or engaged. That only leaves one option: what we do is none of your business. I'd suggest you get your photograph taken too, but it would be a waste of money. Your photograph would come out looking like some embittered ex-wife took a knife and scratched your likeness to shreds."

"It's not that bad, Leonard," Mary said kindly. "I'm glad you're okay. Go dance with Sherry or someone. I'll talk to you later." She added to Paul, "I would like a photograph with you, too."

"Can you excuse me for a moment?" Paul said as he hurried through a crowd of people, wrapping his arm around Gus to drag him away from the lady he was talking to. The excitement in his voice couldn't be contained. "Gus, I had a brainstorm! I am going to harass, push, and ride that Leonard fella who wants to court Mary until he snaps. I have a brilliant idea! Watch and learn, buddy, watch and learn."

"What are you talking about?" Gus asked. "Don't cause any trouble. Bud's already got it in for you."

Paul laughed. "No, it's brilliant. I'll explain later tonight, but I'm going to push that man to his limits and beyond. You'll love it when I tell you."

———

LEONARD WAS STUNNED by Mary's indifference as he watched the two of them walk toward the stage. His irritation grew when Paul placed his hand on her lower back to guide her up the stairs. She did not flinch, sidestep, or seem to mind. Frustrated, Leonard went to the bar, ordered a drink, and then carried it to a spot where he could watch Mary and Paul pose for a photograph. They sat close together, holding hands. Leonard gritted his teeth tightly as a sneer lifted one side of his lips slightly. He noticed a heavy, bearded man suddenly standing at his side, his blackened eyes fixed on them as well. Although the man was dressed in an ordinary suit, Leonard recognized him as the man who played the part of the jester.

"I heard you like her?" he asked, pointing a finger at Mary.

"What's it to you?" Leonard replied, not interested in making small talk with anyone.

"I'm Bud Hennessy, Landy Jandy works for me. That woman is a fool to fall for him. I've seen it everywhere we go. Paul Jandy is a swindler, liar, and cheat. But women don't stand a chance against his charms and sweet talk. He's a magician in more ways than one, or maybe he's more than a magician. Either way, he always gets the lady he sets his sights on."

"What does that mean?" Leonard asked.

Bud took a deep breath and exhaled. "It means I'm doing you a favor. If that lady means as much to you as I heard, you better step in and protect her," Bud said, tapping Leonard's abdomen before walking away.

"Protect her from what?"

Bud stopped and pointed toward the stage where Paul was with Mary. "Him. Do you think he really wants a photograph with her? No. It's just another illusion to get what he wants from her. I've seen it all before. If you like, love, or care about her, you'd better interfere while you can because you don't have long."

CHAPTER FOURTEEN

THE BAND PLAYED A SOOTHING INSTRUMENTAL piece that tugged at the heartstrings of many couples who had come to see the Hennessy Brothers' show to step onto the ballroom dance floor and hold their partners as they danced. Perhaps no couple danced closer together than Matt and Christine. He held her in his arms and gazed into her eyes as they swayed to the music.

"Do you miss dancing here?" Matt asked. Christine had spent a considerable amount of time chatting with her friends throughout the evening at the dance hall.

"I miss dancing with you. I don't miss anything else. The girls are still the same: gossiping about everyone and everything. You remember Mary, the quiet and sweet Mary? Rose and Sherry were quick to tell me that Mary had taken a liking to the magician and had him stay after closing last night. Her friend Leonard isn't very happy about it."

"I remember Leonard," Matt said.

"Nothing's changed, he's still trying to court her. The

girls are snickering because Leonard is moping around Mary while she's trying to talk to the magician. Rose thinks Mary has been put under a spell because Mary has never acted so smitten before. I see Mary dancing with the magician over there." She spoke quietly, "Matt, turn me around slowly to see if I can spot Leonard. He may have left. Nope, there he is by the bar watching Mary. He doesn't look like he's moping, he looks hurt to me."

Matt guided Christine in a slow turn until he could see the bar. "He looks devastated. I can't say I don't empathize with him, though. I probably looked the same way once or twice."

Christine grinned as she said, "That's the cost of falling for a dance hall girl."

"That's true," he said. "But I wouldn't have it any other way. I still don't know what I ever did right to have you as my wife."

"What you did isn't the question. I fell in love with who you are. I'm still in love with who you are."

Matt paused the dance, placed his hands on Christine's cheeks, and kissed her in the middle of the dance floor. "I hope so, because I plan on spending the next fifty, sixty, or seventy years with you."

MARY FELT safe in Paul's embrace. They had danced several times, but now, with the soft music, they could sway rhythmically in each other's arms. For the first time in a long while, Mary felt she could draw closer to a man with whom she enjoyed dancing. She breathed in the scent of the same perfume that Rose Blanchard often wore. She wasn't sure what the name of the perfume was, but the fragrance on Paul's neck pleased her senses. Mary could feel the tempting yearning to look into his eyes and bring her lips closer to his, but she kept her cheek on his shoulder and gazed at the floor, occasionally smiling at a friend or two who were dancing nearby.

Of all the ladies Mary met at the dance hall, she held Christine in the highest esteem for her integrity, faith, and kind nature, despite the tragedies she had endured. Christine had emerged from the darkest tunnel a young mother could face, shining brightly. Mary had never lost her husband to a senseless murder or experienced the death of her only child like Christine had. Mary had never known heartbreak on the scale that Christine suffered. Now, Christine was married to a man who loved her and treated her like a queen. Christine was happy, and it showed not just in her eyes but in the contented expression on her face as she danced with her husband.

Christine was never desperate to find a husband while she worked at the dance hall. She met Matt, and their friendship blossomed into an inseparable love that rivaled any love story she had ever heard or read in fiction novels. It was the kind of love that Mary longed for—the type of love that would honor and cherish her enough to make her the most important person in her husband's life. There was no doubt that Christine and Matt would be married for the rest of their lives, and she was confident their love would shine brighter as the years went by. That was the kind of love that Mary wanted to find.

She couldn't say for sure, but if Paul felt the same yearning and desire to be in her company as she longed to be in his, then maybe after all these years, she might finally have found the one man she had been praying to meet.

Like an answer to prayer, Paul's hand left her back and

cupped her chin, lifting her gaze to softly meet his. Gradually, his lips descended to caress hers with a gentle, tender touch. It was all Mary needed to part her lips, close her eyes, and wrap her arms around his neck in a deep, fully engaged kiss.

Her heart pounded. She had not surrendered to kissing a man so thoroughly in a long time. Mary knew her friends at the dance hall would tease her about it later, but she couldn't help herself. Paul was everything she had been praying for, except maybe he wasn't a Christian. She had asked him if he was the night before, and he had answered the question vaguely, saying that he had been raised in the church and that his father was a minister. For the life of her, she could not remember how the subject shifted to her parents and their occupations. It was uncanny how quickly conversations could change to new topics when meeting someone new for the first time. There was so much to discuss and so much she wanted to know about him, but there was so little time.

His lips were soft, and the kiss felt warm and passionate. If a woman could dream of the perfect first kiss, Paul had just perfected it. The kiss lasted longer than Mary had expected, and when their lips parted, their eyes locked in a silent gaze for a moment. "That was magic," he whispered just loud enough for her to hear over the band.

"Was it magic?"

"No," he said. "That was fate."

"You better kiss me again to make sure, then," she whispered.

"I better." His lips pressed against hers in another passionate kiss.

———

LEONARD HARRIS'S fist coiled tightly as he watched the woman he longed to be with kissing another man. He felt tempted to storm through the other couple's dance, rip her from Paul's grasp, and break the man's jaw with his clenched fist. Leonard had pursued Mary for months, gifting her trinkets, affordable jewelry, and most recently, rabbit-lined hand muffs to keep her hands warm as winter approached. He cared for her deeply and felt profoundly embittered to think she would choose a man she had just met, who was leaving in two days, over him.

He had always been a loyal friend to her. He could tell when she was joyful, sad, or burdened just by the way she walked. Leonard may not have had an education, but he could read her expressions like a well-read book. There was no other man in the building who could understand her the way he could. Even if her smile never faded, the truth was revealed in her eyes, which anyone willing to invest time to know her could easily read, as he had. Mary would have to be blind not to notice how committed he was to her. And still, she closed her eyes and kissed a stranger, her arms wrapped around him like a newlywed bride on her wedding night.

Anger, like a bitter stew, swirled in Leonard's stomach, threatening to erupt, but he held himself back from storming across the dance floor and yanking her from the magician's arms. His eyes hardened as he sipped his drink.

Sherry Stewart was enjoying her evening to the fullest. Rarely did the ladies get a night off work to drink with their companions. She was talking with two men, laughing, flirting, and occasionally dancing. With a playful smile on her lips, she approached Leonard, "Hey, Lenny, the next time you cut a tree down and watch it fall, picture Mary falling for Landy Jandy. She's falling hard and she'll be horizontal by midnight." She laughed while fluttering her eyebrows insinuatingly.

"Sherry, I'm not in the mood to listen to you," Leonard said firmly. There was no humor in his tone.

Sherry laughed as she patted his shoulder empathetically. "Loretta's looking for a husband. She's at the bottom of the totem pole and the next dancer being forced out. She needs a husband, Lenny. She's pretty enough, don't you think?"

Leonard rolled his eyes impatiently. "I'm not interested in Loretta, Sherry. Go bother someone else about marrying her."

Sherry spoke bluntly, "You're wasting your time with Mary. Loretta's more of your woodchopper's kind, anyway. She's hardy, tough, and she would love to live in your lumber camp. You should ask Loretta to marry you tonight, Len. You're wasting your time with Mary. She will never be interested in you. She's an educated, high-class, rich girl, and you're...nothing. Can you even read?"

Leonard had heard enough. His voice sharpened, "Leave me alone, Sherry! I mean it."

"Fine," she whined. "It's your heart that's going to be broken, not mine." She turned and waltzed toward the bar with a drink in her hand, where the men were waiting for her.

Leonard waited for the music to end and briefly feared that Mary would stay on the dance floor for another dance. However, Paul guided her toward the bar, where a crowd of men and women gathered. Leonard politely made his way through the crowd to reach Mary.

He tapped her shoulder. "Mary, could I talk to you in private?"

"Leonard, I told you I'm not working tonight. We can dance next weekend, I promise."

"That would be great, but can we talk for a moment, please?"

Mary sighed. "Fine. Paul, I'll be right back."

"What do you want to drink?" Paul asked.

"Lemonade."

"What?" he gasped. "Nothing stronger?"

"She doesn't drink!" Leonard snapped, his eyes glaring at Paul.

A slow, broad grin spread across Paul's face as he looked at Leonard.

"I don't drink," Mary said. "I'll be right back." Her tone turned to ice. "Come on, Leonard."

CHAPTER FIFTEEN

Mary led Leonard by the hand out of the ballroom and into the foyer, between the roped-off stairs leading to the ladies' rooms and the front door. She turned toward him and asked abruptly, "What do you want, Leonard?"

He glanced at the security guard, Gaylon Dirks, who stood near the stairs before pointing toward the ballroom. He spoke irritably, "Mary, you don't even know that man, and you're kissing him? You have never once kissed me, and I'm the only one who knows how special, beautiful, and truly wonderful you are. He doesn't know you. All he knows is you're giving yourself to him like a harlot!"

Mary's gentle brown eyes hardened like petrified wood. Without a moment's hesitation, she slapped his face with a loud crack. Her voice was venomous, spoken through sneering lips, "I'm not giving myself to anyone, Leonard! Since when is it any of your business what I do anyway? We're not courting. What gives you the right to say anything about what I do?" Angry, she shoved him with both hands. "I think you should go now! Gaylon, he needs to leave," she said to the security guard.

Alarmed by her sudden fury, Leonard raised his hands innocently and spoke honestly, "I care about you, Mary, that's why. That man's boss told me to protect you from him. I don't know what that man may have told you, but his boss said this is what he does in every town they go to. You are nothing to him, you're just another woman, just another number to him, Mary. That's all. But I know how special you are. You're amazing, wonderful, and...beautiful..." He paused short of saying he was in love with her. "Mary, you don't mean anything to him, but you mean everything to me."

Paul Jandy responded from the ballroom's double doorway, "My boss warned you? The short, fat one? The trull-looking jester?"

"Yes, that's him," Leonard replied, his gaze hardening as he looked at Paul.

Paul chuckled as he leaned against the doorjamb. He had followed her without ordering any drinks. "That doesn't surprise me. Bud Hennessy doesn't like me. He never has. He's done this before to provoke a woman's sweetheart to attack me. I think Bud's trying to do it again since he got whipped by one of your locals last night. I'll talk to Ian about that tomorrow morning. I believe that's his motivation for lying to you. But you're wrong, Scribble Face. Even though I have just met Mary, I think she is as beautiful, wonderful, and just as amazing as you do. And she's an incredible dancer, which I'd like to do more of."

"What did you call me?" Leonard demanded.

Paul chuckled to himself as he pushed off the wall. "Listen, I apologize if I caused any offense, but when I look at you with your face all sliced and scratched up and looking a mess, I'm reminded that freak shows are always looking for new talent. You could call yourself the scribbler. Look," he added quickly, "you probably should have stayed home and healed a bit before coming out in public. Oh, but wait..." He paused with a sideways glance. "You sly devil." He laughed. "Were you hoping Mary would take you to a nice quiet room where you two could be alone and let her kiss your wounds and doctor you up? I'm sorry, pal, but Mary's my girl now. So, please, cut your losses and slink away while I take my lady back out onto the dance floor where she belongs."

Mary's cheeks flushed with the awkwardness of being at the center of a growing confrontation between two men vying for her attention. Her irritation at Paul's blatant rudeness was evident in her furrowed brow. "Paul, please go over there so I can finish speaking with Leonard. I don't need your help."

He gazed at Mary fondly. "I'm just protecting my lady."

Mary let out a half-gasp. His words had left her speechless. A glimmer of hope clashed with her apprehension. Leonard had never lied to her, and she didn't doubt his sincerity or his concern for her. However, her attraction to the tall, dark, and mysterious Paul Jandy was stronger than anything she had ever felt. He seemed to embody everything she hoped to find in a man. "I'm not your lady," Mary heard herself say. "I'll talk to you in a minute, Paul. Go over there, please."

"Okay," Paul agreed. "I'll let you and Scribble Face chat."

Leonard had heard enough and stepped toward him. "My face may be scratched up, but I'll turn yours black and blue..."

"Whoa, whoa," Gaylon Dirks said, stepping between

the two men. "There will be none of that in here. Take it outside."

Mary gently pushed Leonard back. "Leonard, please just go. We can talk next weekend."

Leonard glared at Paul and pointed a finger. "If you mistreat her, I'll hunt you down!"

Paul's condescending smirk widened. "Generally speaking, a spider isn't frightened by a fly. You might be physically stronger, but I am far out of your league." He said to Mary, "I'll be at the bar."

Leonard watched him step back into the ballroom as he heard Mary say, "Leonard, please just go."

Gaylon said, "Leonard, if she's asking you to leave, then you need to go."

Leonard nodded in understanding. He asked Mary, "Could you answer just one question for me? Why would you kiss him like that? Honestly, what do you see in him? You just met him, Mary. He's here for two days, and you're falling for him? What's wrong with you? That's not the Mary I know." The anguish in his heart was evident in his expression.

"I'm not falling for him."

"It sure looks like it," he said softly.

"I don't care what it looks like. It's none of your concern." Her tone rose sharply.

"Yes, it is! I want you to be my lady. That's what I want. It's what I've always wanted."

Paul returned and leaned against the doorframe with a grin. "If only I were a poet: Scribble, scribble, scribble. No, I can't think of anything. Listen, she thinks of you as a chalkboard that's been erased. Okay? Chalk isn't permanent. Your time is over, Scribble Face, now please leave. I want to dance with Mary before the band stops playing for the night."

Gaylon darted his eyes at Paul. "You're not helping. Go back to the bar, please."

Paul smirked, unconcerned. He knew he was the star of the show and could get away with much more than anyone else. "You can talk to Bella about that."

Leonard ignored him and spoke to Mary. "When that branch hit me, I was knocked to the ground, and all I could think of was you. Even before I knew if I was hurt or not, I was thinking of you. While I was lying there, I saw this rock sticking out of the ground." He pulled the piece of obsidian from his pocket. "I knew you'd like it."

"Ouch!" Paul exclaimed with a short chuckle. "The old obsidian protective shield, huh? That is touching," Paul admitted. "The next time I stumble and end up on the ground, I'll remember that *thinking of you*, line. Always rise with a new gimmick, I like to say."

Mary took the piece of obsidian in her hand to examine it. "I do like it, Leonard, and I thank you for it. But please hold it for me until next weekend, okay? I'm going to go dance with Paul now."

"Mary," Leonard pleaded, "he implied a moment ago that he's like a spider. If I'm a fly, then you're a butterfly, and he's just waiting for your beauty to fall into his web."

"Hey, that's a good one, Len, thank you," Paul said as he put his arm around Mary's shoulder. "Is that all you can offer her, a rock? No wonder she has no interest in you. Now, if you'll excuse us, shoo, shoo, fly." Paul waved his fingers to shoo him away like a nuisance.

Leonard glared at Paul heatedly. He then turned his attention to Mary. "If you don't believe me, then ask his boss. But don't fall for him."

"I'm not falling for anyone. Now leave before I have Dave and Matt throw you out for good!" Mary exclaimed.

Leonard could see Bella's husband, Dave, and Matt Bannister stepping toward the foyer to diffuse any trouble. "Do we have a problem?" Dave asked.

"Leonard is leaving for the night," Gaylon said. "He's trying to talk to Mary, but this gentleman keeps interrupting." He waved toward Paul.

Dave had a good idea of what was going on. "Leonard, do you want to talk more with Mary?"

"No," Leonard said with a heavy sigh as he returned the piece of obsidian to his pocket. "I guess I've said all I have to say. If that's not enough, then I don't know what is. Good night, Mary."

Paul spoke victoriously. "Ta-Ta, Scribble Face. Remember, freak shows aren't a bad life. Rub some ink in those wounds and wow the crowds, Scribbler."

Leonard lingered a moment to peer at Paul before walking out into the cold and rainy night.

———

"MATT BANNISTER, it's nice to meet you officially. Thanks for your help on the stage," Paul Jandy said, extending his hand to shake. "I've heard a lot about you. But I'm more interested in hearing about your brother giving Bud a beating today. Tell him thank you for me. I can't stand that fat pig."

Matt shook the man's hand. "I'll let him know. You're the magician."

"Yes, I am, without the makeup. My name is Paul Jandy. Did you enjoy the show?"

Matt nodded. "I did. Tell me, how did you do the rope trick?"

Paul chuckled. "I'll tell you the same thing I tell everyone: magic."

"I'm not sure I believe in magic, but it was interesting. I'll watch closer tomorrow night and figure it out. It was a great show, though."

"Thank you. But I never do the same trick twice in the same town, and people like you are the reason why." Paul laughed. "Tomorrow night, I'll leave you amazed, and you will believe in magic. I promise."

Dave asked Mary, "What was going on over here? It looked like there was some tension."

Mary answered, "Leonard was jealous of Paul. He's fine, though."

Paul put an arm around Mary. "He's just a sore loser like a touch of chalk dust under Mary's feet. Now, we're going to step away from what's left of him and go dance. Right, my lady?"

"Right," she said, smiling.

"I don't like him," Gaylon said, watching Paul lead Mary out onto the dance floor. "He's a troublemaker."

"Well," Matt said, "I need to get back to my wife for one last dance before we go home."

CHAPTER SIXTEEN

Deloris Fasana paced the floor of the family room, watching the minute hand of the clock circle the hours as the evening grew later. She had expected Travis to knock on the door, but he had not shown up. His absence was concerning. She was tempted to grab her coat and walk to his house, but she could not think of a convincing excuse for knocking on his door after dark. His wife was not a fool.

She heard the handbell ring from upstairs. She had given Solomon a handbell to ring if he needed anything since he was too sick to get out of bed. She ignored it and continued to pace, cursing Travis under her breath. The bell rang again.

She ascended the stairs and entered the spare bedroom, where Solomon rested in bed. She stepped back as the overwhelming odor of the room flooded her senses. Not only did the bucket need to be emptied because of his vomiting, but his bodily waste had soiled the sheets and bedding. "What, Solomon?" she asked bluntly from the door.

"I can't keep anything down or in me," he said weakly.

"Would you like some more soup? We need to keep you hydrated and put something in your belly. I made a pot of soup just the way you like it. It might help calm the stomach cramps."

"I'm not hungry. Get Dr. Ambrose. I'm sick."

She ignored his request. "Quit whining, Solomon. This will pass in a day or two. Are you thirsty? I'll get you some more water, or maybe some buttermilk will help calm your bowels. I don't know where you picked up your sickness from, probably from one of those dead bodies you touch. I think it's best that you stay isolated for now, though."

Solomon closed his eyes in deep exhaustion. "I need the doctor."

"I'll fetch him tomorrow if you're not feeling better."

"No. Get the doctor tonight. I'm dying," he pleaded.

"You're not dying. You may feel like it, but you'll survive just fine until tomorrow. I'll bring you some soup and water to help keep you hydrated. And then you need to rest. I'll be back."

"I can't keep anything down." He slowly shifted onto one elbow and leaned over the side of the bed to vomit into the bucket. His stomach was empty, and all that came up during the violent contraction of his abdominal muscles was a bit of bile. He fell off the side of the bed and landed on the floor, spilling the bucket as he did. Groaning, he lay on his back in the day's collection of cold, watery vomit. His white bed shirt, which hung to his knees, was stained with diarrhea. Solomon began to weep, realizing he didn't have the strength to pull himself back into bed. The humiliation and helplessness were overwhelming.

Deloris groaned with frustration. "Crying isn't going to help you. Next time, stay in the damn bed," she snapped irritably. With a cringe and a gag, she reached down to help Solomon sit up just enough to place him on the edge of the bed. Deloris pulled his soiled nightshirt off his naked body and helped him into a clean, dry one before he lay back onto his soiled sheets. Solomon's body smelled terrible, and he looked just as bad as he smelled. "Now I need a bath, thanks to you," she said. "You stink!"

"I'm dying," he said weakly as she covered him with soiled blankets. "If I die, tell James the business is his," he said of their only child. James worked on a sternwheeler in the Willamette Valley.

"You're not dying. A week from now, you'll be back at work and appreciate me all the more for taking care of you. Most wives would throw you out on the street and hope the rain would wash your stinking flesh clean."

"I love you, too," he said softly.

"I know." She paused to look down at him. "Are you happy, Solomon?"

"I'm sick."

"I know. But are you happy being married to me?"

"Yeah," he said weakly, his eyes shut.

"I'll get you some more soup and water."

"Thank you."

She sighed with disgust as she looked at the discolored moisture on her hands. "It's my pleasure."

CHAPTER SEVENTEEN

CHRISTINE BANNISTER SAT AT THE DINING ROOM
table, weeping quietly when Matt woke the next morning
and stepped out of their bedroom. The aroma of coffee
filled his senses. He was tempted to grab a cup, but
instead, he sat at the table near his bride and gently asked,
"What's the matter, my lady?"

She sniffled and shook her head.

"Something is. You might feel better if you tell me."

Christine wiped her eyes and sighed. "I don't think I'll
ever be pregnant again."

Matt furrowed his brow, but he stayed silent.

Christine continued, "I had hoped this time I might be,
but..." Her bottom lip quivered. "I started my time earlier
this morning."

"Oh," Matt said. He understood that she meant her
menstrual cycle. "We'll just keep trying."

"That's not the point. I'm not conceiving. I think Dr.
Ryland is right, I'll never be able to have children again."
She sniffled. "I was late, and I was hoping. I was waiting to

tell you that I think I might be pregnant, but my time started at about four o'clock this morning. I was really hoping, Matt." She leaned forward to be held by him as he wrapped his arms around her and held her gently while she wept.

After a moment, Matt responded, "I'm sorry to hear that."

She whimpered, "I was getting so excited. I was a week later than usual. I can count on it. But not this time." She sniffled as a tear rolled down her cheek.

"Maybe that's a sign that we're getting closer." Matt paused and said, "We should go try again."

Christine lifted her head from his shoulder and smiled, gently slapping his arm. "Not right now. You'll have to wait." She wiped her eyes as she gazed at her husband. "I want to have a baby, Matt. I miss being a mother. I miss my daughter. I can never replace my baby girl, but I want another baby." Christine had lost her daughter to influenza on the Kansas plains during a wagon train to Oregon with her first husband, Richard. Her daughter was named Carmen, and losing her was a nightmare from which she thought she would never heal. Time brought a smile to Christine's face, but the emptiness in her soul and the hurt never truly went away. She thought of Carmen often, and even amid all the good things in her life, tears would occasionally fill her eyes from a deep hole that Carmen once filled.

The wagon train heading west brought misery upon misery as it entered Denver, Colorado. Her husband, Richard, went to town with some of the other men and was stabbed several times by a drunken man after accidentally breaking the man's mug of beer. Christine's family was taken from her, leaving her stranded in Denver with nothing to move forward or return to. By God's grace, Bella learned about the beautiful young woman's tragic circumstances and took her into Bella's Dance Hall, providing Christine with a safe place to live and an opportunity to earn a living through dancing.

Christine understood the nature of tragedy and had faced her share of it. There were times when she wondered why her life was so difficult, filled with disappointment and heartbreaking circumstances. There was nothing as unbearable as holding Carmen and watching her fade away until she passed. Burying her child on the great plains, knowing she would ride away without being able to give her daughter a proper burial or a granite headstone to mark where her remains lay, was agonizing. Little did Christine know that she would soon be alone in a world filled with strangers.

Her menstrual cycle could not compare to any of the tragedies she had experienced, however, the disappointment was profound. "I have been optimistic all this time. I keep believing that the Lord will bless us with a baby, and I really thought this time might be it." She raised her brow and smiled emotionally. "There are times..." She hesitated. "No, I better not say it."

"Say what?" Matt asked, encouraging her to continue.

Christine's brow lowered as her eyes filled with thick tears, and her bottom lip quivered. Her breathing grew strained as she said, "There are times that I want to go to the cemetery and piss on Martin Ballenger's grave for shooting me! It's his fault I can't conceive."

"Christine," Matt said gently through an understanding gaze, "Our life together is just beginning. We were only married three months ago. We have time."

"Four!" Christine exclaimed. "Almost four months ago."

Matt smiled. "Almost four, then."

Christine's frown deepened. "I had a dream about Carmen last night. We were playing like we used to, and I could hear her laughing again. I miss her so much." She began weeping and leaned back into Matt's loving embrace. "I miss her so much." She began to sob on his shoulder.

Matt stayed silent as he held his bride in a warm embrace. "I know you do, sweetheart."

———

IT WAS SATURDAY MORNING, and the ladies of Bella's Dance Hall had a lot of work ahead to clean the ballroom after Friday night's activities. The Hennessy Brothers' Traveling Show was hosting another performance that night, bringing a rare excitement to the ladies. They never had a weekend free from dancing, enjoying great entertainment, and doing whatever they pleased within Bella's protective barriers.

Some of the ladies didn't feel as well as they had the night before when they were drinking, but they still had to rise and assist with cleaning, cooking, and preparing for the evening's activities. Most wore simple dresses and let their hair fall freely or gathered it into a quick bun to complete their chores, but Mary once again wore the prettiest of her chore dresses and took extra time to style her hair nicely before going downstairs to help in the kitchen. She knew that at some point, Paul would come to the dance hall to prepare for his show that night. He promised to perform new tricks that hadn't been showcased in Friday night's show.

Sherry Stewart worked in the kitchen, washing dishes, while Mary and several other ladies prepared a large potluck-style meal for the guests to purchase later that night. Sherry paused, closed her eyes, and lowered her head weakly. "I'm never drinking again," she complained. She had spent the evening drinking with a few men who surrounded her.

"I've heard you say that before," remarked a dancer named Susan.

"I mean it this time."

"That sounds familiar, too."

"Yeah," Sherry consented. "Why do I always end up doing the dishes?"

"Because you can't cook," Mary responded.

Sherry paused to close her eyes. A bit of a headache was beginning to form. "That's true. I never had to. I once had a maid to do all the cooking when I was married to my ex. I sometimes wish I was still married to him, and then I wouldn't have to wash dishes. I could tell the maid to do them." She glanced at Mary, who was quietly slicing strips off a slab of bacon for the green bean casserole planned for dinner. "The way Mary was lip-locked to the magician last night makes me think she's about ready to pack her bags and hit the road tomorrow with her new beau."

"Are you going to run off with him, Mary?" Susan asked.

Mary grinned, a bit embarrassed. "No. My parents would be disappointed in me if I did that."

"Parents?" Sherry questioned. "I don't even know what that word means."

Mary glanced back at Sherry with a sincere gaze. "That's too bad, Sherry. We've talked about it before, and I'm sorry that your mother was the way she was. Your stepfather was a horrible man."

Sherry shrugged. "I survived it. I met Hiram, and we

were married. I can't say happily, but I had a maid to do this." She pointed at the dishes. "So, is Landy Jandy going to ask you to leave with him?" She changed the subject to Mary.

Mary rolled her eyes at the absurdity of the question. "No."

Rose walked into the kitchen. "Mary, I was told to come in here and take your place. Bella and Dave want to talk to you."

"Uh-oh, someone's in trouble. You're not supposed to kiss on the dance floor unless you're Christine and Matt," Sherry chided. "At least it's not me this time. I was beginning to think that no one here got in trouble except for me."

"There's usually a reason why, Sherry," Susan replied.

———

"HAVE A SEAT, MARY," Dave said as he opened the door to his and Bella's apartment, which was next to the kitchen. Mary settled onto a davenport near Bella, who was sipping a cup of coffee. Dave took a chair facing them.

Bella glanced at Mary with a stern expression. "So, what are you thinking, Mary?"

Mary felt a chill run down her spine. There wasn't a lady in the dance hall who didn't fear the tone in Bella's voice. "I don't know. What do you mean?"

"You know what I'm talking about. You've been with us for several years, and I've never seen you kiss a man on the dance floor. Not even one of the men you've been courted by. Especially the way you were smacking on that Landy Jandy creep last night."

Mary's face reddened. "Yeah, I don't know what got into me."

"His tongue by the looks of it!" Bella snapped. "Were you drinking?"

"No." Her face reddened. "You know I don't drink anything except water, tea, or lemonade."

"Then why were you kissing him?"

Mary hesitated to take a breath. "I don't know. I wanted to, I guess," Mary replied sheepishly.

Dave spoke bluntly. "What was going on between him and Leonard at the door when Matt and I walked over there?"

Mary sighed. "Leonard was upset that I kissed Paul. I think he was jealous."

"You think?" Bella exclaimed.

"He was," Mary admitted.

"Mary, Leonard has been hooked on you since the night he first walked in here. He has wanted to court you since we opened. You remember when Martin Ballenger murdered Edith? Do you think it's wise to lip-lock a man you just met in front of everyone when the one man who has been pining for you is in the audience? The only reason Leonard comes here is to dance with you. I'm very cautious about that nowadays. I will not lose another one of my ladies like we did Edith, nor will I allow someone's rage to erupt in here. You, young lady, must obey our rules and be more aware of your surroundings."

Mary nodded in understanding. She was friends with Edith Williams and remembered that night almost a year ago very well. "I will be more mindful. The kiss just happened. I don't know what came over me."

"Don't let it happen again. You ladies are supposed to be professional, and you know the rules: no kissing on the dance floor. Ever! I was very disappointed in you last night, Mary. I would expect that from Sherry and some of the other girls who don't value themselves as highly, but not you. You are the one lady here that most of the girls wish they could be like. Don't lower your standards for a man you don't know."

"Yes, ma'am. It won't happen again."

"Be sure it doesn't."

Dave said, "We spent some time talking to Miss Hellee Montrese last night, and she told Bella and me that Landy Jandy does this everywhere they go. He's no good, Mary. To protect yourself, we highly suggest you stay away from him."

Mary's brow furrowed. "That's what Leonard said. I didn't believe him. He said the owner, Bud Hennessy, told him to protect me from Paul. But honestly, there's nothing to protect me from. Paul was a gentleman and didn't suggest anything that crossed any lines."

Bella spoke. "How many times have I told you ladies that every man interested in you will be *nice*, but that doesn't mean they are. Take the time to get to know a man's character before you ever put your lips to his. Respect yourself enough to do that, and you will be thankful you did when his true character is shown. Whether he's a good man or bad, you will be thankful either way. Trust me on that."

Dave said, "Our suggestion is for you to stay away from Paul Jandy. He's leaving town tomorrow, and I'll be glad to see him go. He's already caused trouble for one of our loyal customers, and I don't like that."

Bella placed a hand on Mary's knee. "Leonard works hard for his money, and he spends a lot of it every weekend to see you. I've talked to Leonard several times, and I think he is a good man. I know you come from a well-established family that's expecting you to marry someone more professional, but you may not want to overlook Leonard. I think he'd make a good, faithful, and loving husband."

Mary shook her head. "I'm not interested in Leonard for anything more than a friend, and I've told him that. He knows that. My question is, what happens when I meet someone I want to marry? Am I going to have to worry about what Leonard thinks then, too?"

"Maybe that someone will be a local and not a weekend fling," Bella said with emphasis.

"That's the difference," Dave said. "Paul Jandy is a spark that's here for two shows, then he's gone, and he'll never come back. Mary, my dear, last night you looked like a—I don't know, a..."

"Whore," Bella said bluntly.

"I wasn't going to say that," Dave admitted.

"No, but she did. I expect kisses like that from Matt and Christine, who are newlyweds. I did not expect to see that from you, Mary. Especially with a man you just met. A traveling salesman is all he is. A liar, conman, and, according to those he works with, a terrible human being. You deserve better, Mary. Much better."

CHAPTER EIGHTEEN

FIFTEEN-YEAR-OLD OLLIE HOFFMAN HAD GOTTEN into legal trouble back in July when he broke into the Fasana Furniture and Undertaker Parlor with his friend Nick Griffin to make the corpse of a man known as the Leather Man bite Nick's arm. Ollie was the one who pulled on the dead man's chin to clamp down on Nick's skin. Ollie knew it was wrong to break into the mortuary, but he didn't realize that Nick was guilty of what the marshal suspected. They stole an end table from the furniture store and left the lamp that was on it in the middle of the aisle as an explanation for the broken window. Matt Bannister could have arrested Ollie for several offenses, but instead, he made Ollie work for free at the Fasana Furniture and Undertakers Parlor as punishment.

It had been almost six months, and Ollie had earned a paid position as an employee. He primarily worked in the furniture store but often assisted Solomon in the mortuary. He learned the furniture business and could work upstairs without Solomon's supervision, although he was still learning the mortuary business downstairs. He had been frightened of the mortuary, but over a few weeks, he overcame his fears and could now ride down the elevator with a body without a flicker of anxiety.

What he wasn't used to was opening the furniture store and working alone in the large brick building. Solomon had been sick, and Deloris asked Ollie to run the store and mortuary until Solomon recovered. He hoped there would be no deaths in the meantime because he was still inexperienced with that aspect of the business, but that hope was dashed with the arrival of a mysterious old woman's body that didn't have a name tag or any paperwork in the basement. Solomon often expressed his wish for more employees to help, however, Deloris believed they didn't need to hire additional staff since they were still paying off the building's construction costs and purchasing inventory for the store after a fire destroyed the old one.

Ollie sat in a plush leather chair in the furniture store, wondering what he was supposed to do with the old woman's body when the bell rang as the front door opened. Thankful for the arrival of a customer, Ollie stood from the chair to greet them. His excitement faded upon seeing Deloris. "Good morning, Mrs. Fasana," he greeted her with a bit of reservation. She wasn't usually very nice to him.

"Are there any customers here?" she asked sharply.

"No. Just me. Mrs. Fasana, is Solomon coming back soon? There's a woman's body downstairs, and I don't know what to do with her."

"Leave her there for now. However, I need you to close the store and come with me. I need your help."

"Is everything okay?"

"Everything's fine. Just lock it up and come with me," she ordered.

Moments later, they walked briskly toward Solomon's large Victorian home. Deloris had said very little and kept a quick pace. She had never been overly friendly with him and seldom spoke more than five words at a time unless it was to criticize his appearance. Ollie knew he wasn't the most handsome teenager in town, but he tried to do a good job for Solomon and her.

"Where are we going?" he asked.

"The house. I need your help. Actually, Solomon does. He hasn't been feeling well, and his fever is too high. The doctor said to move him into the basement, where it's cooler, for now. I need your help to set up a spare bed down there before I can."

"Oh. What is he sick with?"

"Nothing you can catch," she replied curtly and continued walking.

Before long, they entered her house and went upstairs to another spare bedroom, where she told Ollie to move the mattress and bed frame down into the basement. Once the bed was placed in the dark basement, Deloris said, "We need to bring Solomon down here. He is very sick and has no energy to get out of bed. I'll warn you that his mattress and the room are soiled. It smells bad, and he looks worse. Listen to me, Ollie. Solomon is a respected fixture around town, and the last thing he needs is gossip about soiling himself. I'll expect you to keep this quiet. And I mean, you had better not utter a word about this to anyone, or he will fire you. And just to reinforce the need for privacy, I'll tell Matt that you stole some money and my jewelry if anyone learns about this. Am I being clear?"

"Yes, ma'am. I wouldn't tell anyone anything that might embarrass Solomon. I won't."

"You had better not for your own good. Now, fill the

boiler with coal for me and come upstairs." The boiler provided some heat in the basement, but most of the heat transferred up through the pipes as steam to the cast-iron radiators in the rooms before returning to the boiler as water.

Ollie followed Deloris into the bedroom, where Solomon lay. Ollie pinched his nose as his eyes watered from the foul stench that was so strong he could nearly taste it. Solomon lay on soiled bed linens, sleeping with his head and arm hanging over the edge of the bed, above a bucket half full of vomit. "What's wrong with him?" Ollie asked with concern. He wasn't sure if Solomon was alive or dead. Solomon's skin was pale, cold, and clammy.

Deloris shot a sideways glance at Ollie. "Nothing you can catch. I promise. The doctor has already looked him over and said Solomon needs a cooler room. The sickness, I forgot what he called it, thrives in warm temperatures. Once we get him downstairs, where it is colder, he'll recover just fine. Now help me move him."

Deloris grabbed one of Solomon's arms and pulled him upward. "Help me!" she shouted at Ollie impatiently.

Ollie timidly approached Solomon to help but said, "Maybe we should take him to a doctor."

"The doctor's already seen him!" Deloris snapped with a viciousness in her expression. "Now, take hold of him and help me."

Solomon groaned in pain as he was lifted.

"Grab him from behind and pull him out of here and down to the basement to the bed. I must get this room cleaned up. Hurry and go!"

"By myself?" Ollie protested. Solomon's white night-shirt was discolored and wet from the combination of sweat and vomit. Stains of watery fecal matter dotted the back of the lower half of his nightshirt. He reeked like some of the bodies that Ollie had helped with in the mortuary.

"You're a man, aren't you? Of course, by yourself. Just drag him down there." Her furious eyes bored into Ollie.

Ollie shifted around and clasped his hands over Solomon's chest, feeling the cold moisture of vomit on his wrists and forearm as he stepped backward out of the room, dragging Solomon's bare feet across the floor. He left the room, moved along the hallway, and carefully descended the stairs, trying to maintain his balance to avoid dropping his employer. After navigating the first flight of stairs and breathing heavily, he dragged Solomon through the house and down another set of stairs into the basement.

The sound of Solomon's heels hitting the wooden steps one after another irritated him, as he expected Deloris to at least help carry Solomon's feet. It took all of Ollie's strength to support Solomon's body weight and drag him to the bed in the basement. Ollie heaved Solomon onto the bed and then kneeled to catch his breath. Sweat poured down his face as he watched Solomon struggle to open his eyes. The man that Ollie knew and respected looked nothing like the man before him.

Ollie explained compassionately, "The doctor says you'll heal up quicker down here. And I hope you do. I miss you at the store and need you in the mortuary. I don't know what to do with that lady."

Solomon's lips were dry and cracked, surrounded by a tan crust of dried vomit. He tried to speak, but his voice was too weak to carry. He struggled to keep his eyes open.

"What's that?" Ollie inquired.

His lips moved once more, but no sound emerged.

Ollie furrowed his brow. Although he heard no sound, Solomon's lips appeared to mouth the word: Doctor. "Do you want the doctor to come back?"

Solomon's eyes opened heavily to meet Ollie's. Solomon barely nodded his head.

"I'll let Mrs. Fasana know."

"Let me know what?" Deloris asked abruptly as she came down the stairs, carrying all the soiled blankets and linens from upstairs. She tossed them onto the floor in front of the boiler. "What did he say?"

"He didn't say anything, but I think he tried to say doctor. I think he wants the doctor to come back."

Deloris sighed irritably. "The doctor has already visited four times. He has a sickness that will heal better in the cold. I already told you that. We need to lower his body temperature to stop the infection, and he'll be fine. Solomon needs to toughen up and get through it like a man. Now, help me bring his crappy mattress down. I need to clean that room. And then I need you to bring me a new mattress within the hour. Did you hear me? Within the hour! That means *immediately*," she emphasized. She didn't think Ollie had the smarts of a turtle.

"Sure."

"Good. Bring that old mattress down here and then return to the store to get me a new one. I'll feed my husband some soup to keep his strength up."

She waited for Ollie to leave the basement and listened to the sound of him going upstairs before stepping over to the bed and peering down at her husband. She sat on the edge of the bed. "Solomon, can you hear me? It doesn't really matter if you can or not. I should never have married you. You took me from my home and brought me out here to this miserable town. For nearly thirty years, I have been married to you, and I have hated every one of them. We were never compatible and never in love. You might have been, but you bore me, Solomon. I'm tired of being bored. Your precious furniture store and mortuary have cost us a fortune to build, and I'm going to sell them, our home, and everything else. I'm taking your life insurance money, and I'm leaving. I'm going back to Boston, where I belong."

Solomon blinked as a hint of moisture gathered in his eyes. His mouth moved, and through a whisper, he said, "James."

Deloris scoffed with disgust. "You would be worried about James, wouldn't you? You're the reason he doesn't want anything to do with me. He's the only son I'll ever have, and he can't stand me. That is your fault. Solomon! You were always the good and loving father, weren't you? You made me look like I enjoyed being the disciplinarian because you wouldn't beat his ass!" She exhaled. "James will come home for your funeral, and then I'll never see him again. Yes, you're dying, Solomon.

"Matt's coming over to tell you that he caught me in a hotel having some fun with Travis, but you won't be home. I moved you down here so I can invite him to check the house to see if you're home, in case he doesn't believe me. I'll say you're feeling better and went to Hollister to pick up a stinking corpse. That should take a couple of days, and by then, you should be dead. To my utter horror, I'll say I found you at the bottom of the basement stairs. You have been sick and weak, so you must have fallen down the stairs. Of course, I'll have to beat your head with a hammer a few times, but you won't mind." She stood heartlessly. "One more day, maybe two, and I can take this ring off my finger and start living again."

Solomon reached out to her. "Why?" he asked in a

feeble voice. Despite the weakness and nausea he felt, the devastation of hearing his honored wife's words was evident in his watery eyes.

Deloris answered with a slight, uncaring shrug. "Because you're worth more to me dead than alive. The only hard part about you dying is I'll have to pretend to mourn until I can sell everything and leave this town." She heard Ollie dragging the soiled mattress across the floor.

Solomon's head lifted slightly as his eyes turned to the stairs with a hopeful glance.

Deloris shouted, "Ollie, just let the mattress fall down the stairs, and I'll grab it. You had better get back to the store and bring me a new mattress right away. Go now!" she ordered sharply.

The mattress slid halfway down the stairs and came to a stop. She heard Ollie holler goodbye to Solomon and listened to the front door close. Deloris glared at Solomon. "He can't help you. No one will. I should throw that stinking mattress on top of you so you can smell yourself as you wither away. I'm not heartless, Solomon, I'll bring you down a bowl of soup and a glass of water for your last meal."

She dragged the mattress down the stairs and let it fall to the floor near the soiled bedding she had brought down. She ascended the stairs and closed the door, locking it behind her. Solomon was trapped alone in the dark basement with only the faint light from the fire in the boiler door window and the sound of the flames devouring the slow-burning coal. The vent allowing heat into the basement was closed. A cold chill enveloped Solomon's damp body without a blanket to cling to. He tried to sit up, but his body lacked the strength, and his head spun like a top.

Closing his eyes, he fell back onto the mattress. A tear slipped from his eyes.

———

DELORIS BREWED a pot of tea and settled down in the reading room with her cup on a china saucer. She felt a tightness in her chest as she awaited Ollie's return with a new mattress. A new mattress could be cumbersome to carry, but Solomon had utilized his backwoods roots to create a cart specifically designed for moving heavy mattresses around the store by himself. If Ollie had the sense of a stork, he would use the cart to transport it. If not, then he deserved to struggle.

Deloris was born and raised in Boston, Massachusetts, in an upper-middle-class family. Her father was an archaeologist who later became a professor at Boston University. However, as an adventurer at heart, he sold everything and secured passage for his family on a steamer sailing from Boston to Oregon, where he was hired as a professor of Archaeological Studies at the University of Oregon. Deloris met Solomon through her father at a community dance while he was attending the university. She was immediately captivated by the tall, dark, and handsome young man.

Solomon was everything he no longer was. She had been smitten with him back then, but that enamored young woman had grown spiteful over the years. Deloris wanted her freedom back while there was still time to enjoy the rest of her life. Soon, she would be a wealthy widow and could leave behind the dust, mud, and filth that Solomon had brought her to. Deloris no longer had living parents and had lost contact with her siblings over the years. One of her brothers, she had not heard from in twenty years, and she had no idea where in the United States he lived or if he lay resting in a grave somewhere.

She wanted to leave Oregon and return to Boston, where she could find a wealthy man to marry who enjoyed mingling in high society while she was still attractive enough to do so. Deloris had always dreamed of becoming one of the elite ladies in Boston's upper society, a woman whom the other ladies admired and respected. She longed to feel important and have a sense of purpose. She wanted her name to appear in the newspaper and draw attention to her charitable works. She yearned for things in her life that Branson and Solomon could never provide. She could divorce Solomon, but then she would have no money and would likely end up marrying the first man who showed interest in her. At fifty-two years old, she wasn't as young and pretty as she once had been. Time was short, her dreams were strong, and it was time to make a change.

Ollie brought a new mattress with the cart and dragged it upstairs to place it on the empty bed frame from which the soiled mattress had been removed. When he finished, Deloris told him to return the cart, close the store, and go home. When asked about the deceased woman's body, she informed him that she would handle the situation. He wouldn't be needed at work until Solomon felt better.

Two hours later, a knock sounded at the door. The sour expression on Deloris's face as she looked up from her book was cold, angry, and resentful. She knew, just from the sound of the knock, that it was Matt coming to inform Solomon about her affair. She opened the door and stared at Matt without saying a word.

"Is Uncle Solomon home? I stopped by the furniture store, and it was closed," Matt said. "Is he still not feeling well?"

She folded her arms over her breasts. "He is feeling better, but he is not home. Solomon and Ollie went to Hollister or some other little town somewhere to pick up a man who died. The family wants him embalmed or something like that. He got word of it this morning. You can come in and look around if you don't believe me."

Matt expected that Deloris might lie to prevent him from telling Solomon that he had caught her in the hotel with Travis McKnight, but since Ollie wasn't at the store, he had no reason not to believe her. Usually, most small-town folks buried their own dead locally in their cemetery, but it was not unheard of for Solomon to be asked to come get a family's loved one to embalm. "He should be back tomorrow, then?" he asked.

Deloris shrugged her shoulders. "Probably. I hope you don't plan on following me around all night." Her lips tightened with resentment.

Matt chuckled. "No, I think I've seen all that I needed to see. Let me ask, did you tell him about Travis?"

"No." Her eyes hardened. "And I don't know why you insist on doing so. It's none of your business what I or your uncle do. We are adults and don't need a yapping dog nipping at our feet every time we make a decision that you disagree with."

"I have a feeling Uncle Solomon might feel differently about that this time. Deloris, you can do whatever you want, I really don't care. But you might not like the consequences, because I do care about my uncle. I'll talk to him tomorrow. Good day."

Deloris closed the door without saying another word. She exhaled, thankful to see him leave.

CHAPTER NINETEEN

Bud Hennessy stood at the bar in the dance hall, sipping a drink while watching some of the women who lived there arrange stacks of plates and glasses along a line of tables against the wall. A dinner was scheduled for later that night, where guests could pay a fee, grab a plate, and walk down a row of tables filled with large bowls of various foods to fill their plates. The previous night's dinner plate sales had been strong for Bella's Dance Hall, but the bar sold a record number of drinks. It had been a good turnout, and Bud was surprised by the number of tickets sold. It showed that Ian's idea of performing in Branson was a solid decision after all.

"It's smart to take the sternwheeler down the Columbia instead of trying to cross the mountain this time of year. Those heavy wagons of yours wouldn't make it through the snow."

Bud raised his brow as he turned to see who was talking to him. It was Dave, the owner of Bella's Dance Hall. "We think so."

Dave lowered his voice. "Hey, between you and me, what's the secret to Landy Jandy's rope standing up on its own?"

Bud shook his head. "I don't really know."

"I won't tell anyone. You can tell me."

"Go look at his rope, and then you tell me. Whatever his secrets are, he hasn't shared them with anyone. As I mentioned yesterday, I have nothing to do with Paul Jandy, except tolerate him. Is it real magic? Of course not. But I don't know the trick to it."

"Bella and I talked to Mary about Paul this morning. I hope what we said sticks and we don't see a repeat of last night's kiss. She's too well-respected by the other ladies to be seen doing that."

Bud took a drink and lowered his glass to yawn. "I warned your dancer lady's friend and you about Jandy. If neither of you heeds my warning, then so be it. That's all I have to say. I can't do much about him right now, but at the end of this tour, he won't be a part of our show anymore. I may not come across as the nicest man, but I don't lie to people the way he does." He finished his drink and set the glass on the bar before leaving Dave to sit alone in a wooden folding chair in the front row.

———

MARY WASHBURN FINISHED ARRANGING stacks of neatly folded linen napkins on the food table and sighed with relief now that the morning chores were complete. She was free to do whatever she pleased for the rest of the day. Some of the other ladies had already retreated to their rooms upstairs to nap or engage in whatever they desired, whether inside or outside the dance hall. Mary noticed Bud standing alone at the bar, having a drink long before any of the other entertainers from the Hennessy Traveling Show arrived. Watching him sit by himself in front of the stage with the closed curtains, she decided to approach Bud and ask him about Paul herself.

"You look lonely," she said as she approached him.

"I'm not." His eyes shifted to hers, revealing his annoyance at the interruption.

"Can I talk to you for a minute?"

He nodded to the chair next to him. "At your own risk."

She sat with a smile. "I enjoyed your show last night. You are hilarious up there."

He exhaled with a downturned frown. "It's just an act. It's what we do for a living."

"You're the funny one, though. It must feel great to hear us laughing in the audience."

He gave a slight nod, and his lips formed a near smile. "My job is to be a fool, an idiot. What did you want to talk about?"

"Did you tell my friend Leonard to warn me about Paul?"

Bud leaned forward, elbows on his knees, and turned his shoulders to look Mary in the eyes for the first time. "Not exactly. I told him he needs to interfere and protect you from Jandy. I told the owners of this place, too. Look, you seem like a very nice lady, so I'll warn you now. You're weekend entertainment, that's all. I hear you're a Christian lady. If so, you need to stay away from Paul because he is certainly not. He's about as far away from that as you can be."

"He told me that he was a Christian. At least, I think he

did." Her face wrinkled as she reflected on their conversations.

"Well, miss, he may have implied it, but he's not. Ian and I were raised in a Christian home, so I have some knowledge of the Bible and its teachings. In all fairness, I'll tell you that the Bible studies and church didn't resonate with me. But I do know that the Bible says the devil appears as an angel of light. So, let me ask you, why wouldn't a man do the same to impress an attractive Christian lady? I won't tell you that *Landy Jandy*"—he emphasized with bitter sarcasm—"worships the devil, but he is a wicked man. I know him better than you do, young lady. You're not the first young lady that I've warned about him, and you won't be the last.

"That photograph you took last night will be mailed to some false address, and he'll never think of you again. Do yourself a favor and stay away from him. Find yourself a good Christian man who shares your values. Those are your people, not men like Paul. Like my father used to say, if you were to marry anyone who doesn't share your faith, your father-in-law would be the devil himself. Again, I'm not saying Paul's a devil worshipper, but if you don't belong to the Lord, then who do you belong to?"

"You sound like you're a Christian."

He let out a small scoff. "Miss, I used to be, but I don't think I have the heart to be a Christian anymore."

"So, according to your words, you belong to the devil?" Mary asked.

He hesitated to answer thoughtfully and then took a deep breath. "Maybe so."

"Then maybe you have forgotten that Jesus said he will never leave us. I believe that once we sincerely accept Jesus as our savior, we are adopted into God's family, and God will never let us go. He may watch us walk away like a little boy wandering away from his parents, but like any parent, God won't take his eyes off us."

"Do you have a point?" Bud asked impatiently.

"I do," Mary answered. "What makes us think God loves us less than we love our children? I don't have any children, but I know my father said he'd die to protect me. He'd jump into a raging river and willingly drown if he could save me from drowning. Is that not exactly what Jesus did for all of us? Didn't Jesus say he leaves the ninety-nine to seek the one that wandered away? I don't know much about sheep, but I'm guessing any lost sheep will run to its shepherd, just like a frightened child runs to his father. The prodigal son is always welcomed home with open arms because he is not a servant or a slave. He is family, God's family. I hope you find your way home, Mr. Hennessy."

Bud squinted his eyes, slightly baffled by the sudden change of subject. "I thought you sat down to talk about Paul, not me."

"Paul is charming, I have to admit. He is also a wonderful dancer. Those are two qualities that I greatly admire. I will admit that I was taken with him, and maybe I still am. But when so many people are warning me about him, perhaps I need to listen. On that note, I am a good listener, and although you say being a Christian did not resonate with you, I believe that it did, and you are doing everything you can to fight surrendering to Jesus. Mr. Hennessy, the unhappiest people in the world are born-again Christians who try to live in the world without Jesus. You won't fit in, and you won't find happiness in anything else because you are part of God's family, and *His* children do not fit into the world. All you'll do is sink deeper into the mire and muck while refusing to take hold of the hand extended out for you to grasp. Jesus is always saying *come home*, Mr. Hennessy."

Bud's lips pressed tightly together as he gazed at the floor, lost in his thoughts.

Mary stood. "Thank you for the warning. Mr. Hennessy, you look like a very broken man. I hope you can change that."

Bud watched her start to walk away. "Mary," he called. When she turned around, he continued, "I don't think God can forgive me for all the bad things I have done"—he gave a short, exasperated scoff—"or currently doing. I've ruined every part of my life. I have nothing left."

Mary wrinkled her nose. "You said you knew the Bible. I can assure you that you have not or could not do more wrong than Samson did. And yet, he is called a hero of the faith in the book of Hebrews. So is the prostitute, Rahab." She paused to emphasize. "It isn't what we have done but what we do when it comes to Jesus that matters. Trust me, that devil you are presently serving, perhaps unknowingly, is lying to you. You've done nothing that can't be forgiven. All you need to do is ask and then pick up your Bible again and read it every day."

––––––––

WILLIAM FASANA, the security guard at the Monarch Hotel, carried a bucket of ice water from the kitchen of the Monarch Restaurant into the bathing room, where four lion-clawed bathtubs were partitioned by pull curtains that could be drawn. Two Chinese ladies worked as bath maids, supplying heated water for the customers' baths. One of the ladies had burned her hand the previous day and was off work until the blister on her hand healed. Taking her place was Barbara Ballenger, a young housekeeper.

Barbara was filling the bathtub when Paul Jandy and his friend Gus Miller entered to bathe. Paul grabbed Barbara and attempted to pull her into the bathtub while exposing himself to her. Frightened, she broke free and reported the incident to her boss, Pamela Collins, who then informed William.

William walked into the bathing room and found Paul Jandy reclining in the now lukewarm water with a washcloth covering his face. Beside Paul's tub, with the curtain open, Gus also leaned back in his tub, relaxing. Their backs were turned to the door.

William sneaked up behind Paul's tub and dumped a bucket of ice-cold water over his head.

Paul shot up abruptly with a loud curse. He turned in the tub, his glaring eyes locked on William's stern expression. "What the hell?" he shouted.

"That's to cool you off. You don't grab our lady employees, and you sure as hell don't expose yourself to them like you did to Barbara. If you do anything like that again, I will personally strip your clothes off and toss you out onto the street where you can show yourself to everyone. Do you understand me?" William threatened sternly. His cold blue eyes didn't show a hint of it being an empty threat.

"Okay!" he shouted angrily. "I get it. You don't need to throw ice in my bath, though, it's cold enough as it is. Could you bring in some more hot water quickly?"

"No," William said pointedly. "Your bath is over. Get dressed and get out of here." Having made his point, William left the bathing room.

"What a..." Paul cursed William. "The water's freezing. I shouldn't have stood up, he looks like the envious type. He'll probably never feel like a man again."

Grinning, Gus grabbed a towel and stepped out of the tub. "I'm glad he didn't overhear you say that. You might have gotten shot for that one. Do you remember grabbing the booty of that woman in Wisconsin, and her husband was about to knock your head off? You'd think you'd learn after all these times."

Paul laughed. "Yeah, you'd think so, but no. I thought that woman in Wisconsin was a waitress, I didn't know she was having dinner with her husband. Ole tough Bud didn't budge to help me, though, did he?"

"No. I think he was looking forward to seeing you get your face beat in."

"Well, fair is fair. I sure enjoyed hearing about him getting beaten the other night. I think we chose the wrong hotel to have any fun. The manager is Marshal Matt Bannister's father, and the security guard is Matt's cousin. His brother owns the building. Even that bellboy Bud hit was the marshal's nephew. Heck, I should've thought about that before grabbing that girl. She might be their niece, sister, cousin, or wife, for all I know. I could've gotten shot."

Gus said, "You better watch yourself and what trouble you do cause because one of these days Ian might get tired of bailing you out of trouble and start listening to Bud and let you go."

Paul waved his hand nonchalantly as he dried off. "Ian listens to Bud about as much as I do. Tonight, after our show, I can guarantee that Bud will go back to his cheap hotel room and stare at the walls, whimpering about his sorrows while we dance the hours away with a couple of lovely dancers."

Gus smiled. "Hey, what was it you were going to tell me about last night? Some new brilliant idea or something?"

"I can't tell you in here. Too many ears are listening to everything we say. Let's get dressed and I'll tell you on the way."

CHAPTER TWENTY

D<small>ELORIS</small> F<small>ASANA DESCENDED THE STEPS INTO THE</small> basement, carrying a lantern and a cup of tea. She held the lantern over Solomon's face to check if he was still alive. Solomon shivered in the cold and barely opened his eyes, only to shut them tight against the light of the lantern. Deloris sighed in disappointment. "You smell dead."

Solomon took a deep breath through his shivering, chapped lips, which were turning blue. "Help...me," he whispered.

"I'm trying to, but you won't die. You will, it's just a matter of time. I'll tell you, though, this tea is nice and warm." She smiled with a devilish grin. "You should finish your soup and drink your water."

Solomon forced his eyes open to look at Deloris in the lantern light. "Deloris...get me a doctor," he struggled to say. "You can have it all."

She snickered. "I know I can have it all. Being a widow is far more respectful than being divorced. I'm thinking of me, Solomon. I would bring you some warm food and water, but you haven't touched your breakfast yet. I don't particularly care, but if you want some warm food, then you'd better finish your oatmeal from this morning. Or you can starve to death, it's up to you."

Solomon shook as he whispered, "I...I'm...c...cold."

Deloris grunted. "I don't care. I would kiss you good-bye, but you stink, just like the life you gave me. I'll come back tomorrow and see if you're alive. Goodbye, Solomon."

Solomon watched her carry the lantern up the stairs and disappear as the door closed and locked behind her. Left alone in the dark basement, with only the faint glow of the coal burning in the furnace and the sound of the flames, Solomon closed his eyes. His stomach cramped with nothing in it to vomit. His bowels had emptied, and severe cramping ached throughout his body. He lacked the strength to leave the bed, let alone stand and try to walk. The nausea swirling through his head wouldn't allow him to stand upright even if he could find the strength to try. His dry throat and cracked lips pleaded for a drink from the glass of water beside the bed, but he knew that if he ate or drank anything Deloris gave him, it would only introduce more poison into his body.

He was already dehydrated and slowly freezing in the basement's frigid air. The furnace burned just a few feet away, providing heat to all the rooms above, but he had chosen not to heat the basement since it served as the cellar. All Solomon could do was lie on the bed and pray that he would be discovered before he died. He prayed that the Lord would soften Deloris's heart, but that prayer seemed to have fallen on deaf ears. He could not remember a time when he had ever experienced such violent chills, nor had he ever felt so cold. His teeth chattered while his body shivered uncontrollably.

The soiled blanket and sheets from upstairs lay on the floor, not far from his bed. It took the strength he didn't have to roll off his bed, land on the bitterly cold concrete floor, and slowly crawl across it to reach the soiled mattress and curl up with the wool blanket. His body ached, and his stomach tightened with an explosive cramp that felt like it was being wrung dry of its last drop of moisture. He tucked his legs into a fetal position, closed his eyes, and prayed as he waited for the blanket's warmth to quell the chills and shivering.

CHAPTER TWENTY-ONE

GUS MILLER LAUGHED LIGHTLY AS HE AND PAUL Jandy walked several blocks toward Rose Street. "I must admit, that is genius. How did you come up with that idea?"

Paul shared his new and brilliant idea with Gus as they walked. He was pleased to hear that Gus approved. He responded proudly, "I just looked at the Leonard, fella, and the idea came to me. I couldn't help but smile, Gus. I think this will be my new gimmick everywhere we go from here on out."

"I love it. Are you going to tell Mary?"

"No. I was interested in Mary until last night when the idea struck me. Now, Mary's just the hook," Paul Jandy said as he and Gus Miller neared a cross street. In his hand, Paul carried a small suitcase containing his Landy Jandy costume and makeup. "If there is anything I like about this town, it is not having to get my boots muddy," he said as he stepped from the wooden boardwalk onto the three heavy beams that crossed the street to keep citizens' footwear from sinking into the mud. A Chinese man carrying a scoop shovel moved from block to block, scraping the mud off the beams. The city had made a deal with the leader of Chinatown to maintain the city streets and walkways. The Chinese man, older and standing to the side, let the two men pass by. He offered them a friendly smile as they approached.

"What I don't like about this town are the rats on the street," Paul said as he unexpectedly shoved the Chinese man down as he passed. The Chinese man fell backward into the mud. Paul laughed as he continued walking across the street without a care. "As I was saying, I've been buttering Mary up for two nights like a Christmas turkey, and it was going well, although Mary's more religious than I'd like. Unfortunately, this is one of those rare times that I actually do like her. She is pretty and interesting to talk to. She's not like most of the women we've met after the shows, who may be pretty to look at but lack brains and values. Mary has both, and her values are strong. She also comes from a very well-to-do family. That helps pique my interest."

"Yeah, but you're not seriously interested in her, are you?" Gus asked.

"No." Paul chuckled. "If I were the marrying type, maybe I would be. But with an unlimited number of fish in the sea, why would I fall for one? Especially when we conquer the sea, so to say, with all the traveling we do. Mary's a nice change of pace for conversation, but I wish I had aimed for the redhead named Rose, Sherry, or one of the other women who weren't so darn pious in their faith. Mary is saving herself for marriage, you know."

"It's not too late to change love interests. This is our last night here."

"No, no, no. I'm thankful I met Mary because I encountered her jealous friend, and that has changed everything. Mary's nice, but now she's just the hook to reel in Leonard. And I am excited to do that."

"Do you ever think about Martha from Boulder? I thought she would make someone an exceptional wife."

"No. Why?" Paul asked.

"No reason. I just think about her from time to time. I liked her," Gus said. "If I settled down and wanted to start a family, I think Martha would be the kind of woman I'd like to settle down with."

Paul grimaced. "You should have told me that then. I would have paid more attention to her friend, whatever her name was. Your gal that weekend." He laughed.

"Coleen. No, Martha was more interested in you. Unfortunately, I'm the one who might have come back for her."

"Oh, you would not have. Martha was too needy and... stop. Stop...stop," Paul said, stopping suddenly on the boardwalk in front of a small grocery store. His eyes narrowed, and a slow grin formed as he gazed through the window into the store. "If there is a god, he must love me, or I have some great luck. Look who is in there. That's my little hen, Mary's friend from last night, Leonard. Gus, I have an idea. Let's go inside and visit Lenny. Don't ask questions, do as I say, okay? I have an ingenious idea."

Gus had seen Paul talking and dancing with Mary the night before, but he hadn't noticed Mary speaking to another man. Paul had told him about Leonard and had just shared an idea he had for Leonard, but now Gus could see Leonard for the first time. The man looked solid as a brick, with broad shoulders and a muscular build that appeared lean, straight, and powerful. Gus had a bad feeling. "Paul, I don't think whatever you're thinking is a good idea. That man looks like a bear to want to fight."

"Fight?" Paul questioned. "I'm not fighting him. Come on."

"Paul, we just talked about causing trouble in the bathing room, not even an hour ago," Gus said, hesitating to enter the store.

Paul laughed as he let the warning slip past him. "Who's causing trouble? I just told you my plans for this man. I'm just going to talk to him. Trust me."

Gus rolled his eyes anxiously. "Your plan, although probably a great one, might get us fired."

"Gus, you worry too much. If Ian fires us, we'll start our own tour. Trust me, it's fine." Paul entered the store.

"Oh, no. Here we go again," Gus muttered to himself as he trailed behind.

———

LEONARD HARRIS WAS BUYING a few groceries that his sister-in-law, Jenny, needed for dinner. When he saw a rack of scarves, he selected his two favorite ones and took them to the counter, where he asked the middle-aged woman behind the register, "In your opinion, do you think the red one is more appealing as a gift or the tan one?" He was leaning toward the tan scarf.

After a moment of contemplation, the lady said, "I find the red one prettier. If I were to buy one of the two, I would choose the red one."

"I'll trust you on that. Could I have you wrap that up as a present for me, please?"

"Certainly..." She paused, glancing at Paul, who stood

behind Leonard with a mischievous smirk on his lips. "Would you like a name tag tied to the ribbon?"

"Yes. Mary is her name."

"Would you like a note added?" she inquired.

"No, I don't think so."

Paul quickly spoke from behind Leonard. "Yes, he would, and I'll pay extra for it. How about: *Roses are Red, Violets are Blue, there is no way I'll ever be good enough to have you. But this scarf will help keep your body warm until Paul returns to you.* Can you write that for us, please?"

Leonard's friendly expression stiffened as he glared at Paul. "I've said all I have to say to you. You'd best remember what was said."

"Of course. And I'm shaking, see?" Paul tightened his muscles to shake mockingly. "Actually, I just want to know what it feels like. I mean, you've been aching to court Mary for so long, and well," he chuckled proudly. "I swing into town like a monkey on a vine and sweep her off her feet, carry her off to my place, and turn your innocent and precious lamb into a used ewe. It's truly my best magic trick." He suddenly pointed at the lady behind the counter. "Miss, let's change that poem to read: *Roses are red, Violets are blue, Mary, I hope you have a great time in Jandy's room.*"

Leonard's chest swelled with indignation. A fuse shorter than a flea's hair ignited within him. Leonard quickly stepped toward Paul, reaching out to grab him, but he froze when Paul swiftly stepped back, pulled a small, silver-plated derringer from his pocket, and cocked the hammer, aiming it at Leonard's face.

"You better stop where you are!" Paul warned. "It may not be a high-powered weapon, but at this range, it will blow your brains out the back of your head." Paul's expression was fierce. The darkness that had briefly shadowed his face faded now that Leonard was standing still and under the derringer's control. Paul smirked. "I'm a magician. I turned your lamb into an ewe, now let's see if I can turn you into a pretty little kitty. Do you want to see a magic trick, miss?" he asked the woman behind the counter.

The storekeeper responded nervously, "Sir, we don't want any trouble in here, please."

"Trouble?" Paul questioned innocently. "Miss, I'm not here to cause trouble. But I do need you to take three steps this way, please. One, two, three. Perfect," he said to the store clerk, positioning her to align parallel to Leonard despite being behind the counter. "I asked, do you want to see a magic trick?"

"I don't want any trouble," her anxious voice replied.

"There is no trouble. The answer to my question is yes or no. Of course, you want to see a magic trick. Why do I even ask? Don't move, miss, or trouble might find you after all. I'm sure you both would like to live long enough to go home. It's just a magic trick. There's no reason either of you should die for it. Right?"

Leonard swallowed to clear his suddenly dry throat. "What do you want?" The nervousness from having a gun aimed at him was evident in his voice.

"Lenny...I hope you don't mind me calling you Lenny. Leonard sounds too formal between friends."

"I'm not your friend," Leonard said bluntly.

"Of course not. I'm taking the woman you love and making her mine like a magician." Paul chuckled. "That part is easy because she's falling for me better than I ever hoped. Now, I want to show you a magic trick. I'm glad you shaved today, Lenny. Otherwise, I'd have to shave your face for you, and you wouldn't want that. Now, close your eyes."

"Are you going to shoot me?" Leonard asked, swallowing hard.

"No, I promise, I won't shoot you unless you force me to. That is up to you, but if I must shoot you, then I'll also have to shoot her. Her life is in your hands, so don't try anything stupid. I am going to hand my gun to my friend, and if you move at all, he will pull the trigger and put a bullet in your head, and then the lady's, too. Her life is in your hands, so I wouldn't move a muscle. Now close your eyes like a good boy and hold still."

Leonard reluctantly closed his eyes while his upper lip twitched.

Paul handed the gun to Gus and set his case on the counter. He gazed at the frightened store clerk, who desperately tried not to cry. "Miss, please relax." He waved his hand for her to step back a few steps out of the line of fire while holding a finger to his lips to signal her to keep quiet. "As long as he remains still, you are in no danger, but if he tries anything, I can't promise you'll live to see my finished work. I think you both will be amazed by this incredible transformation." Paul opened his case.

Leonard opened his eyes to check if Gus was aiming the gun at him. He was.

Gus was quick to say, "I wouldn't try anything, big fella. Just let him do what he wants to do, and we'll all get out of here." He felt uneasy and disliked the way Leonard gazed at him. Leonard closed his eyes.

Paul opened a jar of white face paint he used for his show and began rubbing it onto Leonard's face with his hands. He chuckled as he painted Leonard's face bright white and then closed the jar. He wiped his hands clean with a towel from the case and grabbed a jar of black makeup. Using his finger, he drew three whisker lines on each side of Leonard's mouth and colored his lips black. He stepped back to study Leonard's face before adding black eyebrows and a circle of black on the tip of Leonard's nose. After returning the jar to his bag, he took out his mirror and held it in front of Leonard's face.

Paul spoke proudly. "I'm amazing. It's a perfect transformation! Gus, don't you love it?"

"Yeah. Great workmanship," Gus said uncomfortably.

"Open your eyes, Lenny."

Leonard's lips curled into a sneer as he looked at his reflection. He resembled a cross between a clown and a child's face painted like a cat. His eyes turned to Paul with a steady glare, but he remained silent.

"Ta Daaa!" Paul sang. "You're a very cute little pussy cat! Don't you love it, Lenny?" he asked excitedly.

Leonard's lips lifted slightly. It took all his self-control to stay still. He spoke in a calm voice, "Laugh while you can."

"Oh, lighten up, pussycat. It's just a joke. Miss, don't you love it?" Paul asked the storekeeper. "Don't you just want to take him home and cuddle up with him? He's so darn cute!"

The shopkeeper glanced at Paul, not amused at all. "No."

"Oh, come on," he feigned offense. "I changed him from an ass to a pussycat. That is an amazing trick! Pure magic." Paul chuckled as he closed his case. "It just goes to show that you have no sense of humor, ma'am. I turned a man into a kitty. That's amazing! Huh, audiences can be so fickle." He carried his case and stood in front of Leonard. "Can you give me a little meow?"

"No."

Paul laughed. "That's purr...fect. You obey just like a

real pussy cat." He patted Leonard's arm good-naturedly. "Listen, join a freak show, Scribble Face. Maybe then Mary will show some interest in you. She likes showmen, like me. Isn't it funny how you can love her, and I'm just going to use her, but she'll choose me over you every single time." He paused to smile at Leonard's hardened expression. "Here." He flipped a coin from his pocket that landed on the floor and rolled away. "I would say Mary was worth two bits, but that's a bit too much after last night."

Paul took the derringer back from Gus and gazed at Leonard with appreciation. "Here." He tossed another coin from his pocket, which bounced on the floor. "Buy a cheap ring for Mary. She'll need someone to help her raise my kid after I'm gone." He laughed as he and Gus left the store.

The woman behind the counter carried a towel and handed it to Leonard. "That man is a true ass. Come to the back, and you can wash that off your face. If you want to tell the sheriff, I'll testify as a witness."

Leonard took the towel and wiped his face, smearing the makeup. "Thank you for the towel," was all Leonard said as he watched the two men walk along the boardwalk, laughing at him.

———

LEONARD ENTERED the sheriff's office and closed the door behind him. The Branson Sheriff, Tim Wright, sat at his desk, busy writing something. He looked up at Leonard's face, wrinkling his brow at the scratches and smudges of white and black paint. "You have something on your face."

"Yes, I do," Leonard said irritably. "I want you to arrest

Paul Jandy for holding me at gunpoint while he painted my face. I got a witness. She was held at gunpoint, too."

Tim frowned and shrugged. "Who is Paul Jandy?"

"The magician, Landy Jandy."

"Oh, him? He did that to you?"

"Yes."

"And who are you?" Tim asked.

"I'm Leonard Harris, Fletcher Harris's younger brother."

"I know Fletcher. He's a good man. But I haven't met you."

"I work in a lumber camp five days a week. I live with Fletcher and Jenny on the weekends. Paul Jandy had his friend Gus hold a gun to my head while Paul painted my face. I'm assuming that's a crime, right? You can ask Alice at the Fourth Street Market, she was held at gunpoint too."

"Hey, Alan," Tim asked his deputy, Alan Garrison, "is that the same magician you watched last night?"

"Yeah. He was amazing," Alan replied.

Tim redirected his focus to Leonard. "Why would he paint your face?"

"I don't know why. He doesn't seem to like me. I'm filing charges against him. I want him arrested."

Tim took a deep breath. "This is the second time I've been approached about that group. Isn't he world famous, the poster says?"

Alan said, "Yeah, like I said, he's amazing."

Tim clicked his tongue and said, "Okay, Fletcher's brother, I'll go see him pretty soon and get to the bottom of this. You can go on your way and check in with me tomorrow. Thanks for letting me know."

"Alice is a witness," Leonard said with a nod.

"I'll talk to her and get to the bottom of this. Have a

good day." Once Leonard left the office, Tim returned to the work he had at hand.

Alan Garrison asked, "Are we going to talk to Landy Jandy?"

Tim shook his head. "No. He didn't hurt anyone. Can you imagine the newspaper articles across the country printing that I arrested the world-famous magician for a joke? That's not the kind of publicity I want to be known for. That whole group will be leaving town soon enough. I'm not going to worry about it."

"What if Mr. Harris comes back wanting answers?"

"Well, two minus two equals zero, right? Two witnesses say he held a gun on the man, two witnesses say they didn't. We have nothing else to go on. I can't arrest a man without evidence," Tim reasoned.

CHAPTER TWENTY-TWO

PAUL'S BROW FURROWED AS HE WAS TAKEN ABACK by Mary's halfhearted hello when he approached her. After the kiss on the dance floor and many more that followed once the dance hall closed, he expected her to be more excited to see him. Her glance and averted eyes, along with her slumped shoulders as she walked away, were clear signs that his so-called friends had spoken to her. It wasn't the first time his fellow entertainers had gossiped about him.

"Mary," he called, "why are you avoiding me? Let me guess, you heard some gossip about me?" Although his interest in her had faded, he needed to maintain her interest. It was crucial to his plans.

"What?" she asked, unsure how to respond. They stood in the center of the ballroom, surrounded by rows of chairs. He had met her as he and Gus entered while she was leaving the ballroom to go upstairs. Unbeknownst to him, she was heading to her room to avoid him.

He raised his hands innocently. "Whatever they said

isn't true. I can almost guarantee it. What was it this time? Did I cheat on you already, or do I have a dozen delinquent kids? I've heard it all before. There's been a lot of gossip about me over the years I've been with this group. I swear, the women gossip like hens clucking, and the men are just as bad. So, what did you hear?" His innocent gaze was as pure as a child's laugh.

Her mind told her he might be lying to her about his intentions and faking his sincerity, but her heart melted under his gentle gaze. Swirling like a pulled drain, her emotions found no solid ground to cling to. She sighed heavily. "Am I just a toy to you?"

"A toy?" he gasped. "I don't know what that means. No. Like I've told you, you're an amazing lady whom I never thought I'd feel this way for. Gus, wasn't I just telling you that on the way over here?"

Gus nodded. "Yes, you were." He added to Mary, "I'll tell you, miss, I've known Paul for a long time now. He's my best friend, and he's telling the truth." He waved around the room. "The folks we travel with are good people, but they tend to assume the worst before knowing any facts. They did it to me about eight months ago. I met a lady I would have married right then and there, and before I knew it, it was over. I don't know if it was Bud or who exactly, but she heard some things that weren't true, and she wanted nothing to do with me after that. There was nothing I could say or do." He shrugged. "As they say, the show must go on. These folks we work with care about the show. They don't care if you're sincerely in love with someone or broken like a fiddle string. They just want to make sure nothing or no one gets in the way of the show. Paul's the star of the show, of course, they're going to lie about him when they know he cares about you. I trust

Paul, but very few others among those we travel with. He's not lying to you."

"Maybe you could let us talk for a minute?" Paul asked Gus.

"Sure thing." Gus walked over to the stage to join the band members.

"You, see?" Paul said with a shrug. "You're not a toy. Whatever that means." He chuckled at the absurdity of it.

Mary's large brown eyes locked onto his. Her expression wavered between being hurt by a deception and hoping the gossip was all lies. "They said you do this everywhere you go."

"Do what?" Paul asked, curiosity evident in his voice. His expression was innocent.

Mary sighed and wiped away a touch of moisture from her left eye. "Make some lady fall for you. I know you're leaving tomorrow, Paul. I don't want to fall for you any further than I already have. You're an amazing dancer and an intriguing man, but you won't ask me to leave here with you, and I wouldn't go even if you did. I don't know what came over me last night, but I'm thinking straight now. You should go your way, and I'll go mine."

Paul played indignant. His tone hardened just a touch as the volume remained low, "Oh yeah, we should just forget we ever met! And when our photograph arrives, we can just pretend that it never happened. Unfortunately, the photograph we took last night does exist, and when I get my copy, it's going to break my heart. Because you're everything I have ever dreamed of. You can even dance without making me trip or pulling me to the floor. You're amazing.

"Yes, I am leaving tomorrow. I have to finish the tour we're on. That's true. I couldn't ask you to come with me even if I wanted to. But here's the thing: what if we get along so well and are so attracted to one another because we finally met the one person God made for us? I mean, I have never felt the way I do about you. Granted, I meet people all over the country, and I won't lie to you: I've had some relationships with ladies that lasted a day or two, but none have compared to how I feel about you."

"Paul..."

"No, please let me finish," he snapped. "I can't take you with me, but that doesn't mean my heart isn't left here with you. When this tour is over, I'll come back to collect that piece of my heart, meaning you. I don't have much time left here, Mary. I don't want to waste it because of the lies that were fed by gossip." He paused, stopping her from responding to continue.

"Think about it: you've already made it known that you're saving yourself for marriage. Why in the world would I be pursuing you if my motives weren't genuine? I have no reason at all to pursue you if I wasn't being truthful with you. I'd pursue one of your friends who had fewer values if I were that way. But I'm not. You are everything I have been looking for. Listen, how about we sit down and talk for a while to get all this straightened out before I start preparing for the show tonight? And then afterward, if you are willing, we can make the most of our time together and dance our last dances until I return."

Mary sniffled and wiped her eyes as she responded slowly, "I don't know. I'll think about it."

"That's all I can ask. Shall we have a seat and talk for a little while?" He gestured toward the chairs arranged in aisles on the ballroom floor.

———

MATT STOPPED by the Fasana Furniture and Undertaker's Parlor and tried the door. It was locked. The sign in the window said *Closed*, but he peeked in anyway. He knew it took a day to ride to Hollister by wagon and a day to return, but he had hoped to catch his Uncle Solomon at the store, however, no one was there.

Matt walked to Solomon's house and knocked on the door. Deloris opened the door and stared at Matt with cold eyes. There was a brief silence before Matt asked, "Is Uncle Solomon home yet?"

"No." She started to close the door.

"You know I'm going to tell him. You might want to confess before I can. It might be easier on you," Matt said.

"Why don't you mind your own business?" Deloris snapped with a bitter scowl. "Do you think your precious uncle hasn't betrayed me? He's not the saint you all think he is!"

"No, I don't think he has betrayed you, nor do I believe he would."

"Well, that shows what you know. Doesn't it?" She slammed the door.

————

"DAMN HIM!" she muttered under her breath. She hadn't heard a word from Travis and concluded that he had a yellow streak down his spine, as bright as the white streak that ran down a skunk's back. Unfortunately, they were tied together in the same predicament, but she would deal with him later.

————

MATT WALKED five blocks to Travis McKnight's house and knocked on the door.

Travis McKnight peeked out of the door window and glanced behind him before answering it. He opened the door a few inches and peeked outside. "Matt..." he whispered, keeping his voice low.

"May I come in?"

"No! Get off my property, Matt. I don't want you around here," Travis whispered nervously.

"Is your wife home?"

"No!" Travis slipped outside and closed the door behind him. He led Matt halfway across the yard to speak privately. "Matt, I'm begging you not to cause me any trouble. Okay? I learned my lesson. I have a son, for crying out loud." His quivering voice and moistening eyes revealed the fear within him.

Matt lowered his head and exhaled. "That scar on your forehead reminds me of another lesson you learned, but it clearly didn't sink in deep enough. Perhaps seeing your wife's broken heart and your son's tears will drive that lesson home more deeply."

Travis shook his head slowly. "I'm asking you to let it go. I'll tell her. I promise."

"Now?" Matt asked.

"No! Matt, I made a mistake that could ruin my family."

Matt raised a hand to stop him. "It wasn't a mistake, it was a decision. I think you're calling it a mistake because you got caught. The consequences of that decision won't be nearly as much fun to pay."

Travis swallowed and nearly choked when the door opened, and his wife, Rhonda, asked, "Is everything all right?" It was concerning to see her husband speaking softly to the marshal in the yard.

"Yes, my love. I'll come inside in a minute. He's just asking about one of the men at the mill," Travis explained.

"Okay," she said, closing the door.

"Another lie, huh?" Matt asked.

"Matt, I'm begging you, let me tell her in my own time. She deserves to hear it from me." He gasped. "I've taken my wife for granted for far too long and been unfaithful. What I tried to do to Christine when Bella's Dance Hall opened was unforgivable, I know that. But I'm afraid of losing Rhonda and my son. Your aunt is crazy, and I don't want anything to do with her anymore. Matt, listen, your aunt wanted me to find someone who would kill you before you could tell Solomon, but I want nothing to do with that or her. So, watch your back. She is the one who wants you dead. I just did you a favor by telling you that, so please, do me a favor and let me be the one who tells my wife."

Matt didn't like his Aunt Deloris, but the words he had just heard surprised him. "Deloris wants to hire someone to kill me before I can tell Solomon?" he questioned. "Who is she asking to do it?"

"She doesn't know anyone, that's why she wanted me to find someone. But, like I said, I don't want any part of that. I refuse. I just want to keep my family together."

Matt hesitated thoughtfully. "I'll let you tell your wife, if you tell me, how long has this been going on?"

Travis lowered his head before answering uncomfortably, "Since July. Slater's Independence Day Ball is when it started."

"You can tell your wife, but I'd do it soon because when it gets out, she'll hear about it. Stay faithful to your wife, Travis. She deserves that much from her husband. Your son deserves that much from his father."

Travis felt relieved when he saw Matt walk away. He

entered the house and was greeted by Rhonda. "Who was the marshal asking about?"

"Um, a man named George. Just one of the laborers," Travis explained, hoping to satisfy her curiosity.

"What did he do?"

Travis shrugged his shoulders, trying to think of something to say. "Pickpocket. Not pickpocketing, but he stole something from the store. Matt was asking what time he got off work, is all."

"Isn't that the sheriff's jurisdiction?" Rhonda asked, knowing that the sheriff, Tim Wright, was one of Travis's closest friends.

"It is," Travis admitted. He knew he was digging himself into a deeper hole. "But Matt just wanted to know about it. It was one of his relatives, come to find out."

"What's George's last name? Which family does he belong to?"

"Um, I'm not sure how he fits in. That's a big family, you know."

Rhonda leaned her arm against the counter as she watched Travis with disgust. "Is the marshal trying to get him out of trouble?"

Travis cut a slice of bread from the loaf and spread some butter on it. "I think he is, yes. It sounded like it."

CHAPTER TWENTY-THREE

Fueled by anger at the thought of Deloris hiring someone to take his life, Matt returned quickly to his Uncle Solomon's house and knocked on the door. Deloris yanked the door open and snapped, "He's not home yet!"

Matt pressed his lips together before taking a breath. He raised his brow as he gazed into her eyes, his voice growing firm. "If or when you find someone foolish enough to try to assassinate me, keep in mind that if they fail, I will hold you responsible and arrest you. If they succeed by chance, my deputies will arrest you and make sure you are hanged. Either way, Uncle Solomon will still find out that he married an unfaithful woman."

An annoyed grimace quickly concealed the shock on her face. "What are you talking about? I'm not looking for anyone to kill you."

"That's good. Your lover isn't looking for anyone, either. I guess I'm safe then."

"Don't ever refer to him as my lover!" she snapped.

"You know who I'm talking about. Good. So, what he told me is true."

"No," Deloris protested. She paused to take a breath. "I was scared, okay? You had caught us in the hotel, and I was panicked. It was just idle talk. Do I want you to talk to Solomon? No. I'll do what I can to save my marriage. I love my husband, Matt. He is a good man, and I made a mistake. That's all there is to it. I don't need to condone my actions to you!" The hatred in her eyes was clearly evident as they burned into him.

"It seems you've made a number of mistakes since July, then, right? Travis told me everything. He also wanted me to know that he doesn't want anything to do with finding someone to murder me or anything to do with you. He thinks you're crazy. I have a different view of you. I'll come back tomorrow when Uncle Solomon is home."

———

DELORIS CLOSED the door and held back a scream. If Travis had the backbone of an ewe, he would have enlisted one of his roughneck friends from the mill to take care of Matt, sparing them both the humiliation of the town discovering their affair. Travis was undoubtedly a cowardly shrew hiding behind the skirt tails of Rhonda's dress, like a frightened child.

It didn't change anything. Her plan remained the same. She wasn't the only woman in Branson who had been unfaithful to her husband, but so far, she was the only one who had been caught. It was unfair how men could go to the brothel or have an affair outside of their marriage, and somehow, that was acceptable to other men. Yet, for a woman to have the same desires and act on them, she faced shame, ostracism, and often divorce. The mark of being an unfaithful wife was a stain on her reputation that could never be erased. She wondered how many of the women on Rose Street found themselves in their predicament for that same reason.

When Solomon finally died, she would move his body near the stairs and make it look like he had fallen down them and hit his head. It would be essential to ensure this was done while his body was still warm and freshly dead. If he died in the middle of the night, she could claim he passed away while she slept.

Slowly, a thought came to mind. Once Solomon was dead, Matt would question where the body they supposedly went to retrieve had gone. There were too many loose ends and not enough answers to the questions. She had come too far to back out now. She had involved Ollie and needed a guarantee that he would collaborate with her story and remain silent when people learned that Solomon had died. The fear of being caught added pressure, making her heart flutter with anxiety. However, if the loose ends were eliminated, all her fears would vanish, and there would be no stopping the desires of her heart if both ends, Matt and Ollie, were killed. No one would suspect her of doing anything wrong and would treat her as an innocent grieving widow.

She opened the basement door and went downstairs to find that Solomon had crawled from his mattress onto the soiled one thrown on the floor, wrapping himself in the wool blanket. The effort it took for him to do so might not have been much, but it represented a sign of life, which infuriated Deloris. She yanked the blanket off him, opened the boiler door, and shoved the blanket onto the burning coal before slamming the cast-iron door.

"I...it's c...c...cold," Solomon stuttered, shivering.

Deloris stood over him with a merciless gaze. "You need to hurry up and die! You have nothing to live for, so die. If you're still alive when I come back, I'm taking a sledgehammer and busting your head open." She turned around to leave.

"I...do...too," he said through chattering teeth.

Deloris snickered bitterly. "Oh, like what?"

"M...my...s...s...son. M...my...f...fam...ily."

Deloris sneered. "Where are they then? They abandoned you years ago. Your world is me, and I don't want you anymore. I think of you like one of those disposable rags that I used to throw away during my menstruation cycles. I didn't weep over tossing them out, Solomon. I won't shed a tear for you either." She ascended the stairs and closed the door behind her.

———

SOLOMON GASPED as an overwhelming wave of hopelessness washed over him. If he had any more liquid inside him, he could weep, but his eyes were as dry as the rest of him. It was true, he had distanced himself from his siblings and raised his son, James, away from his relatives. It wasn't that he held anything against them, it had more to do with maintaining peace within his home.

Deloris considered everyone in his family to be low class and did not want him to associate with the Fasana family, which sparked bitter fights whenever Solomon wished to join his family for holiday dinners and gatherings. His brothers, Joel and Luther, raised their families in the same town, but the only times Solomon spoke to them were on the street corner or while ordering a gravestone from the granite quarry. Seldom, very seldom, did he manage to get together to enjoy the company of his siblings. And when he did, Deloris kept James at home.

To his shame, their son James had been raised under his mother's wing and was nearly a stranger to his aunts, uncles, and cousins. They had kept James isolated to prevent the Fasana family from influencing him. Unfortunately, the Fasanas and Bannisters would never know that it was not Solomon's wish to do that, but rather his wife's, at the cost of containing her wrath.

Solomon stared at the dark ceiling and closed his eyes. He felt cold, weak, sick, in pain, and miserable. Death would be a welcome companion to ease his suffering. As a Christian man, Solomon knew heaven's gate was merely hours away. It didn't frighten him, he was at peace with his eternal home. What scared him was the truth never being revealed. He owed it to James to apologize for denying him the chance to know his family. They were not the uncivilized animals that Deloris portrayed them to be. They may have been a rough bunch who worked hard for their living, but James would never meet truer hearts or better people than those who shared his family line.

It was Solomon's fault for not standing up to his overbearing bride. He allowed Deloris to set the standards and rule their home as she saw fit. Solomon earned the money and made business decisions, while Deloris managed the household. His fear of angering her rendered Solomon a feeble voice within his home. If he could go back in time, he would never marry her. Deloris transformed him from an adventurous young soul with a yearning to explore the world into a weak, silent, and cowardly man whose only purpose was to work and support Deloris in fulfilling all her social ambitions.

He shifted his eyes to the yellow glare of the boiler door window, darkened by the coal. "L...Lord, s...s...save me. If...you...will," he stuttered through his chattering teeth. Without a blanket, the cold chill was deep and penetrating.

———

"OH, CRUD," Matt griped as he entered his house. His younger sister, Annie Lenning, sat at the dining table, drinking coffee with Christine. "What are you doing here?" he asked with a sour expression.

Annie stood up and stepped toward him, opening her arms to hug him. Suddenly, her loving embrace turned into two fists playfully hitting his stomach. Matt covered himself with his best protective block. Unable to target his body, Annie reached up, grabbed the back of his head by his long hair, and yanked it back.

"Girls grab hair!" Matt said, wincing.

"I am a girl," Annie said. "But I also have a right fist that I can pound on your face with." She raised her clenched fist above his head as Matt laughed.

"So," Annie said, her smile fading. "What's this I hear that you made Christine cry this morning? What? You can't get her pregnant? Don't you want a screaming baby? Huh?" She tugged harder on his hair.

"Yeah, I do!" Matt said, grimacing.

"Good," she said slowly. She emphasized her words with a threatening tone, saying, "And what are you going to *name* your first daughter?"

"Annie!" he exclaimed with a grimace.

"That's right. Good boy. Yeah, that's all I came over for." She released his hair. "I heard there was a magic show tonight, so Truet brought me to town. Steven and Nora came as well, but they are doing some shopping. Mostly, I came here to make sure we had your daughter's name picked out when you have one. And we do, right?"

"Yes. Yes, we do. It's good to see you, Annie." He hugged his sister affectionately. "Where's Truet?"

"He went to change his clothes. He'll be here soon. I thought we could go to the Monarch Restaurant for dinner. You're paying, of course. Right?" she asked with a threatening scowl.

Matt nodded. "Of course."

She smiled. "I thought so. So, what's this I hear about catching your Aunt Deloris in a hotel with some other man?"

Matt looked at Christine with disappointment. He had hoped to keep that information private until he could inform Solomon. He hated the thought of everyone knowing about it before Solomon did.

Christine gave a guilty grimace. "I had to tell her, Matt."

"She's your aunt, too," Matt told Annie.

Annie scoffed bitterly. "I can't stand the woman. She's not my aunt. I think I called her Aunt Deloris once when I was fourteen, and she said never to call her that again. So, she's cheating on Uncle Solomon? Have you told him? I'll be glad to if you haven't."

"Uncle Solomon went to Hollister to pick up a body. He should be back tonight or sometime tomorrow morning, I'm guessing. I'll stop by his place tomorrow evening. He should be home by then."

"Is Deloris scared?" Christine asked.

"Probably. I stopped by Travis's house and spoke with him. He said Deloris wanted him to hire someone to assassinate me before I could tell Uncle Solomon."

"What?" Christine exclaimed.

Matt continued, "Travis washed his hands of her. He said he wanted no part of that, and she doesn't know anyone she could ask."

"She never asked me," Annie quipped. "I'd do it cheaper than anyone probably."

"Does Travis know anyone?" Christine asked, ignoring Annie.

Matt scowled at his sister before answering Christine, "Travis doesn't want any part of it. I confronted Deloris, and she initially denied it. However, she then explained that she was scared and panicked. I don't think it is anything to worry about."

Annie spoke sincerely, "You better be careful, nonetheless. I don't know her, but she seems to be a ruthless woman. I remember her slapping the stuffing out of James when we were younger for nothing more than stating he didn't like his mother's pumpkin pie in front of the rest of the family. And her pie wasn't good, I do remember that. I believe that was the last time they attended a family gathering."

Christine stated, "They missed some good times then, I'm sure."

"Yes, they did," Annie agreed. "I don't think I've seen James more than once or twice since."

———

LEONARD HARRIS WAS grateful that no other customers were in the store to witness his humiliation by Paul Jandy and his friend. He carried a cloth bag of groceries and a wrapped gift for Mary back to his brother's home. He had to explain to his sister-in-law why his face was smeared with paint. He washed it off in front of a mirror and stared at his reflection. The scratches on his face had been opened by the towel and retained a hint of white paint. He squinted as he rubbed the deepest scratch with the corner of a towel to remove the paint.

"Make sure you get it all, or it may leave a tattoo if the skin heals over it," his sister-in-law, Jenny, said.

He gazed at her thoughtfully. "That's what he said he wanted to do to my face last night."

"Who?" Jenny asked, not understanding whom Leonard was referring to.

"The magician I told you about. Will you help me remove this paint from these scratches before I go talk to Mary?"

"Len," she said, using his shortened name, "you're a good man, and if that woman can't see that, then maybe it's time to let her go and give another woman a chance to hold on to you."

He grimaced slightly as she rubbed the towel into the deepest scratch. "I like Mary."

"You may like her, Len, but if she liked you, she wouldn't be infatuated with the magician you told me about."

"He's leaving town tomorrow."

Jenny exhaled heavily. "And then it will revert back to the way it has been for the past year. She'll gladly take your money and accept your gifts, but she won't give you anything. Len, she won't let you kiss her because she's not interested in you. Not romantically. I don't know why it is so hard for you to see that, everyone else does."

"You don't know her," he argued. "You've never even seen her. So how would you know?"

"Ask her, Len. Come straight out and ask her, and then, for Pete's sake, let her go. She's just wasting your time."

Leonard remained silent as Jenny dipped the towel into a bowl of water and gently wiped away the white paint that had seeped into another deep scratch. It began to bleed just enough to fill the cut.

"My friend Gretchen would be a good lady for you to consider courting. She's pretty."

Leonard rolled his eyes. "Is that why you keep inviting her over for Sunday dinner?"

Jenny grinned. "Well, I'd like to have her as my sister-in-law."

"Forget it. She's nice, but Mary is the one I want."

"Why? She hasn't shown any interest in you except for what she can get from you."

"That's not true. She let me rub her back just last week when I stayed late."

Jenny laughed. "That's getting something from you—a back rub. What do you get from her, Len? Honestly?"

Leonard's brow furrowed in thought. "I don't know. Her company. Her friendship. I just enjoy being with her. I guess that's all I care about, being with her."

Jenny couldn't argue with his answer. "Well, you're a grown man. However, I think Gretchen would be a better fit for you. You should give her a chance."

"No. Mary will someday realize how important she is to me and accept my courtship. I know she will."

"Do you think she'll find it funny when she hears about him painting your face like he did?"

"No, I think she'll be mad about it."

"Len, if she finds it funny, give her up. That will tell you everything you need to know, right?"

He took a deep breath. "I suppose it would."

CHAPTER TWENTY-FOUR

DELORIS FASANA WALKED TO THE FURNITURE store office to search for Ollie's address in the office files. After finding it written down, she walked nearly ten blocks to the Dogwood Shacks, where Ollie Hoffman lived. She knocked on the door.

The door was opened by a woman in her mid-thirties, with blonde hair that fell to her shoulders and a weathered face that bore the marks of her life's trials. "Yes?" the woman questioned. She gazed curiously at the strange older woman standing at her door, who wore a man's long wool coat over her dress and a wide-brimmed felt hat to conceal her face as she walked through the more impoverished side of town.

"Is Ollie home?"

"No. Who are you?"

Deloris put on her friendliest smile. "I'm Deloris Fasana, Solomon's wife."

"Oh! Would you like to come inside?" Ollie's mother invited her in from the gentle rain as she stepped back and opened the door wider. "I sure appreciate you and Solomon for allowing Ollie to work for you and treating him so well. It helps us a lot. My job doesn't pay much, so we are very thankful."

Deloris remained outside. "You are very welcome. Ollie is becoming very valuable to us. In fact, do you know where he is? I'd like to talk to him."

"No. He went off with his friend. He said something about going to Jeff's house, but I don't know where Jeff lives or his last name. Would you like to come inside out of the rain? I could make some coffee."

"No. No, thank you," Deloris said kindly. "When Ollie comes home, will you please have him come by my house? No matter what time it is. If I'm not home, ask him to wait. I will be home shortly."

"Okay. Is everything all right? He's not in trouble, is he?"

"Heavens no. Not at all." She hesitated, peering at Ollie's mother. "What do you do for work?"

"I'm a barkeep and cook at Ugly John's Saloon."

"I imagine there are a lot of rough men there?"

"Oh, yeah. You name it, we get it coming in."

Deloris questioned, "Who do you think is the most dangerous man you've met that lives here locally, anyway?"

She raised her brow. "For me, it was a man named Richie Thorn, who I courted for about four months. He was brutal."

"I'm curious, would you be interested in leaving that job and working in the furniture store with Ollie if we decided to hire someone else?"

Her eyes widened. "I'd love to!"

"Let me talk with Solomon. I'll see what I can do. What is your name?"

"Sheryl Hoffman. I'd be excited to work there if I could. I know I look terrible right now, but I can look better." The desire for a better job showed in her hopeful gaze.

"I'm sure you'd fit right in with Solomon and Ollie. I will have Ollie give you our decision when he comes by later."

Deloris was frustrated that Ollie wasn't home, however, she had the name of a brutal man she might be able to convince to kill Matt for a price if she could locate him. She knew Richie's name but had never met him personally. She knew Richie's brother, Joe Thorn, had three children with Solomon's niece, Billy Jo, but he never had the decency to marry her. Deloris had met Joe Thorn once or twice, but she was aware that the two brothers had led a strike at the Slater Silver Mine and attacked the Slater home while she was there. It was a frightening night, but there was no doubt that the Thorn brothers were fearsome and perhaps exactly what she needed.

———

DARKNESS WAS APPROACHING, and as every Branson citizen knew, Rose Street could be a dangerous place for a woman to walk alone at night. Men of every type came to Branson from all around to spend their pay on drunkenness, women, and carousing. Deloris wasn't familiar with any of the establishments on Rose Street other than Shady Ben's Hotel. She took a deep breath and entered Ugly John's Saloon. Immediately, she felt the eyes of all the customers on her. It was clear that a woman in her mid-fifties, wearing an expensive dress under a man's coat and a wide-brimmed felt hat, did not fit in with the rough and rowdy typical customers of Ugly John's Saloon.

The bartender was a large, heavy man with long, dark hair draping over his shoulders and a thick beard brushing against his chest. His gruff expression regarded Deloris as if she were a two-headed chicken. "Can I help you?" he asked, expecting to receive a tax bill.

She approached the bar and spoke quietly, "I'm looking for Richie Thorn. Do you know him?"

"Richie Thorn is not allowed in here. If you are looking for that wretch, you'll find him and his pals at the Thirsty Toad Saloon down the road. That's where they like to go."

Deloris walked along Rose Street, glad that it was still early enough for the street to be free of drunken toughs harassing her. The Thirsty Toad was just a few blocks down and had a larger crowd than Ugly John's. She entered with great trepidation at the sight of so many men of all ages drinking, gambling, cursing, and being led into back rooms by harlot women. Her stomach turned at the smell of unwashed bodies and soiled clothes mingling with alcohol and smoke. Nevertheless, a hint of excitement sparked within her. The crowd was far below her standards, but the freedom she felt amid the madness was thrilling.

She walked up to the bar and glanced around the saloon.

"Miss, you look about as lost as a beaver in a barren desert. I'm John Briggs, the owner of this establishment. Welcome to the Thirsty Toad. What can I get for you?"

"I'm looking for a man named Richie Thorn. Do you know him?"

"Richie? Of course." John looked toward the far end of the saloon. He cupped his hands to his mouth and shouted, "Richie! Richie Thorn. There's a woman here to see you!"

"Oh, boy, Richie, you should have run when you could!" a man teased.

"At least it ain't her husband this time, right, Richie?" a man shouted.

"Did you give her the ole drip-a-roo, Richie?" A man laughed.

"She looks a little haggard for a twenty-year-old, Richie. I think you've been lying to us about that new lady friend of yours."

Richie stopped six feet away to gaze at Deloris. "That's not my lady. It might be her grandma, but it isn't my doll." He took a drink from the glass he held. "Who are you?" he asked. Richie was tall and lean, with short, dark hair and a mustache.

"Can we talk in private?" Deloris asked. Her cheeks reddened with a surge of humiliation mixed with anger at the men mocking her age.

"If this is about Clara's eye, it was an accident. Are you her mother?" Richie asked.

"No," Deloris said. "This is about...well, could we step outside and talk privately?"

"As long as you're not Clara's mother, I suppose it's fine." He led the way onto the boardwalk. "All right, miss, who are you, and what's this about?"

Deloris hesitated and spoke quietly, not to be overheard. "I am Deloris Fasana."

"Are you related to William?" Richie asked.

"Unfortunately, by marriage. Solomon is my husband. He owns the..."

"I know who Solomon is. You're his wife? So, what do you want?"

She hesitated. "I was told you might be the kind of man I'm looking for..."

Richie laughed. "I'm not that desperate, mame. You'll

have to look for someone else. Is this a joke? Did my brother put you up to this?"

"No. This is not a joke," she said, her friendly expression fading away.

"Then what do you want, miss? My pals are waiting for me."

"What if I offered you a lot of money to do something for me, would you be interested?"

"Maybe. How much, and what would I have to do? Build a fence or something?"

"Not quite. What I have in mind is a little darker and more illegal. However, I heard you might be the right person for the job. Are you interested?"

"It depends, but you have me curious now. What is it you want done, miss?"

Deloris hesitated to speak. She had been observing Richie carefully to size him. In her view, Richie seemed more like a young drunkard than a killer. Disappointed by his lack of being a cold-blooded killer who frightened her, she said, "I can't say right now. I want to check with someone else first, but if you're interested and the job's still open, come to my house between eight and eight thirty tonight, and I'll tell you what I want done. I assure you, I will pay a lot of money if you're man enough to do the job."

Richie scoffed, offended. "Lady, I'm man enough to do whatever you want. Give me your address and I'll stop by. I am curious what a woman like you wants done."

"Come by the house, and I'll give you five dollars just for stopping by in case I need you to do the job. Then, and only then, I'll tell you what I need done and how much I'll pay. But understand this: if you mention a word about what I tell you, I'll pay a great deal more to ensure you never speak again. I may appear like a lady, but rest assured, I can be as hard as a rock. Come alone between eight and eight thirty."

"Miss, I have no doubt that you're as cold as a dead snake when you want to be. You have me intrigued. I'll be there."

———

THE GRAY CLOUDS obscured the sun setting over the mountains as a light mist gently fell onto the wet ground. Leonard Harris had dressed in a pair of new brown wool pants and a matching brown wool flannel shirt. As a lumberjack for the Seven Timber Harvester Company, living in a bunkhouse five days a week, Leonard spent his money on practical work clothing. He didn't own a suit and couldn't dress as fancy as Paul Jandy, but he wore his new clothes to compete for Mary's affection.

He arrived at Bella's Dance Hall early, hoping to see Mary before they opened for the show. Part of him burned with jealousy, but a stronger motive for arriving early was to limit the time the magician spent with her while also reinforcing the idea that he was willing to fight for her. Leonard never used the word love, as it was a frightening term that could scare her away like a startled bird if it came up too soon. However, watching her kiss another man the way she had the night before ignited a fury that could only be attributed to love. Mary was supposed to be his lady, he wanted her to be his bride.

He had not slept well the night before, lying awake filled with indignation, pondering what Mary was doing and wondering if Landy Jandy was with her. Inappropriate thoughts crossed his mind, and the anger burned within him. Paul Jandy's words, *"going to turn your lamb into an ewe,"* haunted him. If he could get away with it, he would beat the famous Landy Jandy within an inch of his life and drag him four miles north of town to throw him into the soiled hole to rot with the rest of the feces. The soiled hole was the first deep hole dug by the Fasana Granite Company to start a granite quarry that had been abandoned years earlier. It was now used by his brother, who bought the Branson Nightmen Company, which worked nights cleaning out privies and dumping the refuse into the hole.

The humiliation that afternoon in the grocery store only fueled his hatred for the man. With that in mind, he wanted to talk to Mary and inform her about the kind of person Landy Jandy really was. The man's intentions for Mary were far from admirable, and she needed to understand what a piece of trash the well-dressed and handsome man truly was. Leonard had no doubt that if Mary knew the truth, she would be disgusted by Paul Jandy and would end her relationship.

He knocked on the door of the dance hall. It took a moment for the security guard, Gaylon Dirks, to open it. "Leonard, we're not open for another two hours," Gaylon said.

"I understand. I was hoping to speak with Mary."

"She's upstairs getting dressed or taking a bath or something. You'll have to come back when we're open."

"Who is that?" Bella yelled from inside.

"Leonard! He wants to speak with Mary," Gaylon shouted.

"Tell him to come back when we're open," Bella replied.

"I already did. All is well." Gaylon turned back to

Leonard. "Sorry, Leonard. You'll have to come back in two hours."

"All right. Tell her I stopped by."

Disappointed, Leonard stepped back from the door as it swung open abruptly. Paul Jandy stepped onto the porch and shut the door behind him.

"Hey, you, let me see that pussy cat face." Paul gasped dramatically when Leonard turned around. "You cleaned your face off? Seriously? You looked so good, too. Hey, listen," he said, lowering his voice and pulling a small brown bottle from his pocket to show Leonard. "After tonight, you might not want Mary. I think Mary will be sleeping in until we're long gone." He chuckled. "Usually, I don't have to use this stuff, but Mary's morals are a bit higher than I'd like. No worries, though. A good dose of this will put her out like a candle's flame. When she wakes up tomorrow, your lamb will be an ewe, or dare I say, bred stock. She'll hate me when she wakes up, but I'll be miles away by then. And the best part of all is"—his face turned to stone—"there is nothing you can do to stop me."

"Do you want to bet on that?" Leonard asked, stepping closer. He felt the wrath swelling within him as his fists clenched tightly. One hit would break the man's jaw. "You're supposed to be in jail."

Noticing Leonard's aggressive approach, Paul stepped back and tried to avoid smiling. He spoke quietly, "Jail? For what?"

"Holding a gun on me. I went to the sheriff."

Paul Jandy's smirk faded into a glare. His voice remained calm. "I painted your face in the grocery store. What kind of a man allows another man to do that? You're a scribble-faced coward, having to run to the sheriff like a crying kid hurrying to tattle to his mother. So, tell me, coward, what are you going to do to stop me? I'm the star of the show, I can buy my freedom from the sheriff, and then I'm taking your woman to my hotel room. And if she ever marries you, you'll be raising my kid."

Leonard had heard all he could take and swung his right fist with all his might. His hardened fist struck Paul on the side of the face, sending him crashing onto the wooden porch decking. Leonard leaped on top of him and began swinging his right fist toward Paul's face over and over, but Paul kept both arms tightly positioned defensively over his face as Leonard's fists repeatedly struck Paul's forearms.

Within moments, Gus was on the porch with Gaylon and Dave, pulling Leonard away from Paul. While Dave and Gaylon restrained a wild-eyed Leonard, Gus helped Paul to his feet and positioned himself between them.

Leonard's fury boiled as he pointed a finger at Paul, shouting, "Stay away from her! Dave, he has a bottle of something he is going to give to Mary to seduce her! He's going to hurt her!"

"A bottle?" Paul questioned, aghast. "A bottle of what? I don't have a bottle. Dave, he hit me for no reason other than jealousy. The man's crazy. I didn't do anything to him."

"He's lying. Search him, Dave!" Leonard shouted. "You know I wouldn't lie about Mary." His heavy breathing, wide eyes, trembling voice, and twisted sneer revealed his outrage. Leonard's chest rose and fell heavily.

Dave warned Paul, "If you have a bottle of chloral hydrate or anything on you, you won't be allowed back inside. I'll cancel the whole show."

Paul turned and raised his arms against the building,

spreading his legs. "Search me. I don't have a bottle of anything. I don't even know what chloral hydrate is. I've never heard of it. Go ahead and search me. I'll prove he's lying. I should press charges. In fact, I will, just to keep myself safe tonight. Dave, I don't feel safe with him attacking me like this. How do we know he won't do the same tonight?"

"It was in his pocket, Dave," Leonard said as Dave began searching Paul.

Dave ran his hands over Paul's body and searched his pockets but didn't find a bottle. He knew all too well that Paul was a magician and that making a bottle disappear wouldn't be difficult with his sleight of hand. Dave was familiar enough with Leonard to know he wasn't lying, yet Paul was one of the stars of the show and didn't have a bottle hidden on him. Personally, Dave didn't like Paul Jandy and believed everything Leonard said, but without a bottle, Leonard's accusation couldn't be proven. Despite his opinion, the fact remained that the dance hall was a business, and he couldn't have a fight in the middle of an event that invited the public to visit their establishment.

"Get back inside, Paul," Dave said. He turned to Leonard. "I'm sorry, Leonard, you're going to have to leave. I can't let you in tonight."

"What?" Leonard stammered. "Dave, he's inviting Mary back to his room tonight so he can drug her!" The frustration and desperation brought moisture to Leonard's eyes as he vented his outrage at Dave. "Who's going to protect Mary if I'm not here? You can't keep me from coming. He's going to hurt her. He told me so!"

Dave spoke calmly. "I searched him, Leonard. He doesn't have anything on him."

"Then search his friend, he has a bottle."

Paul Jandy stood behind Dave and Gaylon, a broad grin on his face as he nodded confidently. "Search Gus, too. Please do. Heck, you can search us both all day long. I don't have anything to hide."

Dave searched Gus for a bottle and turned to Leonard. "I'm sorry, but I can't find any evidence of a bottle. I'm afraid I must insist that you don't bother trying to come here tonight. Go home, Leonard. I will protect Mary. Rest assured of that. She won't be going anywhere with him. You have my word. You can come back next week."

Leonard felt as though his insides had fallen out. "Dave..." He swallowed strenuously as his eyes filled with moisture. "You can't mean it. Mary..."

Dave hardened his voice. "I do mean it. Come back next week. Mary will be fine, I promise."

"Dave..." Leonard pleaded.

"Wait, Dave," Paul said, stepping forward as if an idea had just occurred to him. "I have a better idea. I have a feeling Scribble Face doesn't like me. So, I have the perfect setup in mind. I'm not doing the rope trick tonight. Instead, I'm performing my greatest feat, the magic bullet trick. It's a real bullet, Scribble Face. I want you to try to shoot me, and I'll bet I can catch the bullet. Here's the deal: you aim at my face, and you pull the trigger whenever you want. But you must aim at my face—nowhere else. If I'm killed, it's just an accident. You cannot be charged for any harm done to me. But if I catch the bullet with my teeth, you leave the premises quietly without speaking to Mary or causing a scene. Are you interested?"

Bud Hennessy stepped out of the building. "What's going on out here?"

Paul explained, "You're just in time, hog. I'm inviting Scribble Face to take your place and be my shooter for the magic bullet trick tonight. I have a feeling he'd like to shoot me, too."

Bud narrowed his eyes. "Really?" He looked at Leonard. "Are you willing to do it? All you have to do is aim and shoot. The only rule is, you have to aim at his face to blow his brains out."

A slight upward turn lifted Leonard's scowling lips. "I'm sure it's a fake bullet, right? Just powder?"

Paul answered. "No. I'll have someone from the audience verify it's a real bullet. You can even load it. But you must be man enough to pull the trigger while I'm looking at you and when I'm ready, of course. If I miss it, that's on me. You won't get in any trouble if I'm killed. The risk is all mine."

"I don't trust you," Leonard said with skepticism.

"Dave," Paul said, watching Leonard. "You are a witness to everything I've said. I'll put it all in writing for all of us to sign. Dave, remind me, it's Saturday night, and Mary can leave the dance hall since she's not working tomorrow, correct?"

"She can, but as I mentioned, she isn't going anywhere with you."

"She is an adult, is she not? It seems to me that she can do whatever she wants. I'm afraid you don't own her, Dave. True?" Paul asked pointedly.

Dave didn't like Paul Jandy at all. "That's true. But Bella and I will convince her to stay here. I believe what Leonard told me. I just can't find the bottle."

Paul shrugged. "No one found a bottle, so how could it be true? Where am I going to hide it? I'll strip down naked if you want, you won't find a bottle of anything. Look, the point is Mary has tonight off, Lenny. If you want to stop me from any of the illusions that you're accusing me of, then here is your chance to stop me, *if* you can. Come on, Scribble Face, I have humiliated you, moved in on your woman, kissed your woman, and painted your face. What more do I have to do to get some fire in your spine? How's this? If you don't stop me, I'll prove your accusations true, and Mary will hate you for not stopping me when I'm giving you the opportunity to. Get some fire in that cowardly gut of yours and aim and shoot right here!" Paul pointed at his nose.

Leonard nodded in agreement. "Fine. It will be my pleasure."

Paul laughed. "Great! Bud, are you okay with that?"

Bud nodded. "I am. I'll start writing the agreement up."

"Good. Scribble Face, be here at eight so we can get you ready."

"What kind of gun do you use? Your derringer?" Leonard asked.

"No. It's a ball and powder. I use an 1842 Aston single-shot with a .54-caliber ball. You'll be twenty feet away, and you aim that ball at my face. You can shoot a pistol. Right? You know how to shoot one of those, right? We'll teach you if not. It's so easy a dumb lumberjack could do it."

"I know how to shoot," Leonard snapped.

"That's good. I'll have an agreement written out stating you are not liable if anything happens to me, so feel free to pull the trigger and stop me before I, well, you know."

"Yeah, I know. I'm looking forward to it."

"Good. I'll see you at the show."

———

LEONARD'S SISTER-IN-LAW, Jenny, questioned him as he came home much earlier than she had anticipated.

"You're home already? I figured you'd be gone until late. Did you ask her what I told you to?"

"No. I didn't get to see her. But I did talk to Landy Jandy. He's giving me the chance to shoot him tonight. The magic bullet trick. I'm sure it's not real, but I'll shoot him if I can."

Jenny's tone grew concerned. "What do you mean? Is it a real bullet? You'd better be careful if so. You don't want to kill him. She's not worth that, Len."

"It's impossible to catch a bullet. It can't be real. I'll feel better just pulling the trigger while aiming at him."

Jenny wondered aloud, "Why did he ask you? You're not part of their show."

"I don't know." He refrained from telling her about Paul's bet regarding Mary. He would worry about that after the show if necessary.

"I don't like it, Len. He must have a trick up his sleeve to frame you. Maybe he'll fake his death and have you arrested."

Leonard answered, "No. He's writing an agreement that states I cannot be held accountable if he's killed or hurt."

"Lenny, make sure to read that agreement carefully before you sign it. He has done nothing but hound and humiliate you, so I don't think he's doing you any favors."

Leonard smiled awkwardly. "I don't think so either. But it's my chance to get even. I might shoot him in the shoulder or leg just to make sure he can't dance with Mary. I never told him I was a good shot. Accidents happen."

"But you *are* a good shot."

Leonard's smile faded. "I know. Fletcher and I grew up shooting the same pistol he's using. I know everything about it. I won't miss, and the audience will know if it's a real bullet or not. He'll be sorry he asked me to fire that pistol. He'll be sorry he laid his lying lips on Mary."

"Len," Jenny said firmly, "Don't you dare do something stupid."

"I won't. I'll just do exactly what he told me to do: aim for the center of his face and pull the trigger."

CHAPTER TWENTY-FIVE

TIME WAS RUNNING OUT, AND DELORIS WAS OUT of options. She had returned to Ollie's, but he still wasn't home. One thought kept surfacing, but it was even further outside her comfort zone than wandering around Rose Street after dark: Chinatown.

The former head of the Chinese Benevolence Society, Wu-Pen Tseng, had been contracted to rebuild the mortuary and furniture store after their business burned down. The cost was significantly higher than initially agreed upon, and as Deloris reviewed the cost of materials, it didn't seem right. By the time the project was completed, their bill was nearly one and a half times greater than it should have been for materials alone. She discussed this with Solomon, but he was impressed by the craftsmanship of the Chinese laborers and, in her opinion, intimidated by Wu-Pen, so he refused to confront him. Deloris wasn't afraid to confront anyone, but she had never had the opportunity to meet Wu-Pen in person. Wu-Pen had reportedly murdered a few men and taken Matt hostage in an underground city built by the Chinese. It was unfortunate that Wu-Pen had not managed to kill Matt, however, Matt survived, and Wu-Pen did not.

After Wu-Pen's demise, a new leader, Ah-See, was appointed President of the Chinese Benevolence Society. The Chinese Benevolence Society owed Solomon and her a significant amount of money, and Deloris needed a favor. With that in mind, she entered Chinatown and found herself directed to a red building. She knocked on the door, which was opened by an older Chinese man in a white gown. He vanished upstairs, and a younger Chinese man followed him down.

"Hello, may I help you, miss?" he asked with a Chinese accent, though he spoke fairly good English.

"Who are you?" she asked.

"My name is Ah-See. I am the president of the Chinese Benevolence Society. Welcome. May I ask your name?"

"I am Deloris Fasana."

"Ah! Mrs. Fasana. How can I assist you tonight?"

She spoke bluntly. "Your Chinamen build my husband's building for the furniture store and mortuary. I've done the math, and you all bought enough lumber, bricks, and mortar to build two buildings. I want what you owe me, or I'll take you to court."

Ah-See was taken aback. "I see. I admit that happened before I took over leadership of our society. Please come upstairs, and I will look for the paperwork that should be there to verify it is as you say. Come," he said, leading her upstairs, down a hallway, and into his apartment. He spoke Chinese to his wife as he entered and took a seat in a chair. "Please, sit," he said, waving to a chair facing him. "My wife will find that file in the office and bring it to me. Then we can see if you were done wrong. By all means, I would like to avoid a lawsuit."

Deloris spoke. "The way I figured it, you owe me quite a bit. Hundreds, if not over a thousand dollars. You Chinese thieves bought enough supplies that you could build an underground city, which I am sure is where my money went."

Ah-See was uncomfortable with her hostile tone. "Well, we will investigate that. If that was done, then we will make it right. I know your brothers-in-law, Luther and Joel, very well. I worked for the Fasana Granite Quarry for years. They are good people. I assume you and your husband are, too."

Deloris sighed in frustration. "I'm sure. However, they are not involved in this. This matter concerns only you and me. It's my money that was taken from me, and I want it returned."

Ah-See nodded. "Of course. I will make things right between us if you were done wrong. We are an honorable people, and I strive to lead our community with honor and truth."

Deloris tilted her head with skepticism. "Nice slogan. But I have other thoughts at the moment."

"Of course you do. I understand." A moment later, a stunning Chinese woman in a beautiful gown entered the apartment, carrying a tightly bound folder. She smiled at Deloris as she handed the folder to Ah-See.

He spoke in Chinese and then said, "This is my wife, Ling."

Deloris glanced at her from head to toe with a snide look. She was a beautiful woman, without a single flaw aside from being Chinese.

"Hi," Ling pronounced with a strong Chinese accent.

Deloris offered a forced smile before asking Ah-See, "What does all that chicken scratching say?" She couldn't read Chinese.

Ah-See's brow furrowed as he read and flipped to the next page. He asked Ling a question in Chinese, and they exchanged words for a moment. Ling Tseng was Wu-Pen's courtesan, who had become his unofficial wife and taken his name.

"Hmm," Ah-See grunted, displeased. "Well, it seems we may have overcharged by quite a sum. May I offer you a settlement and resolve our dispute without involving the American court system?"

"That's why I'm here. How much?"

Ah-See nodded with a pained grimace. "Quite a bit."

Ling spoke in Chinese and initiated a brief conversation between the two.

Frustrated, Deloris asked, "What are you two dogs...I mean, people talking about?"

Ah-See looked at her with a kind smile. "No harm done. Finances, to answer your question. The former president of the Chinese Benevolence Society was not as honest as he should have been. Your husband was done wrong. It was very tricky how they did it, but you caught him. You are a smart lady."

"How much do you owe me?" she asked suddenly.

He spoke briefly to Ling before answering. Her pleasant expression remained unchanged. "My offer," Ah-See said, "is seven hundred dollars right now and three hundred more next month."

Deloris hesitated. "A thousand dollars? What if I were to offer you that money back to have one of your people kill someone for me? Is that a possibility?"

Ah-See paused in silence for a moment. "We don't do that," he replied slowly.

Deloris nodded. "Yeah, you all do. I remember your last leader's men doing that. My husband owns the mortuary, and we saw the bodies. Your people may not have gotten caught, but Solomon knew those deaths out at the mining camp were murders. Nobody gets bitten by that many black widows and drowns in their own vomit. He was tied up, the marks were on his body. So don't tell me you don't have access to people who can do that. I'm talking business. Can you help me or not? If not, I want the thousand dollars tonight, otherwise, I'll file charges and make it known publicly what you dogs did to my husband and me on Monday. I'll take it to the Branson Gazette Newspaper, and no one will do business with you folks ever again."

Ah-See shook his head innocently. "What happened before I took over, I know nothing about."

Ling Tseng noticed the stress lines on Ah-See's forehead and asked him what had been said. They had a brief conversation in Chinese. She nodded in understanding, wearing the same pleasant smile as she watched Deloris.

Ah-See spoke with a heavy heart, "We do not have a thousand dollars available tonight."

Deloris leaned forward in her chair with determined eyes as she said, "Then I want a man killed tonight or first thing tomorrow morning. If you can't help with that, which I would find hard to believe, you'll find your community isolated and eventually driven out of town. I have a lot of influence in Branson and will ensure that your reputation is that of thieves and swindlers. Do you understand me?"

"I do. Give me a moment." Ah-See translated to Ling Sheng. She spoke to Ah-See, and he seemed surprised by what she said. He turned to Deloris. He asked slowly, troubled. "Who do you want killed so badly that you would try to blackmail us?"

Deloris spoke slowly. "The marshal, Matt Bannister."

"Matt? Why?" Ah-See asked quickly.

Deloris's voice hardened. "Why doesn't matter! I need him dead tonight. You have two choices: find one of your people to do it or give me a thousand dollars right now. If not, I'll go to the courthouse on Monday and make this thievery public. Your little city here in Branson will disappear overnight, I'll make sure of it."

Ah-See's anxiety escalated. "As I said, we do not have a thousand dollars tonight."

Deloris gazed at him with a victorious smile. "Then I suggest you instruct one of your people to kill Matt and his wife tonight while they sleep. And maybe your man could start a house fire to cover up any evidence of a murder?"

Ling spoke, initiating a conversation between the two in Chinese.

Annoyed, Deloris snapped, "What is she yipping about?"

"I was translating our conversation to her," Ah-See explained. "You leave me no choice. There is apparently such a man that we know who can do as you request, but as the Bible says, at Jesus's court in front of Pilate, I wash my hands of this crime."

"I don't care about that. I just want it done. Can it be done tonight?"

He nodded. "Yes. Our friend is apparently quite talented with what he does. No one will know it was not a natural death."

Ling spoke softly while gesturing toward Deloris.

"Does she ever shut up and mind her business?" Deloris snapped.

Ah-See smiled. "Ling says, guess how old she is."

Deloris frowned. "I didn't come here to guess her age. I came for my money."

"I know, but please guess Ling's age."

"Twenty-three."

He responded in Chinese for Ling. Her face brightened in surprise. She spoke extensively.

"Ling says no. She is forty-five."

"No, she's not!" Deloris exclaimed.

"Yes. Forty-five. Ling says your beauty is fading too fast. She can tell you were a stunning lady in your youth, and you can be again. She can take the years from your face and make you shine thirty years younger if you want."

"How?" Deloris was curious.

"Chinese medicine. It can take years away just like it has with Ling."

Deloris was quickly skeptical. "Wait a minute. Is this a ploy to get out of our deal? I bet it costs just as much as what you owe me, right? Do I have to decide between Matt's death and looking younger? I choose Matt's death. I won't change my mind on that!"

"No. If you insist on paying for his and Christine's deaths, then it will be accomplished as you wish. As I said, I wash my hands of it, and once it is done, there will be no talk of it. No history of it, and no trace of who did it. But Ling's youth medicine costs very little. She thinks you could be beautiful and happy again."

"What do I need to do?"

A moment later, Ling brought her a small vial of green liquid. Ah-See explained, "For six weeks, you drink one vial of this medicine once a week with a glass of water and follow it with another glass of water. Each week, you will look five years younger. Start tonight and come back next

Saturday for another vial. In six weeks, you will look almost as young as Ling. That is what she says."

"And the cost?" Deloris asked, anticipating a high sales price.

"Ten dollars. You can pay next week if you'd like. Your gray hair will be darker by next week. Ling is confident that you like the results and will be back for more."

"And Matt? Can you promise me he will be killed tonight? I'm giving you a thousand dollars and saving your reputation in town for it."

Ah-See nodded. "I promise, our friend has never failed."

Deloris held up the vial to a lantern's light. "Thank you. I feel better already." She snickered. "I'm glad I came here."

"Me too," Ah-See said. "Our friend will make their deaths seem very natural. I will see you out and get you a rickshaw ride home to keep you safe."

———

DELORIS ENJOYED the rickshaw ride home as she directed the Chinese man toward her house. She guarded the vial of Chinese medicine as if it were a fragile newborn in a den of lions. It was the secret elixir that could turn her dream of finding a new husband in Boston into a reality. If she could look thirty again and restore the natural color of her hair, she could lie about her age and marry a younger man with the energy to keep up with her desires.

She knew Richie Thorn planned to come by her house later that night, but she cared little about that. The joy of looking younger outweighed any cost she might incur. Aging was tough enough on her knees and finger joints, but it was her reflection in the mirror that bore the heaviest burden. She remained an attractive woman for her age, but her beauty had faded over the years as the lines deepened around her lips and eyes, while gray crept into her hair like a growing cobweb. For ten dollars a week, she could restore her beauty and become a single woman, with her future shining even brighter. Matt would be dead by morning, and she could literally get away with murder.

She poured the vial of green-tinted liquid into a glass of water, mixed it with a spoon, and gulped it down. She refilled the glass and drank that as well. She looked at the basement door and considered going down to see if Solomon was still alive, but with Matt's life coming to an end by morning, she felt no need to worry about it. She decided to wait until daylight to find him dead.

She went to the family room and sat in her chair. Within a few minutes, she began to feel strange, and then a pain gripped her chest like a blacksmith's vice, squeezing tighter until she could not breathe. She stood and stepped toward the hallway, but collapsed to the floor in severe pain. She stretched out her arm, reaching for any hope of help, but there was no one there. And then, in the family room of her large empty home, her life on earth came to an end.

CHAPTER TWENTY-SIX

ANNIE LENNING WRINKLED HER NOSE AS SHE looked at the white gauze wrapped around her nephew Josh's head due to his injured ear. "So, the doctor said your ear will be deformed, huh? If you want your ears to match, I could hit the other one. It might knock your sense of balance back into...well, balance. There might be some truth in that knocking-some-sense-into-you saying, after all."

"No thanks, Aunt Annie," Josh said with a faint smile.

"Are you sure? If I hit your other ear hard enough, it might fix your bad ear. I'm thinking."

Josh smiled. "One ear is bad enough for right now."

Annie's eyes narrowed. "Hmm. Maybe I just want to hit that ear, though."

Steven Bannister placed his thumbs in his pockets. "I have a small vice. If that ear wrinkles up like a dried-up potato, I can straighten it out just like a woman ironing clothes if I get it tight enough."

"A flat ear would look kind of silly, wouldn't it?" Annie asked skeptically. "I think hitting his other ear with my fist to make them match is the best option."

Steven raised his brow thoughtfully while clicking his tongue. "I bend iron for a living. I'm sure I can manipulate his flesh to bend with some hot steel, pliers, and rivets, if nothing else. Skin and cartilage aren't as hard as iron. How hard could it be?"

"Good point," Annie agreed. "Do you have your vice here?"

"No. I'd have to take him to my blacksmith shop to do that."

"Then we have no choice. Hold him down, and I'll wallop that other ear."

Steven stepped forward and grabbed Josh as he screamed, "Mom! Mom…"

Steven laughed and let go of Josh.

Annie shook her head, disappointed. She rubbed her right fist on her left palm. "I was warming up my fist to give you a good wallop and fix that ear. You're calling for Mama, huh? I'm disappointed, Josh. You sound like your uncles. I expected more from you."

"Annie, quit harassing my son," Mellissa Bannister said as she entered the reading room where Josh sat with some of his younger siblings and cousins. He had agreed to babysit the younger kids for the night while his parents went to the traveling show at the dance hall with the others.

Annie grunted. "I just wanted to hit him and make him better."

Mellissa rolled her eyes. "I'm sure it would work, Annie, but we need to get going."

MATT LED the way into Bella's Dance Hall with Christine on his arm, followed by his brothers and their wives. Matt's sister, Annie, entered with her fiancé, Truet Davis.

"Christine, it is so nice to see you again," Gaylon Dirks said as they entered. "I know you were just here last night, but we miss you around here." He gave her a warm hug before shaking Matt's hand and greeting the rest of the family.

After chatting with Gaylon for a moment, Matt and his brothers went to the bar to get drinks for the ladies and themselves. While standing at the bar, Matt noticed Ollie Hoffman stepping into the dance hall with a friend about his age. Matt chuckled slightly as he watched the two teenage boys' mouths drop open when two of the dance hall ladies, Rose Blanchard and Sherry Stewart, walked past them. He was sure the two boys had fallen in love at first sight, as they couldn't take their wide eyes off the two ladies.

The brothers returned to their seats with the drinks, where the ladies were waiting. Matt handed Christine her lemonade and excused himself for a moment to approach Ollie and his friend, who were watching Rose and Sherry talk to a pair of men at the bar.

"Ollie, you're not even old enough to be in here, are you?" Matt asked with a friendly smile.

"I think so. They let us in."

"Ollie, do you know if Solomon is planning to come here tonight?"

Ollie shrugged his shoulders. "I don't know. He wasn't feeling good this morning."

"Maybe not, then. Just as well. I'll talk to him tomorrow. What time did you two get back?"

Ollie looked at his friend with a puzzled expression. "A couple of hours ago. We weren't fishing for very long." He continued nervously, "Am I in trouble for something? My mother said Mrs. Fasana came by looking for me, but no one answered the door when we stopped by there. That was just thirty minutes ago or so."

"Do you know what she wanted?" Matt asked.

"No. Maybe she needed help moving Solomon again. I don't know."

Matt tilted his head to hear better in the noisy ballroom. "What do you mean?"

"She had me help move Solomon this morning. He's sick."

"You didn't go to Hollister?"

"No," Ollie answered, perplexed. "Why would I go to Hollister? I don't even know how to get there."

"Where is Solomon?"

"In his basement."

"Wait. Wait. Wait," Matt said quickly, trying to make sense of what he was being told. "So, you and Solomon did *not* go to Hollister?"

"No," he answered. "Why would I be going there?"

"So, Solomon is at home. He's just been working in the basement, building shelves or something?" Matt questioned.

Ollie hesitated to speak but slowly shook his head. "I'm not supposed to tell anyone, but he's sick. Real sick..."

"Who told you not to tell anyone? Deloris?" Matt asked.

"Yes, sir."

"What did she say?"

"She said the doctor told her he'd heal better in the basement, where it's colder. I helped Mrs. Fasana take him down there this morning and put him on a mattress."

"In the basement?"

"Yes, sir."

"How sick is he?"

"Real sick. He can't walk and he..." He lowered his voice so he wouldn't be overheard. "He was puking and soiling himself. It smelled bad. Real bad. I told Mrs. Fasana he needed a doctor, but she said the doctor had been there four times and to put him in the basement to keep him cool."

"What doctor said he should be in the basement?"

Ollie shrugged. "She didn't say."

"And he's still there?"

Olie shrugged. "As far as I know."

"Ollie, enjoy the show. I'm going to check on my uncle." Matt searched the audience in the ballroom for either of the town's two doctors but did not see either of them in the crowd. However, he did notice his deputy, Nate Robertson, sitting beside one of the dancers named Angela. Matt stepped around a row of chairs to speak to Nate. "I hate to do this to you, Nate. But I need you to run to Dr. Ryland's house and take him to my Uncle Solomon's house right away. I don't know what's going on, but I have a bad feeling about it. I'm going over there right now."

Nate stood. "Sure. Angela, I apologize, I have to leave, but I'll be back. Save my seat."

Matt's eyes swept the room and met Christine's. She could tell by his expression that something was wrong. She moved to meet him halfway as he approached her. "What's wrong?" she asked.

"I don't know." He explained what Ollie had told him.

"Go check on Uncle Solomon. I'll tell your brothers and sister that something came up and you had to leave. Matt, be careful. Remember, she wanted you dead."

He kissed her and left the dance hall.

CHAPTER TWENTY-SEVEN

IT WAS THE SAME OPENING ACT FOR A NEW audience. Ian Hennessy, dressed in his black suit, ruffled white shirt, and a jacket with a long tail, questioned why his brother Bud was dressed as a court jester. Bud once again wore yellow tights, brown cloth shoes with pointy toes that curled upward, a green tutu, and a tight purple shirt that hugged his belly, exposing his flabby and hairy stomach. On his head, he had a floppy green hat with a pair of bells at the end.

For those who were not at the show the night before, it was humorous and entertaining. However, for those who attended, like Christine, it wasn't quite as funny as it had been the previous night.

Annie and Mellissa seemed to be enjoying the show. Lee, Steven, and Albert had a few drinks before arriving at the show and had a few more at the bar before taking their seats. Albert watched Bud, his face lacking any hint of a smile.

Steven snickered as he leaned toward Albert, "Now

everyone in town is going to know the man you bragged about whipping acts like a fool for a living. That's a half step up from beating a woman, Albert." He chuckled. "Maybe next time you could beat the snot out of a midget and regain some of your manliness."

"Shut up, Steven," Albert said quietly.

The Hennessy Singers performed the same songs as the previous night, accompanied by the same dance routine. A familiar comic exchange unfolded between Ian, the host, and Bud, the foolish jester. The Hennessy Band played the same songs since the show was a repeat of the night before, until Darlene Smith, the contortionist, came onto the stage. She amazed the crowd by standing at the edge of the stage and bending backward until her arms, shoulders, and chin were twisted behind her, resting on the stage floor between her legs. She waved and blew kisses to the audience while comfortably answering questions like, "Does that hurt?"

Gus Miller took the stage with Bart, his puppet, entertaining the audience with a comedic skit that elicited significant laughter. When he walked off the stage to loud applause, Ian Hennessy stepped to the center of the stage and waited as his brother, Bud, dressed in his jester costume, bounced onto the stage like a bunny rabbit. His purple shirt was pulled up, revealing his large belly that hung over his tutu. Every time he jumped, his belly shook like a bowl of jelly.

"Pull your shirt down! Do you think everyone wants to see your stomach hanging out?" Ian scolded his brother.

"I'm doing a science experiment. Watch." Bud jumped and observed his belly bouncing up and down with his momentum. "There! Did you see that?"

"I don't really want to, but yes," Ian answered with a

tone of repulsion. "What kind of a science experiment could you possibly be doing?"

"Well, I heard the mountains surrounding this town were formed by volcanoes a long time ago. So, if a volcano erupted like this..." He jumped up and landed, watching his belly shake. "Earthquakes shook the ground like jelly, and the mountains just bounced around so much that they shot upward and settled where they are. I can conclude by simply watching my belly that I should be a geologist. I bet you didn't know that."

"No, I didn't know that."

"I may not be able to tell you if the earth is flat or round, but I can tell you that it's filled with jelly. That is the only explanation for how the ground moves during an earthquake. Jelly is the only substance that moves like that, dirt doesn't, rock doesn't, and sand doesn't either. So, you tell me if it isn't jelly that fills the earth, then what does? There's only one answer, jelly. It's the same thing that fills my belly. I love jelly, as you know."

Albert Bannister rolled his head and quietly said, "This is stupid." He cupped his hands to his mouth and shouted out in his best pirate's voice, "Blub...blub...blub...blubber! Aye, dead ahead, Captain, thar's a whale ahead! Grab thy harpoon. We's got us fat one!"

"Albert! Stop it!" Mellissa whispered, slapping his thigh.

Albert continued, "Blub...blub...blub...blubber enough to shade thy ship on a summer's hellish day and warm the coldest of seas. Aye, Captain, she's a beast in those yella skimpies."

Steven hollered out in his best pirate imitation, "Aargh! But alas! She's a bearded he. Confused be me! Thou troubled mind by the lack of jewels. Dare I declare a wee poker in thy treasured mine? Tis she is a he!"

"Knock it off, Steven!" Mellissa hissed, leaning over Albert to slap his leg. She had hoped to find some reinforcement from Regina and Annie to control the Bannister boys, but they were laughing with the men.

Lee resisted it for as long as he could, but he cupped his hands around his mouth and shouted with a deep voice, "Bloat! Floating Bloat."

"What?" Annie questioned with a laugh.

Lee shrugged his shoulders. "He's bloated. I don't know, I couldn't think of anything else."

Bud walked off the stage while Ian nodded and waved to the group of laughing brothers. "Gentlemen, do you mind if we finish?"

Albert shouted, "Please do!" He took another drink.

Mellissa buried her face in her hands and then said loudly enough to be heard, "I apologize to everyone."

Ian waited for the laughter to subside and then spoke loudly, "Ladies and gentlemen, in a moment, you will witness one of the greatest acts of magic you will ever have the privilege of seeing. I give you the World's Creepiest Magician, Landy Jandy!"

"Wait!" Bud shouted as he returned to the stage. "Landy Jandy is my magician. I taught him everything he knows. So, introduce him as my magician."

"He's not your magician," Ian argued.

Bud clenched his fist and lowered his voice. "He *is* my magician. Introduce him right or else," he threatened by shaking his fist.

"Or what? You're going to knock me to Chinatown with your fist?"

"No. I'll tell Mom."

Ian laughed. "Ladies and gentlemen, I give you the

Jester's Magician, the Creepiest Magician in the World, Landy Jandy!"

As the night before, the Hennessy Band began to play a soft yet off-key, eerie piece of music as the black curtains opened. The music created an unease within the crowd that intensified when the curtains were drawn back. The background had been transformed into a dark screen featuring shadowy, skewed tombstones draped in spiderwebs.

A man dressed in a black suit and tailcoat stood at the center of the stage with his head bowed. A tall black hat crowned his head. He raised his gaze to look at the audience, revealing his face for the first time. His face was painted bright white, except for his eyes and lips, which were painted black. The expression on his face was stoic, grim, and haunting.

"Ooh, I don't like this," Mellissa said. "He looks evil."

Landy Jandy spoke when the music settled. "Welcome to my show. Tonight, you will be amazed, in disbelief, and mystified by what you see. My life will be in danger, and you might witness my death if I make a mistake. I assure you that statement is true. But first, let's play with a deck of cards."

CHAPTER TWENTY-EIGHT

MATT RUSHED ACROSS TOWN AND APPROACHED Solomon's house, only to find Richie Thorn pounding on the front door. He was accompanied by two friends, Bruce Ellison and Bobby Alper. Richie Thorn shouted at the door, "Hey, are you going to pay me or not?"

"Richie...Matt's here," Bobby Alper said softly, noticing Matt walking toward the porch.

Richie turned and smiled awkwardly. "Evening, Matt."

Matt paused at the bottom of the stairs, scanning the faces of the three men. "What are you three doing here?"

"We just came to talk with Mrs. Fasana. She wanted a piano or something moved, I think. I'm not exactly sure what she wanted done," Richie explained. "But she said she'd pay me just to show up."

Matt had a good idea of what Deloris wanted done, but it didn't seem like she had mentioned it to Richie and his friends yet. None of the three wore a gun belt or typically carried a weapon, but knowing that Deloris was looking to have him murdered, Matt wasn't taking any chances. "I hope the job she asked you to do doesn't put you in any danger." He pulled his coat back, exposing his Colt as he removed the thong from the gun's hammer.

"She hasn't asked me to do anything yet," Richie said with a puzzled expression. "She hasn't answered the door."

Matt waved the three men away from the door as he ascended the three steps to the porch. "Let me knock." He banged on the door and shouted, "Deloris, open the door or I'll bust the window and come in anyway!" There was no response.

Bobby Alper remarked, "I don't think she's home."

Matt grabbed his Colt and shattered the window's glass. Then he reached inside to unlock the door.

"You don't mess around, do you, Matt?" Richie asked.

"No, I don't," Matt said, pushing the door open. "Deloris, where are you? Deloris!" Matt called as he entered the house. He stopped when he looked into the family room and saw Deloris lying on the floor. He went in and kneeled down to feel for a pulse. He glanced up at the three men who had gathered around him. "She's dead."

Matt quickly rose and hurried to the basement door, unlocking it. He descended the stairs, wrinkling his nose at the foul odor, only to find his uncle lying unconscious on a soiled mattress covered by a similarly soiled sheet, shivering in the cold. Matt could barely see him in the darkened basement. "Uncle Solomon, can you hear me?" He grabbed Solomon's wrist to feel for a pulse. It was weak, but he had one.

"It stinks down here," Bruce Ellison said.

"Is he dead, too?" Richie asked.

"No. Help me carry him upstairs."

Richie Thorn and Matt lifted Solomon and carried him up the basement stairs to the family room, where they laid him on the davenport. Matt instructed Bobby to find blankets to cover Solomon with to warm his body.

"Is he dying too?" Bruce asked for the third time. He worried about catching an unknown disease. "What kind of disease do they have? Do you think it's contagious?"

Matt gazed at his uncle and Deloris's bodies. "Dr. Ryland should be here shortly. I don't know what's wrong with him."

Richie glanced at his hands. One was damp from carrying Solomon. He hurried out of the room to find a source of water to wash his hands.

Bobby Alper returned with a bundle of blankets and spread them over Solomon. His voice trembled as he pointed at Deloris's body and asked, "Does anyone know what they have? I don't want to get sick and die."

Matt glanced back at Deloris's body, which lay face down on the floor with an extended arm. "I don't know. She hasn't been sick that I'm aware of." He turned his attention back to Solomon, who barely opened his eyes. His brow lifted slightly to see Matt, and a faint hint of a smile touched the corners of his lips.

Matt kneeled and placed a reassuring hand on the blankets covering Solomon's shoulder. "You hang on. Dr. Ryland should be here soon."

———

TWENTY MINUTES LATER, Nate Robertson arrived with Dr. Mitchell Ryland. The doctor focused on Solomon while Matt relayed what little he knew.

"Matt, help me sit him up for a moment." Dr. Mitchell lifted the back of Solomon's nightshirt to examine the skin on his back. He sighed as he looked at Matt for a moment.

"What?" Matt asked with concern.

Dr. Ryland pointed at Deloris's body. "From what you told me, I believe she was poisoning your uncle. See these blotches on the skin? That's called arsenical keratosis. It's on his hands and feet as well. Those are signs of arsenic poisoning. He seems to have all the symptoms. Matt, I'm going back to my office to grab some medicines. I'll treat him right here over the next few days and pray that it's not too late."

"Do you think he'll live?" Matt asked.

"I don't know. Your uncle's body has been through a lot. I'll treat him as best I can, but right now, I'd give him a slim margin of surviving. Twenty percent, maybe. It just depends on how strong his body is and how much arsenic he has been given. I'll do an autopsy on her tomorrow. But for right now, can you men take her to the morgue?" he asked Richie and his friends. He didn't wait for an answer. "I'll be back. Matt, search the kitchen for a bag of barley. If they have some, boil it until I get back. Do not throw the water away. I'll bring some barley just in case you don't find any. It's going to be a long couple of days, but I'll stay here with him."

"Is there anything else I need to do?" Matt asked.

"Pray. That's all you can do. Just pray for him."

————

MITCHELL RYLAND HAD OBSERVED the effects of arsenic poisoning in patients before. His years in medical school and practice on the East Coast provided him with ample experience to recognize the visual effects of various conditions. The arsenical keratosis and pigmentation changes on Solomon's skin, especially on his back, were the telltale signs confirming that Solomon had been a victim of arsenicosis, or a high level of arsenic in his body.

Unfortunately, there was no cure that guaranteed Solomon's survival or ensured he would not experience long-lasting effects. Dr. Ryland was forced to focus on managing the symptoms and, first and foremost, trying to hydrate Solomon without him vomiting. He hoped that warm ginger tea would calm Solomon's stomach long enough for him to digest barley water and chicken broth mixed with some potassium iodide.

He would consistently encourage Solomon to drink ginger tea and barley water to hydrate his body. Trioxide of iron and hydrated sesquioxide of iron would help absorb the arsenic, while staying hydrated would flush the poison from his system. Other herbs and medicines would also be used. He had employed the same ingredients in the past to treat arsenic poisoning, but Solomon had the worst case he had encountered. If Dr. Ryland knew anything, it was that it would take prayer and a strength that Solomon may not even know he possessed for him to survive.

CHAPTER TWENTY-NINE

THE MAGICIAN, LANDY JANDY, HELD UP A DECK OF ordinary playing cards as he scanned the audience. His gaze settled on Mary, and a subtle smile appeared on his lips. "All through life, we hope that we can find our queen of hearts who will make our lives whole, complete, and worth living. Sometimes we take a chance and find..." He pulled a card from the deck. "A two of spades. Well, we know a two is far below our standards, whether we're just not attracted to her physically, or her voice becomes as irritating as a yapping dog. We know immediately that a two of spades is not the golden heart we're searching for." He tossed the two of spades onto the floor.

"A two of spades isn't the right one, so we try to find our queen of hearts again." He pulled another card randomly from the deck and showed it to the audience. "Well, we're getting closer with a nine of clubs. We may be drawn to the nine of clubs. In fact, the nine of clubs may be very pretty indeed, but as my father used to say when I was growing up, what's in the heart comes out of the mouth.

"Sometimes a pretty face has an ugly heart that's festering with anger, resentment, and bitterness, just waiting to spill over onto us like a predatory lion camouflaged by beauty. And ladies, this is also true for you. A man may be very handsome indeed, charming, and oh so nice at first, but he can have the same poisons festering in his soul. I know you ladies who work here are looking for your king of hearts. Take my father's advice and listen carefully, choose wisely. I can tell you that a nine of clubs isn't the right one for me. I experienced one once, never again." He tossed the card to the floor.

"Might I finally find true love with the next lady that comes along?" He pulled a card randomly from the deck and revealed it. "Oh!" he exclaimed. "A seven of diamonds. Well, a diamond is a lady's best friend, so now we're thinking about marriage. There is a large percentage of men and women who settle for a seven of diamonds and live contentedly enough. Though a seven is not always a winning hand, a ten of diamonds would have been a stronger marriage." He paused to look at the seven of diamonds thoughtfully.

"But what if the universe, God, or whatever you believe in, had only one queen of hearts planned for you, and you settled for a seven of diamonds, a nine of clubs, or a two of spades? I'm forty-three years old and I've traveled this country and met every stinking card in a player's deck." He slowly flung the cards one at a time onto the stage until there was one card left in his hand. He turned it over to reveal it to the audience as he spoke, "But I have never met my...queen of spades?" he questioned with surprise upon looking at the card. He turned toward the side of the stage and yelled angrily, "Bud, did you mess with my deck? This deck of cards is flawed!" He threw the card down with a mild curse and paused to take a few breaths before explaining, "I can't do this trick with a flawed deck. I'm sorry, folks."

"Do the rope trick again," someone in the audience shouted.

Landy Jandy stood silently in contemplation and then said, "No, I don't think I'll do the standing rope. You know, it's time to come clean with you folks. It's time to be honest and upfront. There's a lot of deception and trickery that goes into magic. Sometimes it crosses over into real life as well. I owe one of the dancers here a very heartfelt apology. Mary, will you please come up here, please?"

Mary sat with a few other ladies, watching. She shook her head, refusing to leave her chair. "No," she said while her cheeks turned red. She knew that somehow, he would cleverly reveal the queen of hearts card once she was on stage. They had spent a couple of hours talking before the show, and Mary was excited to enjoy more time with him after the performance, but she couldn't deny that her heart would be broken when the last dance of the night came to an end. If she believed in love at first sight, she'd swear it was true.

She didn't know what word might define her affection for Paul, but if he stayed in town for any length of time, she knew she'd be falling in love quicker than she ever had. She was captivated by him, even though he did not seem to be the most devout of Christian men. Her one rule for being courted was that it had to be by a Christian man who loved the Lord. It was one of the reasons Leonard was not suitable for courting her. She had no idea why she felt the way she did about Paul, but he was winning her heart. She was afraid of having him announce her as his queen of hearts and asking her to leave with him in front of the audience.

On stage, he was Landy Jandy, but when he spoke to Mary, he dropped the Landy Jandy character and stood there as Paul. He placed his hands together in a begging motion. "Please. It's important to me." He turned his head to the side of the stage to see Leonard Harris standing behind the curtain, holding the pistol and patiently waiting for his chance to try to shoot Landy Jandy. Paul fought to suppress the tugging of his upper lip that threatened to smile. "Mary, the show cannot go on until you come up here. I apologize for putting you on the spot, but I must. Folks, can we cheer and urge Mary to join me up here?"

The crowd applauded, and many shouted, encouraging her to go on stage. Mary relented and ascended the stairs to the stage amid loud cheers from the audience. "What are you doing?" she asked with an uncomfortable, but warm smile.

"Mary, do you have anything up your sleeves?" he asked suspiciously.

"No."

"Please show the audience that you have no hidden cards on your person. I don't either, see?" He revealed his wrists and lower forearms.

"Why?" Mary questioned, exposing her forearms.

Paul took her hand in his and kneeled to one knee.

"What are you doing?" Mary gasped with unexpected panic, taking a half step back. A wave of excitement washed over her. She knew the queen of hearts card was about to be revealed from somewhere magically on her body.

Paul gazed up into her brown eyes. "Mary, when I first stepped inside this dance hall, I was stunned to find it filled with so many attractive ladies, but you were the very first one that caught my eye. In fact, what is that?" he asked while reaching for her ear. "It's a card. Before I turn this card over, I just want to say, I knew you were the one for me. I have searched my whole life for my queen of hearts. Mary, if this is the missing queen of hearts card, will you marry me?"

Mary was stunned by the unexpected words and encouraging cheers from the audience. She shook her head. "I...I...we'd have to talk about it...I mean... Yes, no, I don't know what to say," she stuttered.

Paul, still on one knee, showed her the card. Her brow furrowed in a perplexed expression as she looked at it.

"What is that?" she asked.

Landy Jandy rose from his knee, chuckling as he revealed the card to the audience. It was a caricature of Bud dressed as the jester. "It's the jester. A joke! Mary, everything you have been told about me is true. There is no queen of hearts in this deck of cards. I knew nothing was going to happen between us from the moment I met you, but when you told me about Leonard that first night, an idea came to mind. After meeting Leonard, I knew it was a brilliant plan. Every word, every dance, every kiss, and everything else I did from that moment on was to get that man to hate me," he said, pointing at Leonard behind the curtain. He grinned. "I got what I wanted. Now, I have no more use for you. So get lost."

"What?" Mary said, confused.

Landy Jandy slowly waved an arm toward the audience with a slight bow. "You can go, we're done."

The crowd was silent, waiting with expectant smiles for the twist in the routine. Mary shook her head slightly as tears filled her eyes. The coldness in Landy Jandy's eyes sent a wave of fear down her spine. They were the opposite of the Paul Jandy she knew. "Are you joking?"

Landy spoke with a devious smile that seemed to take pleasure in her pain. "I told everyone before I asked you up here that it was time to come clean and be honest. Mary, get it through your head, I used you for my purposes. I have no more use for you, period. Now, get lost."

His words struck like an open palm, however, the sting was intensified by the presence of a large audience. "Paul..." She gasped.

"Mary, you were warned by everyone I tour with, and you still believed me." He laughed. "How stupid are you? Get off the stage and out of my sight! I have a show to finish."

"You're..." Mary's body jerked with an emotional convulsion. She could barely breathe as her chest tightened. He blurred as her eyes filled with warm tears. "We... you... I can't... What about me? Us?"

He held the jester card in front of her face. "It was all an act. I feel nothing for you. You mean nothing to me. The stairs are over there." He extended an arm toward the stairs with a slight bow. "Goodbye. Now go away, shoo fly."

"You...you... I never want to see you again!" she yelled and sobbed as she ran down the stairs, across the ballroom floor, and toward the stairs leading to her room.

Landy Jandy watched her with a wicked grin. "Would you mind giving my medallion back? I need it for the next woman that catches my eye." He laughed.

At the same time, Leonard Harris barged onto the stage and hollered, "Mary!" He watched her run across the dance floor and turn to dash upstairs. Gaylon held the rope open for her and a couple of the ladies who followed, then secured it back across the stairs.

Landy Jandy spoke to the crowd. "I can say this for

Mary, for being a good and faithful Christian lady, she sure kissed like a tramp."

Leonard turned toward Landy Jandy and raised the flint-lock pistol with a true aim at Landy's face. Anger burned in his eyes as he shouted, "You had no right to treat her like that. I ought to blow your face off right now!"

The other dancer's rumblings, shouts, and curses were quickly quieted by Landy Jandy.

Landy laughed. "Boy, you are as dumb as Mary. According to the contract you signed, even a powder burn, when I'm not ready, could be criminal. You have to wait until I'm ready. But more importantly, you can't fire an empty gun, you idiot. I have the ball." He pulled a .54 caliber ball out of his pocket. "You might want to wait until we load it, Scribble Face. You'll get your chance."

Leonard's fierce glare revealed his hatred for Paul Jandy. He slowly lowered the pistol, keeping the barrel elevated to prevent the black powder from spilling out.

Paul spoke to the audience. "Ladies and gentlemen, let me explain. Too often, people think this next trick is fake. I'm here to prove to you that it is not. To prove it, I wanted someone not affiliated with our group pulling the trigger who had a reason to *want* to hurt me. I discovered that the man standing before me was obsessed with Mary. He's been trying to court her for a long time. Dare I suggest he even loves her?" He chuckled as he looked at Leonard, who glared at him steadily. "But then I came to town and swept Mary off her feet with a single dance. I didn't even have to work at it. She fell into my arms like a pushy harlot..."

"Don't talk about her like that! I'm warning you," Leonard snapped.

"I say he loves her. Don't you all think it shows? Unfortunately for Lenny, here, I kissed the love of this man's life right in front of him, and he didn't budge. So, I did it again and again. Mary's kiss is as sweet as sugar, and her lips are as soft as butter. Scribble Face, you ought to try it some-time. She has very soft lips. Listen, all you fellas, all it takes to kiss Mary is knowing how to dance."

"I told you not to talk about her that way!" Leonard said angrily through tightened lips. "If we're going to do this, then let's do it. I won't listen to any more bad talk about Mary."

Paul motioned to Leonard. "This man really wants to shoot me. Good. That is exactly what I wanted. Folks, I wanted Leonard Harris to *hate* me. And I believe he does. Now I'm going to share why.

"My final trick is very dangerous and some say impossi-ble. I am going to perform the magic bullet catch for you tonight. I am giving Leonard the chance to actually shoot me with a real gun and a real bullet. And trust me, I have given him every reason to *want* to shoot me. The shooter, gun and the ball are real. To satisfy any doubts about the ball, I'll prove to you that it is real. Can I ask the marshal, Matt Bannister, to come onto the stage and verify this is a true .54 caliber ball? Marshal Bannister?"

"He's not here," Steven Bannister shouted. "I'm his brother, and I'm a blacksmith. I can check it."

"Better yet. Come up here, Matt's brother. What's your name?"

"I'm Steven Bannister," he declared as he walked down the aisle and ascended the stairs to the stage.

"Steven, is this a true and deadly .54 caliber lead ball?"

Steven took the ball, examined it, and then bit down on it. "I can verify that it sure enough is. Yep." He then returned to his seat.

Landy Jandy held the ball up between his thumb and

forefinger for the audience to see. "Folks, to verify there is no trickery, I'll hold this ball in sight of all of you until I hand it to Leonard. Now, I don't know if Leonard has the jewels to actually pull the trigger or not, but we have one rule, and that's for him to try to shoot me in the face. If I get hit anywhere else, he could face criminal charges for murder, but not if I miss the bullet. If I'm killed doing this trick, that is on me. Leonard will have no fault for my failure. The contract is written as such and signed. Leonard is holding an 1842 Aston .54 caliber single-shot flintlock pistol. Leonard, are we friends?" Landy Jandy asked.

"No."

"Do you like me?" Landy asked.

"Hell, no, I do not like you," Leonard replied plainly.

Landy Jandy smiled. "Good. Then shooting me should be easy for you to do, right?"

"I consider it no different than shooting a rodent," Leonard said. "You shouldn't have done what you did to Mary."

"She doesn't matter to me. I just hope you can pull the trigger like a man."

"You don't have to worry about that."

"Good." Landy Jandy turned to the audience. "The gun is an 1842 Aston with a .54 caliber ball, which your local blacksmith, Steven Bannister, has verified as being real. The gun has already been loaded with the cap and powder. I am going to hand this ball, and if you've been watching, you'll know the ball has remained in the same two fingers all this time. I am going to hand it to Lenny and let him load it. Scribble Face," he said, handing the ball to Leonard. "Please, load and ready the pistol."

Leonard dropped the ball into the barrel and used the ramrod to pack the ball and paper against the black powder. His brow twitched with interest at the sight of fine gray dust floating out of the barrel as he pressed it down. He could feel the ball compressing into powder. For a moment, he considered exposing the magician as a fraud, but pulling the trigger while aiming at Landy Jandy's face would be more satisfying.

Landy Jandy pointed at a chalk line on the floor. "You stand there, and I'll be over here. These lines are exactly twenty feet apart, which leaves me approximately one and a half seconds to react before the ball penetrates my face. When I say I'm ready, you aim at my face and pull the trigger at will. I will be ready. Agreed?"

"My pleasure," Leonard said as he positioned himself on the chalk line.

"Good." Landy Jandy addressed the crowd. "Folks, what I am about to do is extremely dangerous, and I need silence to concentrate. Please, be quiet until I am either successful or dead. My fate rests entirely in my own hands. Scribble Face over there would like to kill me, and I'm giving him the chance to do just that, free of being convicted for it. So, without further ado, I hope you're all smart enough to never try this at home. Don't be stupid. This takes years of training." He walked to the chalk line and faced Leonard. He could see a harsh glare in Leonard's eyes. He smirked. "Take your best shot."

LEONARD POSITIONED HIMSELF, raised the pistol, and pulled back the hammer. He found it curious how Landy Jandy had his right foot back and angled for a fall, his knees slightly bent, and his weight on his toes. His head was lowered, chin tucked, as he stared at Leonard from under his brow. By his posture and focus on the gun, it was nearly convincing that he was determined to catch a bullet that didn't exist. Leonard felt the ball crush with the ramrod and witnessed dust float from the barrel. Whether it was made of chalk or graphite, he didn't know, but the only thing that would fire out of the gun was dust.

Landy nodded. "I'm ready when you are. Don't chicken out now, Scribble Face."

Leonard lowered the gun an inch. "I'm ready. This is for Mary," he said.

Landy Jandy chuckled. "Whatever you say. I'll count to three. One...two...three!"

Leonard pulled the trigger, and the loud bang coincided with the black powder smoke billowing from the barrel.

Landy Jandy fell backward so quickly that his legs crossed when he hit the floor. The silent ballroom was soon filled with the anguished screams of Landy Jandy, who squirmed on the stage floor with his hands covering his face. Blood flowed like water through his fingers as he rolled back and forth, rocking and kicking his feet in agony. His wailing was louder than the crowd's horrified gasps. "I can't see!" he screamed as he tried to stand but fell, squirming like a worm being pressed onto a hook. "I can't see!"

"What did you do?" Gus Miller exclaimed as he rushed past Leonard to help his friend. Ian and Bud quickly joined him.

"Doctor!" Ian yelled at the crowd. "We need a doctor!" Chaos suddenly engulfed the stage as everyone rushed to assist Paul Jandy, who continued to cry out in agony.

Leonard stood frozen in place, watching in horror. He saw Bud rise from kneeling beside Paul Jandy and point a bloody finger at Leonard. The expression on Bud's face was severe as he stepped toward him quickly. His voice boomed, "What did you put in the barrel?"

Leonard saw the town sheriff, Tim Wright, and one of Matt's deputies, Truet Davis, climb onto the stage to investigate what had happened and assist where they could. As panic set in, Leonard leaped from the stage just before Bud Hennessy reached him. He ran through the crowd toward the door, pushing people aside and even striking a man in the head with the pistol still locked in his grip when the man tried to grab him.

"Stop him!" Bud yelled repeatedly from the stage.

Leonard's heart thundered so loudly that it drowned out everything else, including the stunned crowd and the lawmen urging him to stop. He pushed a woman aside and struck Gaylon Dirks, the security guard, with the pistol while desperately trying to reach the door. He burst through it and ran, terrified, into the street before turning a corner and disappearing into the night.

Tim Wright dashed outside with his gun drawn, aiming it at Leonard just as he rounded the corner. He had a shot to take, but Truet yanked Tim's arm down. "There are too many bystanders. We'll find him."

———

INSIDE THE DANCE HALL, silence enveloped the audience, paralyzed by shock and concern. They watched Landy Jandy wither on stage like a child caught in a beehive, covering their ears against his terrified screams.

"We need a doctor!" Ian shouted to the crowd.

CHAPTER THIRTY

JENNY HARRIS SAT ALONE IN THE FAMILY ROOM OF their small home, breastfeeding her four-month-old baby girl. It was a nice, quiet evening with a warm fire burning in the wood stove, and their three-year-old boy slept soundly in the bedroom. She was thankful for the blessings that had come to their home since her husband, Fletcher, bought his own business. The nightmen's business was a filthy and disgusting way to make a living, but it paid well. If their plans came to fruition, Fletcher would be able to hire more men and stay home at night while working during the day to schedule work for his employees. As it was now, however, Fletcher was out doing the work with two other men who would eventually become the night supervisors of their own crews. Jenny missed sleeping beside her husband, but they had everything they needed to survive and no longer struggled to get by month after month.

Suddenly, the serene evening was interrupted when Leonard burst through the door and slammed it shut behind him, startling the baby and causing her to cry. Jenny covered her breast with a blanket.

"Darn it!" she snapped, angry about the door slamming. It was then that she noticed his sweat-covered face, labored breathing, and wide, frightened eyes. The panic in his expression startled her. "Len? What's wrong?"

He leaned against the door, hands on his knees to catch his breath, staring at her. He shook his head silently.

"What happened?"

"I...I...shot him."

"Weren't you supposed to? Is he okay?"

Leonard's eyes filled with frightened tears. His trembling voice seemed higher-pitched. "Jenny...I did something I never should have done."

"What did you do, Len? Did you kill him?" Her breathing grew more rapid.

He turned to lock the door. "Worse." Turning to her, he spoke quickly, "He told me that he was going to drug Mary. He dared me to stop him, so I did. But I didn't know it was all a lie." He sniffled. "It was all a damn lie!" he shouted angrily. "I messed up." He struggled to hold back a sob.

Mary's impatience was becoming evident. "What *did* you do?"

Leonard gasped emotionally. "I was furious. If I had known it was all a lie...I...didn't mean to..." He pressed his hand against the wall to steady himself, suddenly feeling nauseous. "I took a hammer and shattered that piece of obsidian I found." He paused again. "I poured it all into the barrel. It...it..." He shut his eyes and shook his head. "I aimed it at his face."

"Oh, no," Jenny gasped. "How bad is he?"

"I don't know. He was screaming and bleeding everywhere. I've...I've never seen so much blood or heard such cries. I ran." His lip began to quiver. "They're going to come for me, Jenny." His emotions were overwhelming him. "I have to go."

"Len, no. No, you need to turn yourself in. If you run, it will only make things worse."

"I need to hide. They'll be coming for me soon. I have to leave so you and the kids aren't in any danger." He entered his small room, just big enough for a bed and a small dresser.

"Len," Jenny shouted. "Don't make it worse on yourself. The marshal won't have any mercy on you if you run." She laid her baby on the chair and followed Leonard. She paused when she saw him loading his rifle. "What are you doing? You're going to make things worse."

"I don't have a choice. I'd rather be shot than hanged."

The sound of someone banging on the front door startled them both and woke Jenny's little boy, who began to cry in the bedroom. "This is Sheriff Wright, open up!"

"I'm going out the back door. Don't lie to them, Jenny. I don't want you or the kids getting hurt."

"Len..." she pleaded as he turned the corner and dashed out the back door.

The banging on the door continued. "Open up before I break the door down!"

Jenny's hands trembled as she picked up her screaming baby and attempted to soothe her crying son, who clung to her leg, wanting to be held. She opened the door and looked at Sheriff Tim Wright, two of his deputies, and several citizens who had armed themselves to assist the sheriff. She stood in stunned silence when she saw so many men searching for her brother-in-law.

"Where is Leonard?" Tim asked brusquely.

Jenny hesitated, part of her wanted to lie, but lying wasn't in her nature.

"I know he's here!" Tim exclaimed.

Jenny waved her thumb behind her. She nearly choked on her words, "He...went out back. Sheriff, he didn't mean to..."

"Save it!" Tim snapped. "It sure as hell wasn't an accident! He shot the magician in the face with so much obsidian that he hasn't got a face or an eye left. Excuse us," he pushed his way past Jenny and searched the house before going out back to search the barn that housed Fletcher's two mules, wagon, and tools. "He's not here," Tim said when he returned to the house. "If Leonard comes back before we find him, tell him he better turn himself in. Let's meet up with the others before they find him," Tim said to his deputies.

Jenny closed the door, locked it, and sat down with her children to comfort them. Her heart felt as tormented as a flood of torrential rapids tearing through a narrow valley. "Lord Jesus, please keep Leonard safe. Give him the wisdom to turn himself in before he gets himself killed. Please, Lord. That's all I can pray for right now. Please, Jesus, keep Leonard safe."

———

LEONARD HAD neither a horse to ride nor a way to get out of town quickly. He had no place to hide or anywhere to go where he would not be found. He knew that if he hid in Fletcher's small barn, he would be discovered immediately, so he ran. He carried his rifle and hid behind the nearest tree, bush, or structure whenever he encountered someone. The idea of stealing a horse and escaping crossed his mind, but the only saddled horses available were on Rose Street, and there were too many people looking for him to risk revealing himself.

He found himself running toward the Modoc River at the south end of town and crawling under the bridge that led to Premro Island. Premro Island was a large basalt land-mass that separated the Modoc River as it descended in elevation just outside Branson's city limits. The island was flanked on both sides by channels of fast-moving water rushing down natural shoots over a series of turbulent waterfalls and rapids.

Leonard wedged himself beneath the wooden bridge to escape the cold rain and rested on the boulders of the bank. In the silence, he could hear the roar of the falls a short distance away and the heavy current rippling below. The sound of the river's turbulent water was comforting, and for a moment, he felt safe. He sat with his elbows on his knees in the darkness and wept. Remorse filled him as soon as he saw Paul Jandy withering on the ground, wail-ing. The sight of blood seeping through his ten fingers, which covered his face, weighed heavily on him. The amount of blood and the screams were haunting and replayed over and over in his mind. The man may have been many things, but he did not deserve what Leonard had done to him.

Leonard didn't consider the consequences or how much it might have hurt Paul Jandy. All he cared about at the time was ensuring that Paul never had the chance to touch Mary. He knew it was impossible for a man to catch a bullet and assumed it had to be a deception. Participating in the deception and watching Paul walk away with Mary afterward was not an acceptable option.

He had been sitting in his room, rubbing the piece of

obsidian he had found when he sliced his finger on a sharp edge. An idea struck him, and he carried the stone out to the barn, using a hammer to shatter the obsidian into hundreds of small pieces that would easily slide down the barrel of the old pistol. He kept the fragments in his coat pocket until he was handed the pistol, and standing behind the black curtain when no one was looking, he grabbed a handful of the sharp, glass-like stone fragments and slid them down the barrel. He noticed, as he rammed the rod down the barrel, a slight gray dust as the .54 caliber ball broke into fine particles. It was clearly not the same ball that Steven Banister had checked.

He could have ruined Landy Jandy's act right then and there by exposing the fake ball, but with a mean-spirited sense of expectant satisfaction, he aimed the bead at Landy Jandy's painted face. He felt the urge to pull the trigger and make the man pay for the humiliation he had inflicted on Mary and himself. To make Paul Jandy pay for hurting Mary in front of so many people, he pulled the trigger. Leonard cared little for the consequences, all he wanted was some retribution against Paul Jandy.

He had been blinded by his rage and hadn't thought the plan through. Now, the deed was done, and he did not feel the satisfaction he had expected. Suddenly, he realized that the life he knew was over. The freedom to work and earn a living, to come home on weekends to play with his niece and nephew and see Mary, was about to be taken from him. The vision he had of winning Mary's heart and taking her hand in marriage crumbled like a shattered stained glass window before him. The only future that faced him now was standing behind iron bars or, quite possibly, a noose tightening around his neck if Paul Jandy died. He had made a decision that now isolated him from the rest of the world that surrounded him. He was a wanted criminal.

Now, sitting under the bridge, he longed to hold his Bible for the hope and comfort it might bring. It was interesting how a sudden change in life's circumstances could lead a person to seek God's Kingdom with greater fervor than they had ever experienced before. If the sheriff or the marshal walked under the bridge and shot him for his crime, he would be on his knees in the presence of the Lord Jesus, begging for mercy because, quite frankly, he knew too little about the savior of his soul, except for Christmas and Easter sermons and a few Old Testament stories. If Jesus was going to be a stranger to him, then perhaps he was a stranger to Jesus, and the thought of it terrified him.

"Jesus, I don't know if you'd say you know me or not, because I don't know much about you. I just know what I heard. I have a Bible. I can recite every word my father wrote in the inscription, but I don't know one verse of the Bible. I don't want to die not knowing anything about you. I'm afraid of hearing you say you don't know me when I stand in front of you. That could be tonight because I did something terrible. I shouldn't have shot him. They are looking for me and I am scared. I am terrified. I don't know if you can even hear this prayer, but I'm hoping that maybe it's not too late. Will you help me? I made a bad mistake, and I can't take it back. I've lost everything tonight. Jesus, if you are willing, forgive me. Forgive me if you can. I am in a mess. I don't deserve it, but help me, please." He began to weep.

CHAPTER THIRTY-ONE

MATT FOUND A BAG OF BARLEY AND BEGAN boiling it while Dr. Ryland went to his office to retrieve some additional medicines. Richie Thorn and his friends agreed to take Deloris's body to the morgue and returned with the key before leaving Matt alone in the house. When Dr. Ryland returned, he used a small funnel to make Solomon drink a small amount of barley water. Shortly after, Christine entered the house, followed by the rest of Matt's siblings and his two deputies, Truet Davis and Nate Robertson. They shared what had happened to Landy Jandy. Matt felt torn and didn't want to leave his uncle, but he grabbed his coat and hat and left with Truet and Nate to track down and arrest Leonard Harris.

After hearing what had happened at the dance hall, Dr. Ryland realized he was needed immediately to tend to the magician. He instructed Christine and the others who would stay with Solomon to make him drink the barley water, at the very least, until he returned. Barley water was known to hydrate the body more effectively than plain water.

———

DR. RYLAND ENTERED the doctor's office, where the small waiting room was filled with concerned friends and citizens who had helped carry Paul Jandy inside. He then proceeded to the back room, where Dr. Bruce Ambrose had just administered a sedative to Paul Jandy to help him sleep.

Dr. Ryland asked, "What do we have going on? How serious is it?"

Dr. Ambrose was glad to see his friend. "This man's face was cut to shreds by fragments of obsidian fired from a weapon. I'm glad you're here, Mitch. We have multiple lacerations, the right eye is severed, and we're in for a long night of picking out flakes of rock and suturing this man back together as best we can."

Paul's face was covered with paint and blood flowing from multiple deep lacerations and puncture wounds, with one eye severed in half. What obsidian lay behind the eye was still to be determined. There was no doubt about it, the gunshot would leave the man's face severely scarred for life, resulting in an eye patch if he was not blinded in both eyes.

Dr. Ryland grabbed a clean towel and a bucket of water to wash the blood and makeup off Paul's face. "Do you know Solomon Fasana and his wife?"

"Of course. I'm their doctor," Bruce Ambrose said.

"I just came from their home. She was found dead on the family room floor. I had her body taken to the funeral parlor for an autopsy tomorrow. Solomon was locked in the basement and is dying of arsenicosis."

"What?" Bruce was stunned. "Are you sure?"

"I am positive..." He paused, grimacing as he pulled a flap of flesh open as he cleaned the face. "I need another towel."

"Do you think there's arsenic in the well water? The silver mine uses arsenic to separate the silver and then dumps it into the river. I've been afraid of that reaching the wells here."

"No, I believe she was poisoning him. I found it in the kitchen cabinet." He pulled a small chip of obsidian from Paul's cheek. "She appeared healthy with no obvious signs of arsenic poisoning, but I haven't looked at her yet. I thought we'd do it tomorrow."

"You think Deloris was trying to intentionally poison Solomon? No," Bruce Ambrose said, shaking his head in disbelief. "I can't believe that. Is Solomon still able to recover?"

"I can't say one way or the other right now. He is critical. I have his relatives giving him barley water for now. He's severely dehydrated. We'll know more by morning."

Dr. Ambrose said, "I wish I could go over and take care of Solomon. He's a good friend of mine. Deloris, too. Let's get this bloody mess taken care of and go over to check on Solomon." He leaned over Paul Jandy's cleaned-off face. "We're going to have to remove what's left of his eye. We'd better start with that. I don't know how handsome this man was before, but I doubt he'll ever attract a woman again."

"He's in for a shock when he wakes up and looks in the mirror for the first time, that's for sure. But we'll do our best with what's left of his face."

CHAPTER THIRTY-TWO

"FLETCHER! WHERE'S YOUR BROTHER?" TIM Wright demanded, riding on horseback with six other riders behind him.

Fletcher Harris and his two employees were emptying the privies that served the Dogwood Shacks apartments. The owner, John Pederson, who also owned Ugly John's Saloon, had not cleaned out the privies in a long time, which made the job tougher due to several feet of human waste, bottles, and other trash thrown into the holes.

"Leonard? I don't know. Why? Is something wrong?"

"He shot the magician on the stage with a load of something that shredded the man's face. I don't even know if the magician will live."

"Leonard did what?" Fletcher asked in disbelief.

"Fletcher, understand that this magician is famous, and his career was ruined in our town. The whole nation is going to read about this, so I need to find your brother!"

"Wait..." Fletcher's mind swirled as he tried to grasp

what he had just heard. "Did this have to do with that girl at the dance hall?"

"It happened at the dance hall. Apparently, Landy Jandy was interested in the same dancer. Have you seen your brother?"

"No!" Fletcher exclaimed. "I'm just hearing about this. I don't know where he is. He could be anywhere. It doesn't sound like something he'd do, though." He spoke to his two employees. "Fellas, I have to go. You know what to do. Bring the mules and wagon back to my place when you're done dumping this muck. I must find my brother."

"Not with us you're not!" Tim exclaimed. "I have three possies scouting the town. We're going to find him and bring swift justice to let the nation know we won't accept this kind of behavior here in Branson."

"What do you mean by that?" Fletcher asked.

"It means we have a rope, and by the morning's first light, Leonard will be hanging from the Rose Street headgate. I expect the photograph will go nationwide. I'm sorry, Fletcher, but that's just the way it is."

Fletcher spoke frankly, "Sheriff Wright, by law, Leonard deserves a fair trial. You can't just hang him on the street."

Tim raised his voice, "We all witnessed what he did. His guilt is not in question. If you find him before we do, don't you hide him, or we'll hang you or your pretty wife too. I'm not playing around, Fletcher. Split up, gentlemen. If you see him, try to arrest him, but if not, then shoot him. I want to hang him, but dead is dead."

Fletcher watched the men, some on horseback and others on foot, depart in various directions. He hurried home and found the door locked. "Jenny," he called urgently, but quietly so he wouldn't wake his sleeping children. She opened the door and was immediately in his arms. "Where's Leonard? Is he here?"

"Thank goodness you're here. He left. Fletcher, he's so scared. So am I. The sheriff is looking for him."

"I know. I had words with Sheriff Wright. He wants to hang Leonard tonight. I saw about thirty men spread out looking for him on my way home. I thought I might be hung when I came across Joe Thorn and his group. I'm worried, Jenny."

"We need to pray," Jenny said. She and Fletcher both got down on their knees in the small family room. Fletcher closed his eyes as he held Jenny's hands. "Jesus, thank you for providing for us the way you have. Thank you for our home, our children, and the love we have for one another. You have given us a good life. The one thing we ask tonight is for you to watch over Leonard. I don't know what happened or why it did, but I know that no matter what or why he did it, he deserves a fair trial. All I'm asking is for you to let him be arrested and treated fairly. Keep him from being strung up like a common outlaw. That's all I ask. And Lord, be with the man he shot. I pray you'll help him to survive and to heal well." When he finished, he took Jenny in his arms and held her quietly to the sound of the fire crackling in the woodstove.

A knock on the door startled them. Fletcher stood and went to the door. "Jenny, go into the room with the children." He turned his face toward the door. "Who is there?"

"Marshal Matt Bannister. Can I talk to you for a minute?"

Fletcher opened the door to find Matt Bannister standing in the doorway. His horse was tied to a tree out front. "Matt," Fletcher said. "I hope you don't intend on hanging my brother tonight, too."

Matt shook his head. "No. Arrest him, perhaps, but not hang him. I take it he's not here?"

"No. I don't know where he is. Sheriff Wright said he wants to hang him tonight. Please find him before the sheriff or one of his posse members does. They're scouring everywhere throughout the town."

Matt frowned. "I saw them. I won't let them hang him if I get there in time. Fletcher, if Leonard is here, it's better to let him come with me now. It would be safer for him."

"He's not here. We don't know where he is. Jenny said he got scared and ran out the back. They searched the house and barn twice now, Jenny said. So, Leonard really did shoot that man?" he asked.

Matt nodded. "I wasn't there, but Christine was. Apparently, from what I hear, the injuries are quite severe. I can't let Leonard off."

"No, of course not. All I want is for him to have a fair trial. If you can arrange that, that would be a blessing."

Jenny left the bedroom and said, "That magician held a gun on Lenny and painted Lenny's face in the grocery store just to humiliate him. He pushed Lenny, aggravated him, and threatened to seduce that Mary woman Lenny is hooked on, and dared Lenny to stop him. Lenny didn't think he had any other choice to protect Mary."

Matt said calmly, "Unfortunately, he made the wrong choice. If he comes back, keep him here. If he has nowhere else to go where he feels safe, tell him to go to my Uncle Solomon's house and hide there. He'll be safe there. My brothers are there with their wives and Christine. He knows Christine."

"Marshal," Jenny said, "just so you know, Lenny took his rifle with him."

"Oh, no," Fletcher said, feeling a sudden chill run down

his spine. "They'll shoot him if they see him holding a rifle."

"I couldn't stop him, Fletch," Jenny said emotionally. "I tried."

Matt said, "You better pray I find him before they do. I'll stop by later."

"Matt, find my brother," Fletcher said. The worry in his eyes was evident as he held his wife by his side.

CHAPTER THIRTY-THREE

LEONARD FELT A CHILL, COLDER THAN DEATH itself, run down his spine when he heard the voices of several men approaching the bridge. He instantly recognized the voice of Sheriff Tim Wright.

"I want every inch of Premro Island searched. Check the gristmill and every other building for open doors or broken windows. He has to be somewhere. Phil, take your boys and search every inch of the sawmill and other businesses. We'll chase this son of a gun all the way back to his logging camp if we have to."

The sheriff's deputy, Mark Thiessen, asked, "Tim, I don't know where Matt is tonight, but don't you think we should get him and his fellas to help us?"

"No! We don't need him to help us. Just do as I say."

"What about us, boss?" Jack Ingalls questioned. He was a local bartender who worked at the Harrison Saloon and grabbed the shotgun under the bar to quickly join the hunt for Leonard. He could feel the thrill of the hunt consuming him with a yearning to be the man who shot the criminal. It was a growing desire shared by the others.

The sheriff, Tim Wright, had not organized an official posse, instead, he sent groups of men and individuals who wanted to help search wherever they chose to go. Tim pointed at the woods at the bend of the river. "Jack, you and Arnie, peek under the bridge and search along the river's edge and the woods over there. If you boys see anything, give a shot, and we'll all come running."

Jack stepped to the edge of the bridge. "We'll do. But I think if I just empty my bladder, I'll flood the riverbank and force him into town." He unbuttoned his pants and relieved himself over the bridge's edge.

Alarm reverberated through Leonard's body when a strong stream of urine splattered onto a nearby rock. He could feel the spray ricocheting off the rocks, spattering him with droplets. He wanted to move further away across the rocks, but he feared making any noise.

"What have you got, Jack, a five-gallon bladder?" one of the men on the bridge asked.

"Pretty close, I think," he said as he finished buttoning his pants. "All right, let's check this bridge and head down-river. This murderer might be camping in the woods."

The light of a lantern shone on the ground to his right, and the sound of horses and boots echoed across the bridge above him. Leonard moved over the wet rocks that formed the bank under the bridge to his left, where the darkness and the smell of strong urine welcomed him like a kind friend. He maneuvered to the outer edge of the bridge just as the lantern's light illuminated the rocks he had left behind. Staying low, he quietly peeked over the edge of the wooden bridge to see the backs of those crossing it, along with three men now leaving the bridge and walking down-hill to the river's edge.

When it was clear, he dashed onto the road and ran toward town. A shout from the woods, followed by a gunshot, rang out. Leonard's heart pounded as he heard the bullet fly past him. He ran as fast as he could toward the nearest house, seeking a barrier between himself and any guns aimed at him. He could hear Sheriff Wright's horse and the others rapidly catching up to him. He ran behind the nearest house and then cut between two others, searching for anything that might slow the horses down enough for him to escape. He darted under a clothesline and between a shed and another house. He heard Sheriff Wright curse in sudden panic and tumble to the ground when the clothesline yanked him from the saddle.

Leonard climbed over a fence and dashed across the yard to scale the other side. He then sprinted as fast as he could toward home. One of the horsemen fired a shot at him but missed.

He felt like a terrified rat trapped in a barrel, running in circles and trying to jump high enough to escape, but the men on horseback were relentless and intent on killing him. It had taken only one bad decision to turn an honest, law-abiding man into a wanted, dead-or-alive outlaw. Sweat poured down his face, mixing with the cold rain. He wearily ran toward the only safe place he could think of—home.

"Get him! Shoot him!" a man shouted.

A gunshot rang out, and Leonard heard the bullet whiz past him, too close for comfort. His body was exhausted and yearned to stop and surrender, but he knew he could not give in. He had only a few blocks left to run.

Another shot rang out and hit the corner of a house

beside him. Leonard ran as fast as terror could propel him, while the rifle in his arms grew increasingly heavy in his grip as he swung it back and forth while running. He considered spinning around and shooting the nearest horseman, but he did not want to kill anyone.

The Halverson home across the street had a narrow walkway between their tool shed and the fence surrounding their backyard. Realizing the walkway would be too narrow for a man on horseback, he dashed across the street, dodging another bullet, and turned into the tight space, intending to climb over the back side of the fence and sprint for home.

He forced himself to continue through the Halverson yard despite the overwhelming sensation that his chest might explode and that his heavy breathing could come to an abrupt end. He stumbled to the fence, hearing Tim Wright curse as his horse could not enter the narrow walkway. Leonard tossed his rifle over the fence and jumped up to pull himself over the six-foot-tall barrier. His strength was waning, but he rested his belly on top of the fence and rolled over it, landing hard on his back in a way that jarred his insides painfully.

A deep growl, bark, and the sound of a moving chain alarmed him as a large dog chained to the doghouse bit into his lower leg, jerking it around with a vicious snarl. Leonard cried out and tried to kick the dog away, but his kicks had no effect. The angry dog was intent on tearing through his flesh, dragging him across the ground in a ferocious attack while jerking his leg back and forth. Leonard reached for the stock of his rifle and barely grasped it. Gripping it, he pulled it toward him while trying to kick the dog off his leg. As soon as the animal released its bite, it clamped down on another part of his leg with the same fierce intensity as the first bite. Pointing the rifle with one hand, Leonard pulled the trigger. The dog, yipping, released his leg and ran toward its doghouse with loud cries of pain.

Fully aware that the homeowner was now awake and would come outside with a gun, and that a group of hostile men was very close to him, Leonard rose to his feet and hobbled out of the yard as quickly as he could. Despite the throbbing pain in his leg, he sprinted to evade the men closing in on him.

Finally, his brother's house came into view. A bullet grazed his arm, sending a painful reminder that his life was in danger. The stinging burn did not deter him, he could not afford to stop and assess how badly he had been hit. His body had given all it could, and he was about to slow to a stop when he saw his brother, Fletcher, open the front door and frantically wave Leonard toward the house while shouting for him to hurry.

The light inside Fletcher's home drew him like an arrow aimed at a target. Leonard expended the last of his willpower and forced himself to run faster. He dashed past his brother and dove onto the floor like a dead man, just as Fletcher closed and locked the door. "You're hit!" Fletcher exclaimed with concern, seeing blood on his arm and a shredded pant leg soaked in blood.

Leonard struggled to catch his breath, but he got to his knees and forced himself to stand. Sweat dripped from his face like a cascading stream. He picked up his rifle and hobbled toward the back door.

"Len, stop. You're safe now. Matt Ban..."

Leonard had no time to listen. "No, I'm not! Stay here...with Jenny. I'm...going...to the barn," he said through his heavy breathing. Exhaustion was evident on his face.

"Len, wait! Talk to me," Fletcher pleaded as Leonard paused at the back door, bending over to catch his breath. Sweat dripped from his nose onto the floor.

Sheriff Wright pounded on the door. "Open up! This is Sheriff Wright. Open up or I'll break the door down and come in shooting!"

"Fletcher, let...him in before you and...Jenny get hurt," Leonard said. He closed the back door and ran across the yard toward the small barn. He grasped the handle of one of the double doors and yanked it open just enough to enter, just as two of the men from the posse began shooting at him repeatedly. Leonard dove to the ground to get lower and fired a return shot into one of the corner posts, just to let the men outside know that he wasn't helpless. The shooting outside stopped.

Leonard yelled, "The first one to open that door is dead!" He lay on his back and closed his eyes for a moment to regain control of his breathing. A single lantern hung on the wall, casting a dim light in the barn. He knew the small hayloft above him was a safer place to be, but he didn't have the energy at that moment to climb the ladder to get there.

He heard more men entering the backyard and shouted again, "The first man to open that door is dead!"

"Leonard, this is Sheriff Wright. Come out unarmed, and you may survive this night. If not, we'll burn the barn down with you inside! This is your chance, come out now!"

Jack Ingalls listened to the angle of Leonard's voice and gauged it to be near the right side of the barn, down low. He had not joined the hunt to get so close yet remain so far from making the kill. He had run, carrying the heavy twelve-gauge shotgun across town, and sweat stung his eyes. He wiped his eyes, raised the shotgun, and pulled both triggers, blasting a large hole through one of the doors in hopes of guessing right and making the killing shot. The discharge of his weapon prompted three others to shoot randomly at the barn's doors.

"Did I get him? I think I got him!" Jack yelled.

The unexpected blast was too close for comfort, as Leonard was struck by flying wooden debris. He hurried toward the ladder and climbed it more quickly than he thought he had the energy to do.

"I see him! Shoot low!" a man with the revolver yelled to the others while beginning to fire through the doors.

"Quit shooting! Don't shoot!" Tim Wright shouted angrily. "I want him alive so I can hang him, you idiots! Now stop shooting!" He cursed and kicked the ground, frustrated with himself for revealing his plan. He cast a hardened glare at Jack and then paused to lower his tone to sound sincere. "Leonard, we don't want to hurt you. Come on out and we'll sort this mess out. We know you didn't mean to hurt the magician."

"I think I killed him," Jack said proudly. "You're talking to a dead man. Let's go inside and hang him up for folks to see."

"No, I saw him moving after you shot," a man replied.

"That doesn't mean I didn't kill him. He might be bleeding out."

"Shut up, all of you," Sheriff Wright shouted. "Leonard, are you still alive?"

Leonard answered loudly, "I don't want to hurt anyone. But I will if you open that door."

"I don't want to hurt you either, Leonard. Since we're all on the same page, why don't you come on out, and we can resolve this? We're all friends here, aren't we?" Sheriff Wright asked.

"That's hard to believe when your men are shooting at me."

"Yeah, but I stopped them, right? You heard me do that, right? Come on, Leonard, it's getting late, and we all just want to go home."

Leonard shouted, "Why don't you all do that, and I'll turn myself in in the morning."

"You know I can't do that," Tim said, growing frustrated in the cold rain. "Now come on out, and I'll take you to jail for the night. That's all."

After a brief moment of silence, Sheriff Wright said, "Come on out, Leonard."

Leonard lay on the hayloft floor with his rifle barrel aimed at the door. He was afraid to ask, but he had to know the answer. His stomach churned as he inquired, "How is Paul Jandy, Sheriff? Did he die?"

"It looked worse than it is. Trust me, Leonard, everything is going to be fine. Now come on out. Please."

The back door of the house flung open as Fletcher Harris hurried outside and shouted, "Don't believe him, they're going to hang you!" He was struck on the back of the head by a pistol butt as a man chasing him tackled Fletcher from behind.

Tim Wright's enraged eyes narrowed at the man who had tackled Fletcher. He shouted, "How did he get away from you, Horace? I told you to hold him and his wife at gunpoint! Get Fletcher back in the house and keep him there! Walt, Jerry, go help him. For crying out loud, I swear the men of this town are as incompetent as a wingless moth." He sighed, considering his next words.

"Don't you hurt my brother!" Leonard yelled. "If Fletcher or Jenny has even a scratch on them, I promise I'll break all of your heads open!"

Tim had lost his patience. He yelled, "Then step out of there and face the music like a man, Leonard! No more fooling around. Come out or I'm burning you out."

Leonard could hear the rain hitting the roof. "You can try, but the wood is too wet to burn, Sheriff," Leonard said confidently. "I'm comfortable and drying out. I can stay in here all night. Please, just go home, Sheriff Wright. I don't want to hurt anyone."

Sheriff Wright motioned to a man. "Peter, pour your lantern's kerosene on the door. We'll show him the barn will burn."

Peter was uncomfortable doing so. "Um, Sheriff, this is Fletcher's barn, not Leonard's."

"I don't care whose barn it is! If he doesn't want to come out, then we'll burn him out. Now, pour that kerosene and light it!"

"Where is Fletcher?" Leonard asked, his tone urgent. He had not heard his brother's voice since the warning. "I want to talk to Fletcher."

"Fletcher is in the house under guard, and we're not bringing him out. I can't promise my men are behaving themselves in there either. If you want to keep them safe, then Leonard, come out of there unarmed. But if you don't come out here like a man, I'll set the barn on fire. That's not a threat. We have plenty of kerosene." He nodded to Peter. "I'm not waiting any longer. Do it!"

"Yeah! It's about time," Jack said, along with several others.

Peter slowly removed the cap from the lantern's oil reserve. He hesitated. "Sheriff, there is no other way out of this barn. If we start the fire, Leonard could be trapped in there."

Sheriff Wright stepped toward Peter with a wild gaze in

his eyes and yanked the lantern from him. "He's going to die either way! He just blew the face off a world-renowned magician. Perhaps the most famous magician in America and the rest of the country will read about what happened in our town. Everyone will know the name of our town and *how* we handled it. The public will want him dead, and that's what we're giving them. Now burn it down!" He shoved the lantern into Peter's stomach for him to take.

Peter shook his head and raised his hands innocently. "Not me. I like Fletcher, you do it."

Tim took the lantern and began pouring kerosene across the two doors. "Who wants to light it?" he asked.

CHAPTER THIRTY-FOUR

"Hell, I'll light it," Jack Ingalls said, stepping forward to volunteer.

"If you strike that match, you're a dead man!" Matt Bannister shouted as he walked into the backyard, holding his revolver in his hand. His deputies, Truet Davis and Nate Robertson, also had their revolvers ready.

Jack Ingalls suddenly lost his willingness to light the match and froze with a cold chill at the sight of Matt Bannister's Colt .45 aimed at him. The match fell from his fingers.

"All of you can go home now," Matt shouted.

Outraged by Matt's intrusion, Sheriff Wright shouted angrily, "This is my arrest! This is my jurisdiction, and I won't allow you to interfere. So, take your deputies and go home! We're doing this my way, not yours!"

"Tim, I'm not going to let you hang this man without a trial, and I'm here to ensure that doesn't happen. I'm taking charge. If anyone has an issue with that, well, here I am. Now is your chance." He scanned the faces of the men, most of whom he recognized. No one dared to argue with him.

Sheriff Wright's upper lip twitched with indignation. "I'm the sheriff, and this is my jurisdiction. Not this time, Matt. I'm standing firm on this one."

Matt's voice turned icy. "Okay, Sheriff Wright, Tim, if you want to fight over it, choose your weapon: guns or fists. Either way, I'm taking charge. Now, step aside or go home, but stay out of my way! You all can leave now," Matt said, scanning the area as he watched the sheriff's posse gradually disperse.

Sheriff Wright stated, "You're interfering with my arrest for the last time. I'm taking this to the city council."

Matt smirked with a light chuckle. "That's fine, they hired you, not me. I'll tell them you should have arrested him rather than telling everyone you were going to hang him. I'm sure they'll take your actions into consideration."

Tim pointed at the barn and yelled, "The whole nation is going to read about what happened. They're going to expect justice. If anyone understands that, it's you. You've killed more people than all of us combined!"

"That's why I am going to arrest him and save you the burden," Matt replied.

Matt removed his gun belt and handed it to Nate Robertson. Turning toward the barn, he spoke loudly, "Leonard, this is Matt Bannister. I am unarmed and stepping through the door. I know you have a rifle, please don't shoot. Can I trust you not to shoot me?"

Leonard shouted, "You're unarmed?"

"I am. You can verify that when I step through the door. Does that sound fair enough?"

"Okay, Marshal Bannister, you can come in. But just you."

Matt opened the door and stepped into the dark barn, where a dimly lit lantern hung from a nail on the wall. "I'm unarmed, Leonard. Just as I said." He turned around slowly to demonstrate that he had no weapons. "Mind if I have a seat? Then we can talk."

————

MATT SAT against the wall next to the double doors, which were closed but unlocked. He leaned his head back against the wood to see Leonard lying on his belly in the hayloft. "How are you doing, Leonard?" he asked.

Leonard's voice quivered nervously. "Not too good. I didn't mean to hurt him like that. I did, but I didn't mean to blow his face off." He gasped. "I am so sorry that I did that. Am I going to be hung, Matt?"

Matt sighed. "Leonard, you shot a man. I don't know what's going to happen. I don't know if that man will survive or how bad the damage is. I won't lie to you, though. Attempted Murder is a serious charge."

"But I wasn't trying to kill him! I never wanted to kill him. I was paid ten dollars to shoot him. I signed a contract stating I would. I would have shot him in the face for free, but they paid me to do it. The contract said I wouldn't be held liable if he missed the bullet."

"But it wasn't a bullet that cut up his face. You know very well that obsidian cuts like glass, and when it's fired from a gun, it isn't going to scratch a man's face. You can't tell me you didn't know that. Therefore, you can't say you didn't mean to hurt him. Because you did."

"Of course I did!" Leonard snapped. He took a few deep breaths. "He showed me a bottle of something that he was going to use to put Mary to sleep. He implied he was going to force himself on her tonight and dared me to stop him. I knew there had to be a trick because nobody can catch a bullet with their teeth. That's just common sense. So, yes, I stopped him. You'd do worse if someone threatened to do that to Christine. I know you would!"

Matt's mind raced back to the time when he took the place of Christine and met Travis McKnight, Tim Wright, and Josh Slater in a Monarch Hotel room and beat the hell out of all three of them for what they were trying to do to Christine. Matt understood what Leonard was experiencing, but what Leonard chose to do was not a fistfight, but a potentially fatal gunshot that could kill Paul Jandy or, at best, leave him severely deformed for life.

"Maybe so," Matt answered Leonard's statement. "But that doesn't justify what you did. Look, these men loitering around outside like vultures want to hang you tonight. It isn't so much about what you did but to whom. Sheriff Wright sees an opportunity to get his ounce of fame in every newspaper in the country by lynching the man who shot the great Landy Jandy. Come with me and I'll take you to my jail, keep you safe, and make sure that you get a fair trial."

"You know, all this time, I just wanted to win Mary's heart and have her as my bride. Then Paul Jandy showed up and ruined everything! She was close to saying yes to me, Matt. I'm sure of it."

Matt shook his head. "I know what it's like to fall in love with a dancer at Bella's Dance Hall. I experienced it as well. But those girls dance with men for a living. It's just a job. You can't get jealous of her dancing with Paul Jandy."

"She kissed him!" he spat out bitterly. "I wasn't jealous, I was furious. She has never kissed anyone like that. Never! Especially not me. I wish she would. I hoped she would, but she never did. I would have given my life for her." He scoffed. "Maybe I just did to keep her safe from him. And do you know what? Paul Jandy wasn't even interested in her. He was using her to get to me just so I would shoot him! I wish he had just asked me. He's the one who dared me to stop him from hurting the woman I'm in love with!" He paused as the words filtered through his mind. "Hmm. Maybe I should have told Mary that."

"Maybe so, but it doesn't sound like she loves you, Leonard."

"I suppose not, since she seemed to love him. I've wasted my time chasing after her, haven't I?"

"I'm afraid so. Luckily for you, you still have time."

"No, I don't," he replied, turning to his side and resting his head on one arm as he gazed down at Matt. "I'll be arrested, sentenced to hang, or spend years in prison for what I did. That dream I had of marrying her is over, isn't it?"

Matt hesitated thoughtfully. "You know, Leonard, we can dream about many things. Most people dream of having riches. It was one of the temptations with which the devil tempted Jesus. We all have dreams for the future, but unfortunately, life is full of unfulfilled dreams. I think of Jacob in the book of Genesis falling in love with Laban's daughter, Rachel. She was beautiful, and she was all Jacob wanted. He asked Laban for her hand in marriage, and Laban told him that if he worked seven years herding sheep, he could marry Rachel. So, Jacob stayed there and labored each day as a shepherd for seven long years.

"Then the day came when all he had worked for and dreamed of was going to come true. It was his wedding day, and he was excited to marry Rachel. They were married, and when he lifted her veil to see Rachel's beautiful face, he was horrified to find that Laban had snuck his oldest and least attractive daughter, Leah, into the wedding gown. Jacob had married Leah. Laban then told him that if he loved Rachel and wanted to marry her, he would have to work seven more years. Jacob truly loved Rachel and willingly stayed there, working for seven more long years, until the day when he got to marry her.

But the story doesn't end there. Jacob and Rachel had a firstborn son, whom they named Joseph, and a short time later, they had another son, whom they named Benjamin. Rachel died giving birth to Benjamin. I would say Jacob had an unfulfilled dream of spending his life with Rachel. He labored for fourteen years for her, and if that's not love, I don't know what is. However, their time together was short—she died." Matt paused. "God promised to be with him, but Jacob had many unfulfilled dreams. We all do. It can be very disappointing, but that's not unusual. King David, Moses, Apostle Paul, and everyone else mentioned in the Bible had unfulfilled dreams. And yet, they rose above them and changed the world. Your life is not over. It might be scary right now, but you have time for a full and happy life ahead of you. You won't be hung, Leonard, unless Paul Jandy dies, and from what I heard, he should survive."

"I sure hope so," he said with a relieved sigh.

Matt stood and dusted off his pants. "Leonard, here's the deal: come with me and you'll have the time to write to Mary and explain why you did what you did. You'll have a fair trial, and you can explain it to Judge Jacoby, and maybe the jury will understand your reasoning, too. But if you refuse to come with me, then I'll walk out of here and leave you to fight it out with those men outside. You won't win. They'll burn this barn down and shoot you when you come out gagging over the smoke." Matt paused. "Listen, I have other urgent matters to attend to. You have a choice to make, and time's short because I'm leaving with or without you."

Leonard said, "I don't have much of a choice, do I?"

"No. You may have run into a wall that seems unpassable, but it's not. You'll get through it and have the chance to rebuild your life. Your best option is to come with me and pray that Paul Jandy isn't scarred up too badly. Lay your rifle down and come with me. I'll keep you safe."

"All right. I'll trust you." Leonard set the rifle on the loft floor and climbed down the ladder.

CHAPTER THIRTY-FIVE

It was past three in the morning when the two doctors entered the waiting room, where three members of the Hennessy Brothers' Traveling Show were still there.

Ian Hennessy stood. "How is he?" he asked. Bud remained seated but raised his head to listen.

Dr. Ryland yawned with exhaustion. "The good news is he will survive and recover for the most part. It took several hours to pull as many obsidian fragments out of his facial tissue as we could. It was a daunting task, but we did our best. There are a few pieces that are too deep and embedded into the bone. Those, we'll never get out. He has well over a hundred facial wounds, and several of the wounds around the mouth and nose needed sutures to close. The scars, unfortunately, will be disfiguring. His right eye was severed, so we had to remove it. He'll have to wear an eye patch for the rest of his life. The fragments of obsidian that pierced his eye lodged in the bone of the eye socket, which we were able to pull out. As far as we can tell, no fragment of obsidian penetrated the brain, but there were so many small fragments that it is still a possibility and could cause problems for him in the future."

"Can he travel?" Ian asked. "We're supposed to be leaving town to catch the next steamboat west."

Dr. Ryland shook his head. "I wouldn't recommend it for a week or two. He needs to rest and let his wounds heal. Right now, we have his face bandaged with gauze, and he'll stay that way for the next few days."

Bud scoffed. "Ian, I told you we never should have come to this town."

"I don't want to hear it, Bud!" Ian snapped, tiredly.

Bud persisted, stating, "It felt wrong from the beginning."

"He's going to live," Gus Miller said. "We should just be thankful for that."

"Thank the Lord for that," Ian agreed.

———

THE TWO DOCTORS, Mitch Ryland and Bruce Ambrose, stepped out of the cold rain and mud into Solomon's home. The atmosphere was solemn. "How is he doing?" Mitch asked as he entered the family room. Several other family members were present, most of whom were crying.

Matt spoke softly, "Uncle Solomon is still the same. He was throwing up the water at first, but I think it's holding now. He hasn't thrown up in a while. We're all praying his body will start functioning and digesting the water instead of rejecting it."

"Good. What about solid food? Have you tried feeding him the barley?"

"Not yet."

Dr. Ambrose kneeled in front of Solomon, holding his wrist to check the strength of his pulse. He placed his hand on Solomon's shoulder to wake him. "Solomon, it's Bruce Ambrose. Can you open your eyes for a moment? There you go, buddy. Hey, listen to me, you have to fight this. Okay. As your doctor, I'm ordering you to shake my hand and promise me that you'll fight to stay alive until we can get the poison out of you. Your family is here, so you better show that Fasana blood and fight for your life."

Solomon's older brother, Luther, kneeled beside Dr. Ambrose. "Little brother, you better fight this with everything you have because if not..." He choked on his emotions. "I don't know that I'll ever be the same. I need you, Solomon. James needs you. We all do."

Solomon's eyes, tired and heavy, opened just enough to gaze at Luther, and a twitch at the corner of his lips suggested a smile. Then, his eyes closed again as he drifted back to sleep.

"How much of the barley water has he kept down, would you say?" Dr. Ryland asked.

Mellissa Bannister raised two fingers. "Two cups, so far. The last one was about an hour ago." She looked exhausted and seemed ready to fall asleep.

"Good. Let's do a cup every hour for the next few hours. I'll be staying here with him, so why don't you folks go home, get some rest, and come back when you're refreshed? Then you can watch him for a while. He needs to rest, and he'll do it better if it's quiet."

Solomon's two older brothers, Joel and Luther, were present, along with several of Joel's adult children, including William Fasana. Joel asked, "Doc, the kids say you gave him medicine. Is it just too little, too late?"

"I wish we had found him much earlier. Right now, he

is at death's door, but Lord willing, we can stop him from going through it. If he is digesting the water, that would be a good start. Had we not found him tonight, he would not have survived another day. I'm hopeful we can get him hydrated and start a series of iron treatments to pull the poison out of him. The key is getting him hydrated first. Even barley oats will help pull the garbage out, and that's what we need. There is far more arsenic in him than we'd like."

"Deloris, the old hag, got what she deserved," Luther said with a cold sneer. His eyes were moist with tears. "If anyone ever starts telling me what a good woman she was, I'll slap the crap out of them. You could throw her body out back and let the rats and vultures eat her as far as I'm concerned."

William had been sitting quietly beside his sister, Karen. His eyes flashed with a coy smile. "Now, Uncle Luther, we all know that you secretly coveted Aunt Deloris. I think you're just upset because she's gone and now she'll never be yours."

Luther bit his lips as he glared at William, his eyes blazing with anger. "William..." He pressed his lips together tightly, refusing to say what he wanted to.

"William, it's no time to tease," his sister Karen said.

William grinned. "Well, after the recent attempt on his life, I don't think Uncle Solomon will mind burying her next to you, Uncle Luther. Her name is Fasana, after all, and future generations will think she was your wife. I mean, that's something lasting."

"William... That's it!" Luther stormed toward the davenport, his fist tightening.

William's eyes widened as a fearful expression transformed his grin into sheer terror. He quickly covered his face with his arms and turned toward his sister. Luther leaned over William and slammed his hardened fist down into William's thigh.

"Ow!" William yelled, clutching his leg and rocking painfully on the davenport. "That hurts! Oh, my...dang... I was only teasing! For crying out loud. You didn't have to hit so hard!"

Luther smiled, feeling a touch of satisfaction. "You're lucky I love you, kid," he said, joining William's father, Joel.

Joel nodded with approval. "I probably should have done more of that myself when he was growing up."

"Damn, Uncle Luther, my leg is numb. How are you going to feel if I can't walk straight because of you?"

"I'll feel fine. I couldn't stand that woman, and you know it!"

William laughed, still grasping his thigh.

Joel added, "We're not putting our Fasana name on her tombstone. Nor will she be buried anywhere near the Fasana plot. We'll bury her in the Chinese section of the cemetery, or maybe we can talk Ah-See into sending her halfway to China before dropping her overboard to feed the fish."

William Fasana exhaled heavily. "I don't know what you people had against Aunt Deloris, she was a sweet lady."

Luther pointed at William. "One more word and I'll hit you so hard that you won't be able to stand for a week. Try me?" he warned.

William laughed.

William's sister Karen stated, "We need to let Aunt Mary and Uncle Charlie know what happened."

Joel nodded. "I'll send them a wire in the morning. Hopefully, I'll have more good news than not to share."

Lee Bannister said tiredly, "Uncle Joel, when you do that, ask if they want me to send my driver over there to pick them up. It's a hard trip for Aunt Mary in a buckboard. My coach is more comfortable for her. I'm sure she'd like to be here."

William said, "I'm using your driver and coach to go to Eastman Forks to pick up Maggie. Remember?" He planned to take Lee's carriage east to Eastman Forks to fetch his sweetheart from the riverboat station when it docked on Tuesday.

"That's right," Lee said, recalling.

"I can send mine for them," Albert volunteered. He yawned.

"We need to notify James that his mother is dead and his father is sick," Joel's daughter, Georgina Dalton, stated. Her husband, Ron Dalton, affectionately rubbed her shoulders.

"I'll wire him in the morning. We stay in contact," Karen Longo stated, her heart visibly heavy on her worn face. Several months ago, her oldest daughter, Hanni, was murdered, and the grief for her firstborn lingered, particularly with the holiday season fast approaching. Her husband remained at home with their other children.

"James Fasana," Joel said while shaking his head. He exhaled. "How many years has it been since you've seen James, Matt?"

Matt yawned and shrugged his shoulders. "He was a kid, four or five years old maybe."

"Well, he's about twenty-five now. He doesn't come home too much. He graduated from college and stayed in the valley to teach school, but then decided he didn't like the pay or the kids. He's working on a riverboat in the Salem area, the last I heard. James's refusal to come home hurt Solomon a lot, but James didn't like his mother. Who did?"

William lifted his head and quipped, "Travis McKnight."

Joel frowned, not finding it funny.

Luther said, "I suppose Solomon is in good hands with the doc here. It won't do me any good to be up all night just to watch him sleep. I'm going home and will be back in the morning."

"Yeah," Joel agreed. "I'd better get some rest myself. We prayed, and we can't do much more than that. Doc, you'll let us know if anything changes?"

Dr. Ryland nodded. "I certainly will. You all should go home and get some rest."

———

MARY WASHBURN COULDN'T SLEEP, so she walked downstairs to the stage. The blood had been cleaned up, but as she scanned the area with a small lantern from her room, she noticed a piece of obsidian lodged in the wall of the stage. She went to the kitchen to fetch a knife to help retrieve the flake of obsidian. She sliced a small section of wood from the wall to get a better grip on the glass-like stone.

"Mary, what on earth are you doing?" Bella asked abruptly. She and Dave had been awakened by the sound of a pan crashing to the floor after Mary accidentally knocked it off the counter in the kitchen. Bella wore a robe, and Dave held a revolver in case someone had broken into their establishment.

Mary sniffled. "There's a piece of the obsidian in the wall."

"That can wait until tomorrow. Go to bed," Bella scolded.

"I can't sleep. Bella, how could I fall for a man who felt nothing for me?"

"Oh, geez." Dave rolled his eyes and went back to bed.

Bella stepped onto the stage. "Sweetheart, some men are no different than dogs. Trust me on that. He is a bad one. Just be thankful he didn't use you for more than what he did. A lesson to learn is to never fall for anyone before you know their character. It takes time, but it will save you from heartbreak and hardship later on."

"I should have listened to what you, Dave, Leonard, and even Paul's boss were saying to me. Paul was right, I was warned."

Bella frowned. "Sometimes we don't want to hear what is being said when our heart believes it is right. Feelings and emotions can lead us down the wrong path if we let them. That's why we have a brain, sweetheart. It's the reasoning part of us. Our eyes and ears are closer to the brain than our hearts, but even so, we can become blinded and deaf to anything we don't want to believe. Even if the gossip is true. I know he hurt you, but that just shows his character, not yours. You are an outstanding lady and deserve much better than that creep. And you will find that special man, and this night will become a distant memory."

"Leonard should not have done what he did," Mary said sadly.

"He did it for you."

She swallowed emotionally as her eyes filled with tears. "I know. He shouldn't have. Bella, two men's lives were changed tonight, neither for the better because of me. Leonard was right all along. But I didn't listen, and now he's in trouble. I can't do this anymore. I'm to blame. I'm going back home, Bella. I don't want to dance anymore." A pair of tears rolled down her cheek.

Bella exhaled heavily. "Maybe after a good night's sleep, you'll change your mind about that."

Mary shook her head. "No. I'm going to see Leonard and say goodbye to him, and make arrangements to go back to Denver. I was going to keep this piece of obsidian to always remind me of tonight. I can't stay here any longer. I'm going to miss you, Bella."

"We'll miss you," Bella said as she hugged Mary. "If that's what you want to do, we'll let all the girls know tomorrow."

CHAPTER THIRTY-SIX

Travis McKnight convinced Rhonda on Friday night that he needed to work that evening to avoid taking her to Bella's Dance Hall. He spent the night in the Monarch Lounge, gambling and having a few drinks. Although he promised Rhonda he would take her to see the Hennessy Brothers' Traveling Show on Saturday night, he knew he needed to find an excuse not to. He had used so many excuses in the past that he couldn't find one he hadn't already used. While talking with his friend Josh Slater, Josh suggested taking some Calomel powder that his mother used when she was constipated. Travis went to the Slater mansion and drank two glasses of Calomel, and when he got home, he drank some mustard powder that made him vomit. Faking being sick, he didn't have to pretend for long.

He spent a miserable night running to the privy and swore he'd never use that same excuse again, but Rhonda compassionately forgave him for missing the Hennessy Brothers' show. Instead, she took care of him.

It had been a restless night, and Travis was still feeling the effects of his decision that Sunday morning. He swore he'd have to go down a suit size if the Calomel didn't leave his system soon. Josh said one glass would be sufficient, but Travis didn't want to take any chances, so he took a heavy dose. He regretted that now. He sat on the edge of the bed after getting a few hours of sleep, feeling exhausted and rubbing his belly as it stirred.

The bedroom door opened, and Rhonda approached to rest her hand on his forehead. "How are you feeling? You don't have a fever. Are you feeling better?"

"I'm not sure. My stomach is still rumbling."

"I have some breakfast for you downstairs. The marshal is here and wants to ask you more questions about his relative, I think. He's downstairs waiting for you. Travis, don't let yourself be used as a pawn to free his relative if he's guilty. You don't owe him anything."

Travis nearly wet himself as a chill crept up his spine. "Tell him I'm sick. I don't want to talk to him right now."

"I did, but he said it won't take long. I'll let him know you're too sick to come downstairs. You should get some rest."

"No! I'll talk to him. I'll be down in a moment." He paused as he watched his wife turn toward the door. "Rhonda," he called.

"Yes," she said as she turned to face him. His heart fluttered. Sometimes it was too easy to take her for granted and overlook how pretty she was. She was a good mother to his son and had been a good and faithful wife to him. "I love you."

A warm smile lit up her face. She had heard those words several times, but it was pleasant to hear them when they were heartfelt. "I love you, too. Get dressed." She turned around to leave the room and jumped back with a frightened cry of alarm. Matt had come upstairs and stood at the door.

"I'm sorry to startle you, Mrs. McKnight. Your young man downstairs was hitting me with his wooden sword…"

"Oh, I'm going to take that away from him. I apologize, but Travis is not feeling well, Marshal Bannister."

"I heard, yes. Unfortunately, I am on official business concerning an attempted murder, which could become a murder that your husband may be connected to, so I insist on seeing him."

"What?" Rhonda gasped, stepping aside to allow Matt into the room. Travis's face had gone pale as his eyes widened at the sight of Matt.

Travis's hands started to tremble. He spoke quickly, "I told you I wanted nothing to do with that. If anyone tried to kill you, that's all, Deloris's doing, not mine. I told you that yesterday. I had nothing to do with that."

"That's not why I'm here. Travis, did you know Deloris was poisoning Solomon? She's been giving him arsenic. Were you aware of that?" There was no friendliness in Matt's voice or his hardened expression.

"No!" he shook his head innocently. "I had no idea. She told me he was sick, but she never mentioned anything about poisoning him. I swear it!"

Matt stayed silent, observing him closely.

The uneasy silence prompted him to continue talking, despite Rhonda's concerned expression. "Did Deloris say I knew about it?" he asked incredulously. "If so, she's lying. I had no idea. I swear that to you."

"Deloris is dead."

"What? How?"

"I don't know yet. Dr. Ryland thinks her heart gave out. Did you know she put Solomon in the basement?"

"No! I have no idea what you're talking about. I knew he was sick, that's all."

Rhonda was confused. "Why would he know about that? He doesn't even talk to that woman."

Matt hesitated to answer and looked at Travis. "Maybe you'd better tell her."

"Tell me what?" she asked. "Travis?"

He lowered his head in shame. He knew that if he didn't say the words, Matt would. His heart pounded in his chest, and an uncomfortable pressure choked his throat. "Rhonda, I have been having an affair with Deloris."

Rhonda's expression fell like a stone tumbling down a cliff. The pain of his betrayal was visible on her face. Rhonda gasped as a hand rose to her breast to keep her heart from shattering into pieces. "You what? No...how long has this been going on?"

"Since July," Travis admitted quietly. He avoided making eye contact with her.

"The Slaters' party?" she scolded while nodding her head. The anger in her eyes intensified. "You took her home that night, I remember. Solomon had to bring me home that night because you were talking to that old, drunken hag. I should have known, but I didn't believe you'd be tempted by her! She's old." Her head shook with disgust. "Why am I surprised, though? I know you've been unfaithful, but I couldn't prove it until now."

Travis stood and stepped toward her with open arms. "No, sweetheart, I made a mistake," he said.

"No! Keep your disgusting hands to yourself. I hope you enjoyed her, Travis, because you will never touch me again! We are done!" She burst out of the room, leaving Matt awkwardly staring at Travis. She sobbed as she descended the stairs.

Travis sat heavily at the foot of his bed. "Well, you got what you wanted, you might as well go."

"It's not what I wanted, it's what you owe her: the truth." Matt turned and stepped out of the bedroom.

———

ONE WEEK LATER, Solomon Fasana, covered by blankets over a heavy coat, sat in a wheelchair next to the coffin containing his wife, Deloris, in the cemetery. Standing beside him was his son, James, who held his father's hand while Reverend Painter delivered the eulogy. It was a bitterly cold day with an inch of snow on the ground. The mountains surrounding Branson looked beautiful, adorned with a thick layer of snow, but Solomon's gaze was fixed on the headstone that his brothers had already engraved and set. It read:

DELORIS KING
UNFAITHFUL WIFE AND ATTEMPTED MURDERESS
DIED 1884

She was being buried like a vagrant on the back side of the cemetery in Potter's Acre, where unidentified bodies and the poorest of the poor were laid to rest to dispose of their remains. Unlike the other graves that surrounded her, she already had a full-size tombstone engraved and set, thanks to Luther and Joel. They used Deloris's maiden name instead of Fasana.

"She didn't want anything to do with us or our name when she was alive, why should we make her carry our name in

death?" Joel had explained to Solomon earlier that morning.

Solomon's legs and feet were damaged by arsenic poisoning, rendering him unable to walk as he once did. His skin appeared ashen, and although he was recovering, his health had been compromised by the amount of arsenic in his system.

Solomon looked at the family members gathered around him. It was strange how desperately Deloris longed to be significant in the city's upper society while so few of her so-called friends attended her funeral. The people she despised formed the largest group surrounding the coffin. It was a peculiar feeling to know a woman for so many years, to love her and then hate her, to despise her at times and love her again. Emotions rose and fell like a butterfly's flight pattern on a summer day.

Their marriage had never been stable for more than a day. Yet, he loved her despite her flaws. She was his wife and the mother of his only son. She now lay in the coffin after attempting to kill him. It turned out that the small vial found on the kitchen counter contained a poison that mimicked a heart attack called Aconite. What was thought to be a heart attack was, in fact, a suicide that claimed her life before she could write a note. Solomon never suspected she would take her own life. It didn't make much sense unless she knew she would be caught. Where she got the poison was a mystery, as it wasn't sold in stores.

"Now, we commit her body to the grave and conclude our service for today," said Reverend Painter. "I'll remind everyone that there is a memorial service at the Branson Community Hall where we can share stories and eat some good food." Reverend Eli Painter did not know Deloris very well, he only recognized her from the furniture store and occasionally at church. She never struck Reverend Painter as a particularly religious lady, and he could not say she was in heaven during the funeral service because he was not confident of it. The funeral service felt strange to him, as he had never attended a funeral that lacked emotion but had angry scowls, a bit of laughter, and everyone anxious for it to be over, including her husband and son.

"Ready to leave, Father?" James asked. He had not shed a tear during the service. No one had shed a tear.

"Yes," Solomon said. He held no flowers to offer as a token of his love.

Luther Fasana snorted up some phlegm and spat on the coffin as a parting gift. "Sorry, James, Solomon. I was offering my respects," he said, noticing that they were watching him.

Solomon offered a faint smile. He was exhausted. He knew there would be no empathy for Deloris from his family, as she had severed those ties and expressed her feelings about them many years earlier.

James replied, "Potter's Acre encapsulates the family's feelings toward her quite well, Uncle Luther. I lacked respect for my mother, but she may have deserved a nicer engraving and plot."

Luther waved his hand. "I'll keep my thoughts to myself about that. No, I won't either. She tried to murder your father, and we're blessed, very blessed that he is even here today. I have no respect for your mother. She's exactly where she deserves to be. That's where I and everyone else here stand on it."

Mary Ziegler hugged James. "I'm sorry you had to come home to all of this. How long will you be in town before you go back to the valley?"

"I'm not going back, Aunt Mary. I'm going to stay here

and help my father run the business and take care of him. I'm home for good."

She smiled warmly. "I am glad to hear that. We can look forward to having you around more often."

"Yes, mame." James had always known that Matt Bannister was his cousin, but he didn't have many memories of him growing up. He could see Matt holding his beautiful wife, talking to a lady who was weeping, a young boy stood close beside her. James had met Matt briefly the day before but had not had the chance to speak with him. "Excuse me for a minute, Aunt Mary."

He left his father with Mary and Charlie Ziegler to approach Matt. "Excuse me, Matt. I don't mean to interrupt, but I wanted to thank you for finding my father when you did. He wouldn't be here if it weren't for you." He found it almost unbelievable that a man with such compassionate and kind eyes could be as dangerous as Matt apparently was.

"I thank the Lord that I found him every day. You could also thank Ollie, the young man who works for your father. He's the one who told me where Solomon was. Our town is blessed to have Dr. Ryland living here because he is the only one who knows what to do. He stayed with your father for three days to pull him back from death's door. He prayed right along with the rest of us, and Jesus answered our prayers."

James nodded in agreement. "Well, I'd better get my father out of the weather and to the community hall. I'll see you there."

"James," Matt said, stopping him. "I want to introduce you to Rhonda McKnight."

"Miss, I'm James. Solomon's son. It's nice to meet you."

Rhonda sniffled as she wiped her eyes. "It's nice to meet you, too. My condolences for your mother."

"Thank you."

Matt said, "James, I have an idea you and Solomon might consider. I was just telling my idea to Rhonda, and I told her I'd speak to you about it. Rhonda has encountered some domestic issues and is seeking employment and a place to live with her son. She can elaborate further if she wants to, but I was thinking she might do well as a care-taker for Solomon while you're running the business. You know, to watch over him, cook, and clean—the things you won't have time to do."

"Really?" he asked, glancing at her. "I was just wondering how I could watch over him and run the business too. My father only hired one person to work for him."

Matt continued, "Her biggest priority right now is finding a place to live. Do you think she could stay in the house with you and Solomon?"

"I would need to talk to my father, but it would be fine with me. In fact, it would be a blessing because I can only cook canned beans and similar items. One of the reasons I quit teaching to work on the sternwheeler is because they fed me."

Rhonda said, "I am a very good cook. Whatever you want, I can cook. And little Edwin here is very well behaved. We're having a hard time right now, but we'd treat your home with the utmost respect and try not to become a burden to you or Solomon." There was a hint of desperation in her eyes.

Charlie Ziegler pushed Solomon's wheelchair over the snow-covered grass toward where James was speaking with

Matt. Charlie spoke firmly, "Matt, James, we need to get Solomon out of the weather."

"Yes, we do," James said, turning his attention to Solomon.

Solomon gazed at Rhonda. "Rhonda, are you waiting for us to leave so you can dance on her grave?"

"Father!" James said, surprised by the rude comment. "That is the rudest thing I have ever heard you say."

Rhonda's lips tightened and trembled as she fought to hold back tears. She shook her head and turned to walk away.

Solomon spoke quickly, "Rhonda, I didn't mean it. Please, don't walk away like that. I know you're just as hurt as I am, if not more so." He paused to catch his breath. "Forgive me. Everyone here would like to dance on her grave, and I took my frustration out on you. Please, forgive me and join us at the community hall."

Rhonda looked at Solomon, her heart heavy with emotional turmoil. She had no home, no money, and Travis was threatening to take Edwin away from her if she didn't return home. If she didn't find a place to live, she would have no choice but to go back to a marriage she no longer wanted. Her friends had turned against her, and her decision to leave her husband was pushing her closer to Rose Street. She had come to Deloris's funeral to offer her sincere condolences to Solomon. He had always been a gentleman and never deserved to be treated the way he was. She had come to wish him well.

"No," Rhonda said softly. She sniffled. "I did not come to dance on her grave. My rage is at my husband, not your wife. I came to tell you I'm thankful you survived, Solomon. I was praying that you would. You've always been so kind to me. I appreciate you. You're forgiven. But I must go."

Christine comforted Rhonda with her arm as she spoke to Solomon. "Matt brought up the idea of Rhonda becoming your caretaker, clean and cook for you and James. She needs a place to live because she's divorcing Travis."

"I was going to talk to you about that," James told his father.

Solomon's eyes brightened at the idea. "Absolutely. Bring whatever you have or want to keep. We have extra rooms for you and your son. James and Matt can assist you with moving in. I could use the company now that I'm not able to work for a while."

"Today?" she asked with trembling lips, her eyes brimming with tears. She had no more money left for a hotel and was moments away from being forced to take Edwin back home to escape the weather.

"Yes. The sooner, the better. We could use your help."

Rhonda began to cry. "Thank you! Thank you," she repeated as he hugged Christine, and then went to Solomon to hug him. "Thank you!"

EPILOGUE

Alex Wentworth finished the last sentence of the paragraph he was writing. He glanced at the framed Hennessy Brothers' Amazing Traveling Show poster, which leaned against the wall. "Do you know whatever happened to Landy Jandy?"

"Yeah," Matt said. "Paul Jandy stayed in Branson for about two weeks and then left a broken man. His face was all scarred up, and he never looked the same. I felt very bad for him. But a couple of years later, he became one of the most famous magicians in the world. He wore a lot of makeup and toured the country and Europe, selling out large theaters. He never came back to Branson, though. I understand he became quite rich and famous for about ten years or so. Then, I read that he died of syphilis around 1903."

"Did you ever figure out his standing rope trick?" Alex asked with a grin.

Matt chuckled. "No. I never did. He was very good at what he did. Amazing, really."

"I take it he didn't take Mary with him?"

"No," Matt said with a slight chuckle. "Mary went back home to her family. Paul Jandy left on a stagecoach with his tail tucked between his legs. Nobody around here wanted anything to do with him once the paper reported what he had done to Mary and Leonard."

"I take it she did not end up married to Leonard?"

"Nope. I remember she came to the jail to say goodbye to Leonard. They talked for a while, and she was crying when she left. He was, too. I don't know what they said, I left them to talk privately," Matt said. "They were friends."

Christine added, "Mary was my friend and we stayed in touch for many years through letters. She married a fine gentleman who worked for her father's company in Colorado, and they raised a large family. She had a wonderful life and passed away about seven years ago. I miss her letters, she was such a happy lady."

"And Leonard Harris? Was he found guilty or let off the hook?" Alex asked.

"Leonard was found guilty and sentenced to five years in state prison. He returned home and resumed logging. Eventually, I believe he moved to the coastal range of Washington and logged there. That's the last I heard of him. No, if I remember correctly, Fletcher once told me that Leonard was married and had a son. That's the last I heard of him."

Alex shifted in his seat. "As you told this story, I didn't quite catch on at first, but it is the history of the Fasana and Sons Funeral Home, isn't it?"

Matt rubbed his nose. "Well, I suppose. Uncle Solomon started the business, and James took it over, and now his sons run it today. Three generations so far. I think Solomon would be excited to hear that if he were still here."

"Did Solomon fully recover from being poisoned?" Alex inquired.

"To an extent. He had to use a cane to walk from then on. He never remarried and lived for another ten years or so before passing away. He died peacefully in his sleep."

"Well, we almost have everyone covered. Do you know what happened to Travis McKnight and his wife?" Alex asked.

Christine smiled, "Alex, as Matt told you, Rhonda divorced Travis and moved in with Solomon to take care of him. As it turned out, even though she was ten years older than James, they fell in love and eventually got married. She married into the Fasana family, and they had two more children in addition to her son, Edwin. Edwin and his younger brothers became morticians, which is where the name of our local funeral home comes from. James adopted Edwin and legally changed his name to Fasana as well. He wanted nothing to do with his father, Travis McKnight."

"Travis," Matt continued, "remarried and divorced several more times. The older he got, the more he drank, and although he remained the saw mill's manager, he was probably the most unhappy man you'd ever see. I think losing Rhonda and Edwin cut him much deeper than he would admit. But it didn't change him at all. He just could not be faithful and gambled away all the money he'd earned. He ultimately drank himself to death in 1895 due to alcohol poisoning."

Alex asked, "Did he ever forgive you for Rhonda finding out about Deloris?"

Matt grunted. "I couldn't tell you that. I don't know. He didn't like me, but he never had. Our interactions never changed. He knew he was wrong. Forgiving others is sometimes easier than forgiving ourselves, and I don't think he ever forgave himself. Once you condemn yourself, you have no reason to want to change. It's like being blinded by your own sorrow and never taking the time to realize that the hole you're digging only gets deeper unless you look up and see the light. He never looked up." Matt paused. "So I tell you, if you're ever in a situation that you can't forgive yourself for something, look up. When Jesus forgives you, you're free, and all you're holding onto is a ghost of a memory. Let it go and be free of it. That's where you find joy in life."

Alex closed his notebook. "I think I have the story in hand." He hesitated and spoke carefully, "Listen, I don't want to impose or cross any lines. I appreciate every story you tell me. The community loves it too. There are stories floating around about how Christine ended up in a wheelchair. One says it was an automobile accident, while another person in the office swears it was caused by her falling off a horse. Do you think it's possible to hear the true story sometime?"

Matt took a deep breath. "In time. I can tell you it was neither one of those. Come back next Sunday, and I'll share another story. I think you'll find it entertaining. When I run out of stories, I'll share how Christine lost the use of her legs, but that will be the last story I tell. So, when you want to stop coming up here, I'll share it."

IF YOU LIKED THIS, YOU MIGHT LIKE:
Willow Falls (Matt Bannister Book 1)

Welcome to Willow Falls. The town young Matthew Bannister ran away from fifteen years before. Now famed U.S. Deputy Marshal Matt Bannister is coming home to reconcile with his family. He prayed he wouldn't see his ex-best friend Tom Smith nor the only girl he ever loved, Tom's wife, Elizabeth. However, old feuds unsettled never die and spark a powder keg of action when the desperate Moskin Gang kidnap Elizabeth and leave a murderous trail behind them. In anguish, Tom, the Willow Falls sheriff, turns to his despised old-friend to help get the woman they both love back alive, if they can. Sometimes God's greatest blessing is unanswered prayer.

AVAILABLE NOW

ABOUT THE AUTHOR

Ken grew up in the small farming community of Dayton, Oregon, where he worked to make a living. But his true passion always lay with writing.

Having a busy family, the only "free" time Ken has to write is late at night—getting no more than five hours of sleep every day. He has penned several novels that are being published, along with several children's stories.

Ken Pratt and his wife, Cathy, have been married for over twenty years and are blessed with five children and six grandchildren. They live on the Oregon Coast where they are currently raising the youngest of their children.